THE TROUBLE WITH SOULMATES

ELKE FEUER

ELKE FEUER LLC

DEDICATION

A huge thanks to my beta readers, Corissa, Cate, and Kim. This book wouldn't be what it is without you.
Thanks to my ARC readers and TSWAG authors whose support means everything to me!

CHAPTER 1

Rachel Miller gawked at the man standing in the conference room doorway. Dressed in a blue pinstriped jacket and a red tie, he was a replica of the man in her dreams three nights ago. This moment was inevitable since most of her dreams became reality, so his appearing in her life shouldn't be a surprise. She was still unsettled, though, because their encounter in her dream was...different.

That's an understatement!

She blinked to make sure she wasn't daydreaming or hallucinating. Maybe she was still asleep? She pinched herself. *Nope. I'm awake.*

Just moments ago, she was watching staff pour themselves cups of coffee with shaky hands because of the rumors of a merger that had been circulating around the office for months. Everyone was already on edge before the announcement of this emergency meeting. Like everyone else, she worried about what a merger meant for the firm, the staff, and her future. Now all she could focus on was the man in the doorway.

"This is Michael Doherty. He'll be overseeing the merger." Rick, head of the accounting firm, stated dryly.

Michael sauntered in with an air of confidence that heightened the tension. He smiled curtly and took the empty seat at the table, across from Rachel.

"Good morning, everyone." His thick Irish accent flowed over her, reminding her of his voice against her ear—low and seductive.

Mumbles welcomed him.

"I plan to make this as painless as possible, I promise. I'll start by meeting each of your departments and in some cases, individuals."

When she finally got the guts to look up, he was watching her. *Oh God! He knows it's me. Relax, Rachel. It was **your** dream.*

The rest of the conversation passed through her, her thoughts too chaotic to focus on what was being said, and she hoped for once thorough meeting notes were taken. Moments later everyone was exiting the room, and she stood to leave with them.

"Ms. Miller, I'll speak with you first."

Everyone stopped and looked at her. She was the best accountant at the firm. If she was being laid off, then none of them stood a chance. The shoulders of each employee drooped as they shuffled out of the boardroom.

Crapity, crap, crap! Rachel wished the boardroom walls weren't made of glass. The eyes of every employee with a cubicle would soon appear at the top of dividers. Rachel placed her hands in her lap and resisted the urge to wring them.

Michael stood and walked around the table to sit next to her. Her heartbeat thundered like oversized speakers in a car. *Can he hear it?* The familiarity of him crashed into her, tingling every nerve, bringing back memories of their experience in her dream. Not to mention the smell of his intoxicating cologne: exotic and masculine.

"I'm told you're the best accountant the firm has."

She nodded, certain only babbling would tumble out if she tried to speak. What the hell was wrong with her?

"We'll need to work closely during this merger, you can show me the ropes and who the go-to people are."

Why do Irish accents have to be my weakness? She nodded again.

Michael gave her a strange look. "You do speak, right?"

"Of course, I can speak," she retorted. *Oh god, he's going to think I'm a complete idiot. Get it together!*

He studied every inch of her face as if he wanted to make a mental log. His hand reached out to her, but stopped short before he abruptly withdrew. "Pick an office. We'll meet in an hour to discuss the next steps," he requested and put some distance between them.

"Yes, sir."

"Call me Michael."

"Okay...Michael."

Their gaze locked. This wasn't the first time his name was on her lips, but experiencing it while awake was like tasting a sweet familiar wine. Her heartbeat escalated the longer their gazes held. *Did he have the same dream?*

"Are you finished?" Rick interrupted the moment from the doorway.

They quickly shifted away from each other.

"Yes." Michael stood and headed out the door, nodding to Rick as he passed.

The knotted tension that was coiled within her stomach relaxed.

"What was that about?" Rick asked.

"He wants my help with the merger."

"Good. I want you to find out all that you can."

"What do you mean?" *You know what he means, Rachel. He wants you to spy.*

3

Rick stepped closer. "They're trying to push me out," he said quietly.

"Really?" Rachel feigned surprise. She'd do the same thing. Rick was difficult to work with and it was no secret he was doing a poor job of running the company.

"Don't pretend you don't know, or even suspect, Rachel," he hissed.

In the eight years she'd worked with him he'd become cantankerous, which spoiled the rugged jawline that once made him attractive, and his gray eyes now exuded irritation instead of sparkling humor.

"I'll do whatever is in the best interest of the company and the employees, Rick." She spoke coolly as she stood and left him alone in the boardroom.

Rachel leaned against the door of her office and released the breath she'd been holding since the moment Michael walked into the boardroom, or the last night she saw him, if she was honest. He showed no real signs he'd had the same dream, only hints in the close way he studied her and his intense gaze when she'd said his name.

She moved to her desk with shaky legs and suddenly had the urge to say, "Of all the offices in the world, he had to walk into mine." *That's stupid and cliché, Rachel!* The result of watching too many old movies with her parents as a kid.

Michael was real and she had the chance to know him outside her dream even with the awkward circumstances. He came all the way from Ireland, and she lived on Grand Cayman. The chances of meeting him in person after seeing him in her dreams were too rare to be considered slim.

Fear gurgled in her throat. Sharing an intense experience during a dream was one thing, but facing that person in real life? Painful memories of rejection crawled beneath her skin. She knew all too well people didn't respond well to her gift, one she suppressed whenever possible.

Three days had passed since her dream, giving her an experience that had touched a part of her she hadn't realized was dormant and yearning to be cracked open and released. *Get a grip! You sound like Skylar.*

Rachel tugged at her light-blue shirt and squared her shoulders. They had a job to do, and she was good at it. Grabbing her phone, she opened her notes app and added a list of things she'd need for her meeting with Michael. For now, this merger needed to be her focus. Their dream connection would have to wait, or better yet, be ignored.

CHAPTER 2

T HREE NIGHTS EARLIER

The lights of the city twinkled like stars amid glass and concrete as Rachel gazed out the window. In the room around her there were faceless people. Their reflections in the window panels laughed, drank, and moved about carefree. Rachel longed to join them, but part of her wanted nothing to do with them. She pressed her back against the wall next to the window. She was happy there in the corner. Alone.

This dream wasn't new, but it did feel different. *Is that a good thing or bad?*

The clinking of glasses was sharp and clear. The silk dress was soft and cool against her skin, sounds and sensations that were usually dull or unnoticeable. Only what her dream wanted her to know in the moment was vivid and detailed.

"Hello," a man said, startling her.

Beautiful blue eyes pierced her brown ones along with a smile she was certain had crushed a heart or two. *Who the hell is this?*

"Hello."

"You here alone?" He leaned against the glass panel window. The words rolled off his tongue in a soft Irish brogue.

Seriously? "Come up with that line all by yourself?" The Irish brogue was nice. She adored that accent, but not the cheesy pickup line.

The man laughed. "Actually, that's the best one I have."

"It needs work." *A lot of work.*

"So, I've been told, but it hasn't failed me yet." His eyes twinkled with mischief.

"That has nothing to do with your line." She gazed over his body tightly hugged by a black shirt and brown slacks. What was he doing here? Was he the focus of her dream? What could he possibly signify? *Wait? Am I really analyzing my dream while I'm dreaming? You've reached a whole new level of control, Rachel.*

"Really? I didn't think you noticed." His eyes never left hers.

"I didn't. Just making an observation." Rachel grabbed a glass of champagne from the passing tray to distract herself from the shivers of anticipation his gaze introduced. Another new sensation.

"Why are you here alone, then?"

"This is a dream."

"True, but aren't dreams meant for indulging in fantasy?"

Rachel snorted. "Spoken like a true man." But he was right. Looking up at him was nice, she was usually the tallest woman in any room. His chiseled jawline and face were as attractive as his lean body and his eyes, but it was his smile that stood out. The kind that caused your pulse to stop and then accelerate.

"I'm Michael." His hand extended.

She glanced down at it. *Who shakes hands in their dreams?*

The intensity of the touch created a warmth in the palm of their hands. This was what she'd felt when their eyes met. Familiarity.

"It's a pleasure to meet you." He stepped unnervingly close, the heat from his body vibrating against the thin fabric of her dress as his lips pressed against her wrist.

Oh my! Maybe this dream was just a fantasy after all. What are you going to do about it?

The noise from the crowd dulled in the background. He held onto the hand he'd kissed and linked their fingers. His other hand went into her hair, caressing the back of her neck.

Rachel's breath stopped as his lips lowered to her face. Outside her dreams she'd never allow a man to kiss her this soon or in a public place, but the man next to her didn't feel like a stranger. The intense emotion and physical reaction when their lips touched pulled a moan from deep inside her, a place she didn't know existed. With each caress of their mouths, Rachel had to grip his shoulders to keep from falling into a puddle on the floor. Cliché, but it was the only way to describe it.

She held his face and deepened the kiss to another level—to one she'd never experienced, but always wanted to share with someone: soft, intimate, and deep. The kind you saw in movies and fantasized about at night alone in bed.

The kind that stirred not only the corners of your body but touches you to your core. Your soul.

Fear gripped her tightly and she broke the kiss. Michael's bewildered expression reflected hers. "I think it's time for me to go now." Rachel's voice trembled.

"Sweet dreams," he whispered.

Sweat had made tracks down her neck when she woke up. Rachel glanced around to make sure she was in her room and in her own bed.

"What the hell was that?" The dream was so real. More real than any she'd had in her whole life. It was strange, exhilarating, and terrifying all rolled into one. What she knew for sure was the man she'd just kissed was going to show up in her life. What she didn't know was when...or why.

CHAPTER 3

*H*oly shite! Rachel looked just like the woman in his dream. She didn't say her name. Or had she and he missed it? The intense attraction drowned out everything else but her. Was she the same woman? He studied her during the meeting and when they were alone, but she just appeared nervous like everyone else in the room, something he was used to when buying a company. Her face showed no signs she recognized him. *Is it just my imagination?* No. Her face was as clear to him in the dream as in real life.

She resembled the woman from his dreams, and the attraction he felt sitting next to her was going to be a problem. Michael didn't mix business with his personal life, especially with someone he'd have to work with so closely. Maybe Rick could recommend someone else who was just as good. Doubtful. Most of the high-end clients spoke highly of her, more so than Rick. *Damn!*

This merger was a big enough problem with having to deal with Rick. The last thing he needed was this kind of distraction. Michael squared his shoulders. Once they started working together, he'd be fine. Neither she nor their connection would matter in three months when he returned to Ireland. The only hitch in his plan was if he dreamed about her again. The tension between them was palpable in and out of his dreams. Maybe scratching that itch in his dream would make their working relationship easier? They'd turn out to be completely different people and then he could focus on work.

With a plan firmly in place, Michael called his father to let him know he'd arrived safely, and all was in play.

Rachel poked at the salad on her plate, wondering why she'd agreed to lunch. Time with her best friend Arlene usually made her feel better, but for some reason it wasn't doing the trick today.

"All right. What going on?" Arlene asked, her dark brown eyes assessing Rachel. "I haven't seen your lip this far on the ground since Ronald didn't ask you to prom."

"It's work."

"You know you can't lie to me, Rachel. Not to mention you suck at it."

"There's a merger at work." *And the new owner appeared in my dreams.* She couldn't say that last part. Not yet. She usually told Arlene everything, but this was different. Although Arlene knew about her gift, Rachel didn't want to talk about it in public.

"Okay. Does that mean you're losing your job? You didn't like working with that prick Rick anyway so what's the problem?"

Rachel grinned. Leave it to Arlene to only see the positives in the situation. "I haven't lost my job, but it might be a possibility, if he has any say."

Arlene snorted, and pushed a strand of her jet-black hair from her face. "That man couldn't run one hundred yards let alone that company without you. You should have that job, not him."

Rachel shoved a forkful of salad into her mouth to keep from saying what she really thought, fearful that if she started talking, the words would never stop. Her relationship with Rick was a complicated one that started with them dating briefly.

"You can always get another job or break out on your own."

Arlene had been urging her to start her own business for a couple years now, because it was something Rachel wanted a long time ago. But she wasn't ready for that kind of risk or change.

"You could start small," Arlene said as if reading her mind.

"Let's change the subject." Although Rachel knew there wasn't anything she would feel comfortable talking about right now.

Arlene touched her shoulder. "Look. I know things seem stressful right now with your job, but whatever happens you'll figure things out and come out on top. You always do, and if not, I'm here for you."

Rachel wasn't sure she agreed one hundred percent, but she was certain about one thing: Arlene would be there for her, and that was more than what a lot of people had. Rachel was a good accountant, and even if she lost her job, she would find another one, with or without a reference from Rick. Her clients would come through with praise for her good work and recommendations. The weight of the stress that followed her to lunch lifted slightly, but Michael was another story. What would happen if he showed up in her dreams again? Maybe a visit with Skylar was what she needed.

If the attraction continued between them in and out of her dreams, she wasn't sure she could handle it until the merger ended. *Will Michael try to take advantage of our attraction? Eww!* Maybe his turning out to be another Rick would do the trick. He hadn't been far off in her dreams, except for the sparks she felt when they touched. Would touching him be different in real life? Sure, there was an attraction between them—at least on her part—but there was no guarantee it wasn't because of her dream.

Rachel pulled herself out of her thoughts and returned her attention to her friend to finish their lunch date. After paying the bill, she said goodbye to Arlene and headed back to the office.

With her luck, he'd turn out to be like Rick and try to hit on her, or other girls in the office. The professional façade was just that, and the real him would come out, either in her dream—if he showed up again—or in the moments they'd work together. Rachel was smiling when she reached the office, relieved everything would work out. It didn't last long. The office was buzzing with questions and accusations about the new owner and what it meant for everyone. Although they were assured of their jobs for the moment, there was no guarantee what would take place after the merger and beyond.

If Rick had shared the news about the merger sooner, she could've researched Michael's company to have an idea of the damage he might've caused with other companies. Something. The only advantage she had over the others in the office was knowing his next steps before anyone else. Rachel shuddered. She'd be working closely with Michael. The confidence she'd had returning from lunch evaporated.

She took a deep breath. Work had always been her savior during difficult times in her life and this merger would be no different, regardless of the outcome.

Her phone rang. She answered to discover it was Michael on the other end requesting her presence. She squared her shoulders and headed to his office. The jump of her pulse when she saw him surprised her. It was expected the first time she saw him, but now? "What can I do for you Mr. Doherty?"

"Michael is fine," he reminded her.

"Michael."

He rattled off what he needed, not glancing up from the papers before him.

Not having his daunting stare focused on her was nice, but it was a little insulting that he didn't even look her in the eyes. His gaze focused on the documents and files spilled across his desk.

"By the way, can you order me some lunch? I'd do it, but I'm not familiar with the restaurants around here."

"I'll have the receptionist order something for you. Anything in particular?" Be damned if she'd let him think she was his personal assistant. She was a top accountant at the firm and would've been a partner by now if it weren't for Rick.

Michael glanced up from his desk, his steely gaze settled on her before replying, "Chinese works. Anything that's not spicy."

"I'll get started on those reports. IT should be up here shortly to give you computer access. Do you need anything else?"

"That's all for now."

Rachel headed to the door.

"Wait."

Her heart jumped to her throat, her hand on the door handle.

"Leave the door open. And I'd like us to meet again later today. Does six o'clock work for you?"

"Six is fine."

"Good. Please have the receptionist make dinner arrangements. You decide."

Rachel nodded and left the room, her mind racing as she headed back to her office. Would this be the moment he'd prove himself to be just like Rick? She shoved down the disappointment burning in her chest.

CHAPTER 4

B irds chirping and the wind rustling through leaves greeted
Rachel when her dream started. Looking around, she found
herself surrounded by tall grasses that resembled fields of wheat. In
the distance were huge groups of trees blocking the scenery. There
were no people around, at least none that she could see. *Perhaps
they are hiding in trees waiting to ambush me,* Rachel joked.

The first sensation was the weight of her hair and the feel of
it against her neck and arms and then her clothing. Her attire
was straight out of the *Braveheart* movie or maybe the *Outlander*
series.

Footsteps crunching leaves caught her attention. Michael was
standing merely feet away, dressed in a blue and green kilt, his dark
hair blowing against his face and shoulders. Her stomach lurched
and her breath stilled.

Rachel was mesmerized.

In regular clothes he was handsome, but in a kilt, he was devastating and shocked every sense and nerve in her body.

During the past few days, they'd found each other in dreams that
had moved from the room where they first met to outside and with
different clothing. She'd chalked up the change in scenery to either
a shared past life, or perhaps her subconscious taking her out of
her comfort zone because of Michael. Who the hell knew? Rachel

was just grateful to be out of the party scene she usually dreamed about. The dream had changed and she was grateful for it.

Michael's gaze devoured her as he closed the distance between them.

She blushed.

"Hello again," he murmured.

"Can't you find something more original?"

"Of course; however, I'd rather not be slapped." His eyes filled with laughter when she blushed again.

They had kept their distance in the previous dreams, and Rachel suspected it was because of the strong connection they'd felt from touching and their first kiss.

"Walk with me," he offered.

A simple request and act for a dream, but it was easier than saying out loud what they were thinking: *Are you the person I just met?*

Although she doubted those were his thoughts, the notion of him being in her dreams would never occur to him. Unlike her, who was plagued with endless questions.

She nodded and they walked side by side through the tall grass until they reached the forest. Soon the narrow paths opened to a clearing with large boulders surrounded by a stream and enormous trees that shaded the beautiful space and the lush landscaping. "It's stunning."

"It was one of my favorite places to come as a child."

"You just thought about it and now we're here?" *Can he control his dreams? Is that how we met in our dreams?*

"Sort of. I was thinking about it before I feel asleep, and I have this dream often, so here we are."

"I can see why you like it so much." Rachel knelt and stuck her fingers in the water. Surprisingly, it wasn't freezing.

"Want to go for a swim?" Michael asked, as he began unbuttoning his shirt.

"I'll just dip my feet in." She lifted her skirts and slipped off her shoes.

"Suit yourself."

Rachel watched as he removed each article of clothing until he was nearly naked. *Turn around!* She couldn't move. He was gorgeous. Taller than her 5'8", and not as lean as she thought. Muscular without the impression he lived at the gym. He obviously lived in a country without sun, but she wouldn't describe him as pasty.

His hand paused on the sides of his boxers as if remembering she was there and left them alone.

"I thought men were naked underneath kilts," she blurted out. *Real smooth.*

"Usually, but I didn't have control over what I wore. I can remove them if you like."

"No!"

He grinned.

"Why don't you come in with me? I'm sure there's something suitable underneath all those layers." He waded into the water before diving in.

It did look inviting. *A sexy man is asking you to go for a swim. In your dreams? What the hell are you waiting for?* Arlene's voice said. She was right. This was a dream. Even if her subconscious was trying to tell her something, it didn't mean she couldn't enjoy herself.

Rachel was partially undressed when Michael turned. "Hooray!"

Unlike Michael who had boxers, she had some contraption for underwear. She didn't know how she was going to swim in it without the weight pulling her to the bottom of the pond, and there was no way she was going naked. She wanted to be adventurous in her dream but not that adventurous.

She waded in slowly testing how much weight the undergarments would be when Michael came up beside her and pulled her in quickly, soaking her from head to toe. *So much for going slowly.*

They were both laughing when she came up. It felt good. She hadn't laughed in a long time.

"You should laugh more. It lights up your whole face. Makes you more beautiful."

Rachel gave him a sideways glance.

"I'm serious."

No one had ever called her beautiful before. Cute, attractive? Sure. But beautiful? Especially not men who looked like him.

Michael pulled her against him, brushing wet hair away from her face. His thumb caressed her cheek. "Your eyes are a unique shade of brown with specks of gold surrounded by eyelashes most women pay to get. Your mouth's snarkiness is adorable, especially since it doesn't reflect the words that come out." His fingers traced her lips. "But it's your lips that I like most."

She expected him to elaborate on other body parts, but instead he kissed her. It was nothing like their first dream. This was one was filled with passion, and so much fire, Rachel was sure the water would either start bubbling or turn to steam.

He leaned in and devoured her, his tongue conquering her mouth as if laying a claim that no other man could take away. A kiss that seared her from head to toe and filled her with so much heat, all she could do was cling to him, wrap her legs around him, and hold on for dear life.

"I want you." His voice was raw in her ear.

The words and sensation took her by surprise. She'd had sex in dreams before, but she never remembered the guy saying those words. Everything usually happened so fast she didn't have time to think about it. But these dreams were different. Every moment was clear and vivid. Every sensation and emotion were heightened, making them amazing and unnerving simultaneously. She couldn't believe how comfortable and natural being with him felt.

"You do realize this is crazy. You're not even real." Not the best response, but her nerves and thoughts were a jumbled mess.

"I'm as real as you. You feel it just as I can," Michael said softly.

She did know it, more than he did.

"You never told me your name, so who's the scared one?"

She shifted from him in the water, their intimate spell broken. "It's better this way. That way neither of us is disappointed." Or the truth revealed.

A warm hand rested on her shoulder. "That has nothing to do with it," he assured her.

Fathomless eyes focused on her, and she longed to ask him what it was, but then what? How would it affect their working relationship? How would she explain how she knew he'd show up in her life? Memories of people's reactions over the years, including her parents, told her all she needed to know. Sharing that truth wasn't an option.

"It doesn't matter," she whispered and shook her head.

The dream ended and Rachel woke up staring at her ceiling and an aching sensation in her chest. For most of her childhood, people and events she dreamed came true in her real life. She hadn't realized she was the only one until she saw the expressions on her parents' faces when she mentioned it casually as a child. As if it wasn't something every kid experienced. Her classmates and teachers thought she was lying, which made school a difficult place.

Grabbing her phone from the nightstand, she called Skylar. She and Arlene were the only people in her life who knew the truth and hadn't called her crazy when they found out. For Arlene it was because she'd saved her life and Skylar had known immediately because of her own unique gifts.

"It's three o'clock in the morning, Rachel. It had better be good."

Rachel wasn't sure where to start. "I manifested a man from my dreams."

"Someone who doesn't exist?"

Only Sklyar would ask that question. "He exists."

"So, what's the problem? You dream about people all the time."

"This is different. The dream felt like real life. Not to mention the connection we felt."

"I see. Give me a minute." Random muffled noises came from the other end of the call.

Rachel knew she was reaching for one of her cards. "Can't you give me an answer as a psychologist?"

The shuffling of cards in the background paused. "Believe it or not, this is the foundation before that answer. You're soulmates."

Rachel wasn't expecting that answer. "What does that even mean?"

"It means it was time for you to connect, heal each other from the pains of your past lives. Your gift of having vivid dreams and them manifesting into real life intensifies the experience."

"Great. So, what do I do? I can't just tell him."

"Why not?" Skylar asked before quickly responding. "Sorry, I forgot."

"For one, he's the new owner of the company I work for." Not that she could tell him either way. Rejection was something she avoided in all areas of her life.

"That means you're in close contact with each other, and you have the chance to talk with him. You don't have to dive into the details, but you must be open to sharing more about yourself, your fears, and to the possibilities of growth."

So, basically my worst nightmare? "And how do I explain this sharing and unloading to him?"

"I sense he's ready to do the same. If he wasn't, you wouldn't have connected in real life and your dreams."

Is this going to affect our working relationship? And that he'll leave the island in three months?

"Stop overthinking, Rachel. This is a good thing. You're opening up to a whole new world."

"What if I like the old world?"

"You're a terrible liar!"

"I hate that you and Arlene know me so well."

"No, you don't. Now, get some rest. You've got a long journey ahead of you."

"Thanks, Sky."

Rachel couldn't decide if she felt better or worse. The last thing she wanted was their weird relationship to mess with the merger. Or worse, to lose her job. *You might be losing your job anyway.*

The realization knocked her in the gut along with the fact she knew nothing about Michael and his intentions for the company and the staff after the merger. That's what she needed to focus on.

CHAPTER 5

"Rachel?"

Michael was waving a hand in front of her.

Blushing, she straightened in her chair and pulled the notepad closer. "Sorry. I didn't get much sleep last night," she mumbled. Truthfully, she'd slept like a baby. It was the next morning that was proving to be the problem. In her dreams she could talk, laugh, and hold him, but at work she had to keep her distance and act as if they hadn't shared intimate moments. The tension between them was excruciating. And "talking" to him as Sky suggested wasn't going to come easy.

"Why don't we take a break?" Michael suggested after looking at his watch. "It's nearly lunchtime. How about a bite to eat?"

Shivers ran down her back as she remembered his mouth on her skin and his teeth nibbling at her shoulder blade before he whispered, "I want you."

"O-O-Okay," Rachel stammered. *Dammit. I should've said no.* It was getting harder not to drop her guard around him. Then what? "Talk to him." Sky's voice intruded.

"Where do you normally eat?" He pushed the chair away from the boardroom table.

"At my desk, but there's a restaurant around the corner we can walk to that has good food."

"Lead the way."

Rachel walked out the door and wished she couldn't feel his eyes on her. Silence followed them to the restaurant and stayed while they waited for their lunch. The restaurant was quiet because it wasn't quite lunchtime. Two waitresses stood by the bar chatting and rolling up silverware while the bartender leaned against the bar. This was one of her favorite restaurants, but she usually had her lunch delivered. The looks she got when sitting alone made her uncomfortable. Those gazes were filled with pity and questioning, as if they wondered why she was eating alone.

The décor of dark-blue walls and underwater scenes reflecting an island theme always calmed her. Her family lived on the beach when she was growing up...before things changed.

"I hope your boyfriend isn't upset by all the long hours you've been working."

Rachel nearly choked on the bread she'd bitten into but was grateful for the question to pull her away from the direction of her thoughts.

"Sorry, is that question too personal?"

"No," she replied although it was. "I don't have a boyfriend."

"Really?"

"I was engaged, but..." *Why are you telling him that? It's way too personal!* Skylar said she should start sharing, but talking about Shawn right out of the gate?

"But what?" Sea-blue eyes, still and intense, inquired.

"It didn't work out," she mumbled.

"Sorry. Who called it off?"

"I did." Sweat started to pool under her armpits. *Stop talking! Stop talking!*

"Really?"

If he said that word one more time, she was going to throw a piece of bread at his head. He wasn't the Michael from her dreams—their relationship in real life was very different. He had never asked if she was seeing someone, and she hadn't asked him either. The question seemed ridiculous.

"Do you have siblings?" Rachel asked, changing the subject.

"Yes. I have a sister who got the looks in the family," he chuckled.

His laughter affected her the same as in her dreams: shivers across her skin and through a part of her heart she kept carefully locked away. "I find that hard to believe."

Lips moved across perfect white teeth into a knee-melting smile. "Thanks."

"Does that mean you got all the brains?"

"No, she lucked out in that department too."

"Some people have all the luck," she mumbled.

Michael laughed and then reached to touch her hand. Warmth raced up her arm. "I think you're doing fine on your own."

Rachel's mouth opened to speak, but no words came out. While his thumb caressed the top of her hand, her mind screamed for her to move it away, but it was the last thing she wanted to do. This touch was a glimpse of the man in her dreams. The strong reaction was the same.

"Can I take your order?" The petite waitress asked.

Rachel jerked her hand from his. Surprise lit his eyes, as if he hadn't realized he'd been touching her.

Awkward silence hung in the air after the waitress left, making her wish she hadn't agreed to have lunch with him. She enjoyed his company, and watching him...when her stomach wasn't in knots, or when she wasn't wary he or someone else might catch her staring.

"So, how is your girlfriend handling the distance?" she asked as casually as she could. *There is no way he has a girlfriend after the way he just caressed my hand. Right?*

Cool eyes met hers as he contemplated her question.

"You can't be the only one allowed to ask personal questions." She grinned, hoping to ease whatever made him hesitate.

His stiff posture relaxed. "I don't have a girlfriend."

Why did his answer make her feel so wretched? He could've said he was seeing someone, something. Rachel knew it was ridiculous, but a small place inside her had hoped. "Ever been married?"

"No, and no broken engagement or serious relationships," he said with a grin, as if answering her next questions.

That should have made her feel better, but it didn't. "So, you're all about a good time, then? Aren't you a little old to still be running around?" The contempt in her voice was harsher than she could control.

Michael laughed. "Since when is thirty-eight old?"

She met his question with silence before shrugging.

"I never met the right woman, I guess. Until recently..."

"Oh?" Her voice trembled. *He's talking about me.*

Michael sipped his water. "It's complicated."

"Relationships often are." *Tell him, Rachel!* No words made it to her mouth.

"Are you seeing anyone?"

"I..." What could she say? Yes, I'm seeing you—you just don't know it.

He grinned. "It's complicated right?"

She laughed but stopped when his smile disappeared. "What?"

Intensity scrutinized her. "Are you sure we've never met? Your laugh is...familiar."

Oh God! Oh God! Not wanting to lie, she said, "You've never been to Cayman before and I've never been to Ireland, so how could we meet?" *It's too soon to tell him the truth.* "Who does my laughter remind you of?"

"Someone special," he replied without hesitation.

Butterflies fluttered in her stomach. "The one that's complicated?"

The waitress set their food before them, preventing Michael from answering. They talked about work between bites and avoided any personal questions for the rest of lunch.

Silence followed them on the walk back to the office.

"You should laugh more." Michael stated as he pulled the door open for her.

"So should you," Rachel shot back.

"What do you do for fun?" he asked after the elevator door closed.

Rachel's mouth opened and closed. *Don't say stay home and read. That'll sound pathetic.*

"How about letting me take you to dinner this weekend?" He smiled brightly, devastating her senses.

"I don't think that's a good idea," she stammered.

"Why?" His eyebrows knitted.

"We work together." And being around him more would make it harder to keep up a professional façade—at least on her part, and if they were out of the office and in an intimate setting...Rachel's heartbeat skipped.

Michael turned and took a step closer until his cologne assaulted her senses, and shivers raced to her toes, something it couldn't do in her dreams. Her heartbeat thundered as he leaned even closer.

"It's not a date, Rachel. Just a coworker who doesn't know the island, or anyone who lives here, asking for some company."

25

Her name on his lips soft and low reminded her of the man in her dreams and she suppressed the urge to throw her arms around him and kiss him. "Okay," she murmured.

"Excellent!"

It's just dinner. What's the worst that could happen?

CHAPTER 6

The moment she walked into the restaurant, Rachel was grateful for the noisy and busy atmosphere emanating from two large tables that were decorated for a birthday and anniversary. Michael's insistence that tonight was not a date had rattled her in ways she hadn't expected, from relief to annoyance. A professional relationship was a necessity given the merger, but didn't he feel their connection? Rachel didn't have time to contemplate further as she noticed Michael waving to her from a table in the back of the restaurant in a dimly lit space.

Michael stood as she approached. "Hi. I thought you changed your mind."

"Why? I'm on time." Nerves made her bump into the table as she sat. The glasses and silverware rattled but nothing fell.

He glanced at his watch. "Right. Mine is still on Irish time."

"That must make meetings interesting," she joked.

"Huh? Yeah."

No smile, nothing. Something was bothering him. Was it work? Her? Rachel found it difficult to believe this was the same man who nights earlier had shared intimate physical and emotional moments with her.

The waiter came to take their order and silence settled around them until he returned with their drinks. Rachel grabbed her glass of wine and took a deep swig to relax her nerves. They were racing faster than a car in the Indy 500.

"Nervous?"

"A little. You?"

"Why?" He sidestepped answering her question.

"Let's see. I'm out on a not-date with kind-of my boss."

"It isn't the first time," Michael shot back.

Great. Rick had opened his big mouth. The man wouldn't know the meaning of the word discreet if it bit him in the ass.

"I've never dated a boss. Just someone who became a coworker later, yes, but I don't usually mix business with my personal life if I can help it."

Her statement must've pacified him, because he relaxed in his chair and the tightness that creased his face when she first arrived dissolved. Was that the reason for his nervousness? Because of the personal question he had to ask about her and Rick? While it wasn't related to the merger, it did affect the company and might have him questioning her integrity.

"I'm glad you're keeping all our staff," Rachel stated, guiding the conversation back to work and not on her. There was one person she thought needed to go, but it was necessary for Michael to come to that conclusion on his own.

Michael's evasive gaze left her wondering if maybe he had. The company would be better off without Rick, but who would fill his position? Her heart skipped, thinking that Michael might decide to stay. *Stop dreaming. If he stays to run the company, our relationship would remain the same.*

"It's why I like to be on-site when a merger is taking place—to reassure owners I will take care of their business and their staff."

"What happens when you can't keep the staff?"

"I look for jobs with our other companies for them, or make sure they're well taken care of."

The casual way he responded made Rachel smile. Not all business owners believed those words and it warmed her that he did. He wasn't just a lackey who worked for his father. He cared about the businesses and people his family acquired.

The waiter placed their food before them.

"What made you decide to become an accountant?" Michael asked between bites.

Safe question. "Both my parents are, so I guess you could say it's in my blood." Numbers were something she was always good at and enjoyed for the most part. "What about you? Did you always know you'd work in your family business?"

Michael nodded. "Yes, whether I wanted to or not. My sister manages the charity side of the business, so the other was pinned on me."

"No desire to change roles with your sister?"

"Definitely not! She has the patience of a saint dealing with the boards of all the charities and companies that approach us, running fundraising events, and being in the spotlight."

Rachel smiled, imagining him standing in front of cameras in a tuxedo during a charity event and giving speeches. Definitely not him.

"Why the smile? Are you seeing me in a monkey suit?"

"I was. Giving speeches in front of a camera. You were terrified, but you looked good in the suit." *Really good.* Images of undoing his tie with her teeth invaded her thoughts along with biting the buttons off his shirt and running her hand over his bare chest. Heat rushed to her cheeks and other body parts.

"What else are you imagining?" Michael's voice interrupted her thoughts.

"Nothing," she mumbled, avoiding his gaze, suddenly remembering their last dream and everything they'd shared physically and emotionally. She wished their dreams weren't so vivid. Some people forget their dreams once they wake up. Did he? She lifted her eyes.

No. His heated gaze screamed that he remembered everything.

A caress on her skin broke their moment and she glanced down at her hand to realize Michael was holding it. When had that happened? This was the second time they'd discovered their hands together, only this time Michael didn't pull away when he noticed, but continued caressing her hand with his thumb. The air sizzled as their gazes shifted from eyes to mouths, and every caress against her skin stoked the fire already burning between them.

"Rachel?"

The question from above was a bucket of ice water on their moment, especially because she recognized the voice.

She glanced up to see Shawn, her ex-fiancé standing by their table with a beautiful blond on his arm. *How cliché.* Rachel didn't recognize the woman, so she must've either been new to the island or not from their old circle of friends...all of whom deserted her for him.

"Shawn. Nice to see you." she lied, but her emotions failed to erupt the way they usually did around him, making her realize all the animosity she'd felt after their broken engagement was gone.

"Nice to see you too. This is Amanda, my fiancé."

The word fiancé snapped her and Michael to attention. She took a closer glance at the woman she'd dismissed as a pretty decoration on Shawn's arm. Amanda was obviously more, from her perfect hair, makeup, and a soft blue dress that hugged her curves. The warm kindness staring back at her generated hope that Shawn would rise to be worthy of that kindness.

30

Shawn's eyes shifted to Michael.

"I'm Michael." He failed to mention their connection.

The adoring way Shawn gazed at Amanda said he'd earned a place at her side and planned to stay there. So did the giant rock on her finger.

"I'm happy for you both." Rachel realized she meant every word.

"Thank you. I just wanted to say how sorry I am for what happened. In the end, you were right. I just wasn't ready to hear it." Shawn rested his hand by Amanda's waist.

"Apology accepted. I wish you a wonderful life together."

"Thank you. Same to you," they returned in unison.

Silence became their companion long after Shawn and Amanda left, although Michael's questions screamed in that quiet.

"Are you going to ask?" she inquired.

He straightened his body. "I didn't want to pry. Besides, you did mention you broke off the engagement, so I know that much."

But what he didn't know was the details and the why. *Time to start sharing, Rachel*, Skylar's words intruded. Tightness started in her stomach and raced to her chest.

"Why did he apologize? You broke off the engagement, right?"

Rachel nodded. "He was hurt, became angry, and turned all our friends against me with lies that I cheated on him and that he was the one who broke it off. Arlene, Skylar, and my parents were the only people who believed me."

"Wow. That must've been hard, and hurt you deeply." His hand appeared on the table, a welcome comfort if she wanted it. She resisted. "If they cut you off, then they weren't real friends."

Rachel smiled. "I know." They were his friends originally, but for two brief years, it had been nice to be part of a group who accepted her as one of their own. Making friends didn't come easy for her. Other than Skylar and Arlene, who'd been her friends since childhood, there was no one else. No coworkers who developed into more. No one.

Michael paid the bill and followed her outside the restaurant to her car. The humidity in the air swirled around them, but Rachel was used to it. The lights from the parking lot blocked out the stars, but the moon was up and shining brightly as if for her.

The tension was thick with everything that happened and didn't happen between them both in her dream world and this one. Normally she'd shut down. Sharing was intimate. Terrifying. But standing next to her was Michael. Someone she'd already experienced so many intimate moments with: physical, emotional, and spiritual. She stood in a place she hadn't been in before, and she wanted to reveal everything, even as her chest ached, and lead filled her stomach. Rachel wanted him to know.

"How about a walk on the beach?" Michael offered as if reading her mind. "We'll drop your car, head to the beach, and I'll take you home later."

Rachel nodded and got into her car when he opened the door.

As she drove home, her mind went over the scene at the restaurant with Shawn. Seeing him had taken her by surprise. Once the initial shock wore off, his words, specifically his apology, were a soothing balm she hadn't realized she was waiting for. When their relationship ended and things went sideways, she allowed Shawn's words and actions to go unchecked, because she felt guilty about their broken engagement and thought his anger was warranted.

Rachel pulled into her driveway and Michael's car lights came up behind hers. She locked her car and headed to his, getting inside. Soft tunes flowed through the speakers as they headed to the beach. *What are you doing?*

Her early thoughts of wanting to share everything with Michael about her relationship with Shawn dissipated, fear and doubt replacing her earlier confidence. Sharing meant an intimacy that scared her, especially when the person would no longer be part of her life. That should make it easier, but didn't. Nothing about her relationship with Michael was easy.

"Did you enjoy the food?" Michael's voice broke through the music.

The question was a redundant one, but it was better than opening with the obvious question: *What the hell happened between you and Shawn?*

Michael parked the car and got out. She slipped off her shoes and exited as well. A blast of salty wind accosted her face, and she welcomed it, along with the sound of the waves lapping against the sand. When they reached the sand, she dug her toes deep in with each step bringing her closer to the ocean. Rachel breathed deeply and unsettling emotions were replaced with peaceful ones. The beach was always the magical calm to her body and senses.

"Feel better?" Michael asked, a smile on his own face, indicating the beach was good for him too.

"Much. Thanks for suggesting it."

He shrugged. "Being an island girl, I figured the beach would make you feel better."

Rachel grinned. "You figured right. I love the beach...always have. My parents and I spent most weekends swimming or lying in the sand soaking up the sun. It was the way they unwound after a long week. I used to hate them waking me up early in the morning to go, but I loved it once I got there, put my toes into the sand, and started swimming. Those were fun times before my parents' relationship went sideways and we stopped socializing as a family or spending weekends picking wild mangoes and hanging out at the beach." The last part slipped out. Thankfully, the dark hid her embarrassment.

Michael's gaze remained on the ocean as they continued strolling down the beach. "What happened with your parents?" he asked after a few minutes, as if he'd used the time to deliberate. This walk on the beach was meant to be about her relationship with Shawn, not her family, and not about her parents' complicated relationship with each other and her.

The sounds of the ocean hummed in the background, and she tried to think of how to answer. There was only one way to answer, with the truth. *Deep breaths!*

"There was no specific event. Just a small series of little events that tore us apart because they didn't try to fix them. Nothing dramatic."

"Are your parents still married?"

"Yes. They're dedicated to spending the rest of their lives tormenting each other—and me."

"Must be hard."

"Sometimes, but we've morphed into a comfortable bitterness no one wants to shake."

"It's never too late to change things."

Rachel wished that were true, but her parents deflected every attempt she made to mend their relationship with each other and her. They were too old to change, and "This is our life now," was their motto. She still had trouble believing it whenever she looked at the photos from her childhood. They'd been smiling. Happy. "What about your parents?" she asked, desperate to talk about something else as her eyes began burning.

"My mother is a saint, and my father is...difficult. Somehow they make it work, but I suspect that has more to do with wanting to keep up appearances."

That sounded about the same as her parents. In private they barely spoke but in public they appeared to be a happy couple. They were never overly affectionate, but they played the part around other friends and family. Rachel never wanted that for herself. Ironically, she almost ended up that way when she accepted Shawn's proposal.

"So, what happened with Shawn?" It sounded like he too wanted to shift the conversation away from their families. Although to her, past relationships weren't a far enough shift.

"At the time, I thought it was because I wasn't ready, but to be honest, I knew we weren't a good fit. On paper he was, but deep down something was missing. I craved a more profound connection. One that we both deserved. The moment I said yes to his proposal, I knew I shouldn't have. Everything with our relationship went downhill from there. I hoped we could remain friends, but the truth was we were never friends to begin with, and that was a big problem. I didn't feel comfortable enough to share my real dreams with him, and how I really felt about things that were important to me. In the end I felt like it was my fault because I hadn't been honest about who I was and what I was looking for."

"Breaking off the engagement took a lot of guts." Michael's hand rested on her shoulder. "A lot of people get married to people they don't really love or aren't their true self with until it's too late. They've spent years of their lives with someone they never really loved or pretending to be someone they weren't and get divorced once they realize it. Some never divorce and live in misery."

Rachel knew it hadn't happened to him because he said he'd never been married. Or had he and just kept it private? "Thank you." She longed to rest her head on his shoulder, but refrained. He removed his hand moments later. Michael had always been honest with her, so she doubted he'd keep something as big as a marriage from her. Or would he? They'd never had that conversation in their dreams and while she'd never gotten anything but an honest vibe from him, the truth was she really didn't know Michael well to assume anything.

That revelation saddened her as she thought of the intimate moments they'd shared and her mind raced with what else he could've lied about. Did he really have a wife or a girlfriend back home, or at each location his family had a business? He could and no one would be the wiser, least of all her. Her stomach churned thinking about Michael not being the man she thought. Could he really hide that much from her?

Why not? Rick had for months before she discovered he was manipulating their entire relationship, making her think she was the only woman. In fact, he was dating two others in the office. She should've called it off the moment she found out they'd start working together, but Rick had convinced her they would be fine if they kept their relationship secret from other employees. Turned out he made the same arrangements with the other women.

They left the company when they found out, but she only stopped her relationship with Rick. She wasn't about to give up a job she loved because of him. After trying multiple times, he became upset when she rejected him so quickly and wouldn't give their relationship another chance. Shutting people out was always easy for her since she didn't let anyone in. Once Rick gave up trying to rekindle their relationship, he shifted to trying to make her life a living hell at work, but she didn't let it get to her.

No, Michael was nothing like Rick. And while he might keep personal secrets from her because of their working relationship, she was one hundred percent certain he didn't keep anything from her in their dreams. He was open and shared every detail with her as much as she did with him. There were no secrets—no walls or barriers between them in the dream world. Everything about her was an open book for him to read and learn whenever they were together.

Rachel's heart clenched, wishing the same was true when they were awake. The walls she always had were firmly in place, and not just because he'd be leaving soon. The possibility of a real relationship with Michael was terrifying. People had long-distance relationships all the time, and while Ireland was a long way away, she'd seen people give up their lives in other countries to move to Cayman with someone they loved. *Could we do that for each other?* No answer came.

CHAPTER 7

Rachel watched her coworkers from the edge of the bar during the company monthly social, although it hadn't happened the last few months because Rick thought it cost too much money. Thankfully, she managed to convince Michael it was a good idea, to ease tensions due to the merger. *Go join!* Grabbing her champagne glass from the bar, she took a deep breath and a step in their direction.

"Enjoying yourself?"

Michael's voice startled her, nearly causing her to spill the champagne.

"I'm sorry. You were over here by yourself, so I thought I'd join you."

Rachel laughed. "At least you didn't say 'Do you come here often?'"

Michael gave her a strange look before smiling.

Did his reaction mean he was having the same dreams? Hell if she knew. They'd been tap dancing around each other for a couple of weeks now and Rachel didn't know if his reactions were because of a shared memory in their dreams or part of their growing attraction. The experience put a strange atmosphere on their interactions, and a familiarity that confused her at times. She took a sip from her champagne glass. "Thanks again for saying yes to this social. Everyone really needed it."

"Agreed. It's a nice break from work." His gaze shifted to the staff scattered about the room before settling on a woman in the corner with bright purple hair. "Who's that?"

Rachel's gaze followed his. "She's a tarot reader. I thought it'd be fun." Skylar would be insulted at such a simple label for what she did, but psychologist didn't really fit her role tonight.

"Does she have a crystal ball?"

Rachel laughed. "I don't think it works like that anymore. Do you want to give it a try?"

"I will if you do."

Rachel shrugged. "Sure." Maybe Sky would sense something from Michael.

They strolled over to her table and took a seat.

Skylar was close to her own age of thirty with almond-shaped eyes that radiated wisdom, giving the impression she was much older. She wore a simple black dress that hung on her slim body and one of her hands was covered with a henna tattoo, something she did when hired for events which wasn't too often now that she had her practice.

"Hi. Please have a seat."

"Hi, Skylar." Rachel greeted with a smile.

"Rachel."

"You two know each other." Michael stated the obvious.

"We went to school together," Rachel answered.

"Aww. So, you know all of Rachel's secrets?" he joked.

The women grinned, but neither responded.

"So, how does this work?" Michael asked, taking the hint.

"That depends on you and what you're looking for. I can do a reading with cards, or an energy reading."

Energy reading? Sklyar rarely offers those in this kind of setting. What is she up to?

"What's an energy reading?"

Skylar beamed. "Well, I read your aura and give you advice based on what I uncover. A card reading is less involved."

"I'll take the card reading," Michael said quickly.

"Good choice. Readings can be very personal, but an energy reading is much deeper." Skylar's gaze shifted to Michael and then her.

Rachel glanced at him. "I can leave if you like?"

"Stay."

Skylar took several deep breaths before reaching for the cards and starting to shuffle them. "Some of your energies are blocked from past pain, but I see they have been clearing up since you met someone. In your dreams. The connection you have with this person is special. You called each other in now because you're ready to heal the pains from your past lives together and be joined in this lifetime."

This isn't the time or place, Skylar. He'll definitely pick up the hint. Glimpsing at Michael revealed his expression didn't change and Rachel relaxed a bit.

Three cards jumped out as Skylar was shuffling. "I'll be able to tell you a little more from the cards. Perhaps give you the answers you seek."

Now we're talking!

"The lovers. The sun. The tower."

"What do they mean?" Michael asked.

"For you they mean the person you're dreaming about is your soulmate. They're dreaming of you too. You have the chance to find the kind of happiness you've always wanted, but there will be a tower moment. You both have a lot to learn still about how to love yourselves and each other."

Rachel glanced at Michael, but his gaze was fixed on the cards, as if trying to see something in them that Skylar hadn't seen. *What is he thinking?* She couldn't tell from his expression. It was the same one he had in meetings when he was digesting everyone's conversation before speaking. That could be bad or good.

"Let me pull cards for the other person." Skylar shuffled the deck again. This time more cards jumped out. She flipped them over in front of them but studied the cards for a moment before answering. "This person is as torn as you. They want to be with you, but they're afraid of how that will change your lives. Hmm. I think it's because you don't live in the same country."

The tension between her and Michael radiated, and she sensed his urge to bolt was as strong as hers. Sky has mentioned they were soulmates before, but what did that even mean? Rachel hadn't been brave enough to ask.

"You both care deeply for each other, but something is blocking you from joining in the earthly plane and keeping you stuck in the dream world. Wait. No. You do know each other here—you just don't realize it."

Those words hit a nerve. Michael stood. "I need a drink. You want something, Rachel?"

She nodded and watched as he strolled over to the bar, ordered a drink, and knocked it back before signaling for another one.

"He is the man you're dreaming about," Skylar stated.

"Yes." Rachel's head was still reeling from everything Skylar said to Michael and the reading she did for his person. Her.

"You've got a long difficult road ahead of you, Rachel, but you mustn't let anyone stop you from reaching for your dreams or keep you from being who you want to be."

41

Before Rachel could respond, a group of staff rushed to the table. Everyone wanted to have a turn. Sky gave her "we'll talk later" glare.

Should she use this moment to talk to Michael about it? She glanced around the room. Not tonight. *When? Tomorrow at work? Over dinner?* There was never going to be a good time, not with their work relationship. Looking at the counter, she realized he'd forgotten all about the drink she asked for and walked over.

"Sorry about that. I was distracted." Michael said when she lifted a glass of champagne.

"It's okay," she mumbled. *Who can blame him after Skylar's reading.* It was no doubt deeper than he imagined.

The silence that stretched before them was as excruciating as a drill during a root canal, neither making eye contact but glancing at the staff interacting.

"I need some air." Rachel's words broke the silence.

"I'll join you...if you like."

His hesitant expression matched her own as she debated. Would his presence make things more awkward? "Sure."

They headed outside the balcony doors, but if the staff and Rick watched them leave, Rachel made sure to stayed in a well-lit area. The last thing they needed to further complicate their relationship was rumors of a romance.

Outside, Rachel deeply inhaled the scent of the salt air from the ocean across the road, which combined with the fragrant trees in the surrounding landscape. A soft breeze caressed her face, and she closed her eyes, pushing aside the tension coiling inside her tight frame.

"Feel better?"

She smiled and took a sip of her drink. "Much."

The outside light from the building cast shadows across his face and a lump lodged in her throat. She had the urge to touch the smile that creased the edge of his mouth. Seeing him, being around him, especially when they were alone, filled her with dread and excitement that clenched her gut and sent shivers racing across her skin.

"That was a strange reading," Michael stated.

"I'll say." Rachel's heartbeat stuttered in her chest, waiting for his next words.

He dug his fingers into his hair. "Look, Rachel. I think we both know there's an...attraction between us, but given our working relationship, pursing anything would be a bad idea."

"And you're going back to Ireland after the merger."

"Exactly. Long-distance relationships never work."

Rachel arms crossed and gloom seeped into her bones, causing her chest to ache. If they did admit they were dreaming about each other, then what? He was leaving. The air between them stiffened and both of their shoulders slumped. Michael's gaze at the landscape below the balcony was as blank as the feeling in her stomach.

"Good. Then we both agree?" His tone was flat.

When their gaze met, the same expression reflected in each other's eyes.

Sadness.

CHAPTER 8

Across a field, Rachel walked toward him. Layers of a tartan kilt brushed against his bare legs, while the long folds of her dress pushed against the tall grasses and flowers blanketing the field. Her hips swayed provocatively as she approached. Was it on purpose? *Beautiful.* That was the only word to describe her. Her dark wavy hair blew wildly, and he couldn't wait to dig his fingers into the folds.

Rachel smiled and touched his cheek. He picked her up and swung her around until they fell on the ground laughing.

Michael caressed her cheek. "I missed you." *God she smells good.* He never remembered smelling in his dreams before, so it was an unexpected sensation. But around her every sense was heightened.

"I know." A cocky grin tugged her lips.

He pinned her when she tried to move. "Say it."

"Say what?" She looked up coyly.

She laughed when he tickled her, then attacked her neck with nibbles. "Okay, I give! I missed you too." She traced his lips with her finger.

Michael shivered. Being so close to her and not touching every inch of her skin was torture. He wanted to make her his in every way, but he didn't know what would happen. They were in a dream, but their connection was different. Their dreams were unique. He knew that, but what he didn't understand was why now? The reader had said they'd called each other, but Michael wasn't so sure. He didn't remember calling in love. He'd been too busy with work and traveling. The revelation by the reader had surprised him, especially the word *soulmates*. Once the shock wore off, and reality sank in, sadness had filled him, knowing that she was the person in his dreams, and he'd have to leave her behind.

That first night they met in his dream, and he saw the empty sadness in her eyes, he knew he had to introduce himself. He'd seen that look reflected in his own eyes. In that instance he had connected with her, and when she looked up at him with those beautiful soft brown eyes, he was lost.

Her nibbling his ear broke through his thoughts. "You keep doing that, and I'll have to ravish you right here."

"Promise?" She gazed up with dark eyes.

He groaned. There was nothing he would like more. He settled instead for a kiss, softly at first, but it became heated, as their tongues sucked, danced, and licked.

He unlaced the strings of her bodice and pulled it down to reveal her naked flesh.

"Beautiful," he whispered, caressing her neck and lowering his head to nibble her shoulders.

Rachel moaned and dug her nails into his back as he captured one of her nipples in his mouth.

Michael pushed up the folds of her dress and pulled at her underthings. He needed to feel her warmth. He looked up to see her hair spread out around her, her eyes closed and from her mouth came moans of pleasure as his fingers dipped into her wet, soft warmth. She shivered and shouted her release, sending the birds in the trees above scattering like butterflies. He shivered too. Their minds were joined and he experienced each wave of pleasure that rocked her body. It was like nothing he'd ever experienced.

He kissed her forehead and pulled her close. The reader said they were soulmates, and their unique connection said as much. His emotions were strong, undefinable. But love?

"There's something I need to tell you. Something I've wanted to tell you for a long time, but..."

"You can tell me anything," Michael assured her, tucking a stray strand behind her ear.

"I'm Rachel. The one you know outside of your dreams."

"I know. The reader told me."

"No. You don't understand. We're in my dream, not yours."

Michael laughed. "That doesn't make sense."

"I know it doesn't, and I wish I could explain in a way that made sense, but there's no way."

The smile on Michael's face wavered. "I knew something wasn't right with our attraction."

"I planned to tell you."

"Really? Why didn't you tell me when I showed up at the office?"

"Seriously?" Rachel pulled her garments together. "That's exactly what I want to say to the new owner of the company I work for. 'Oh, I'm the woman you met in your dreams and made out with.'"

"What about later when we were alone, at dinner, lunches? There were other opportunities!"

"It's not the kind of topic to bring up at the office, or any time. I didn't know you well enough."

"And after we got to know each other in the weeks we worked closely together?"

"I was scared."

"Of what?" He paced around her, kicking up the grass.

"Of what you'd think of me knowing you were in my dream. People don't react well when they find out."

"I'm not just anyone, Rachel."

"I know that, but I couldn't take the risk."

"You lied to me this whole time, Rachel. That's what really hurts the most. We were getting to know each other both in and out of our dreams—your dreams—and you weren't honest enough to tell me the truth. I was beginning to fall for you, Rachel." His voice croaked. "Inside and outside of our dreams. And every day you saw me, felt our connection, looked me dead in my eyes, and continued to lie to me. I just don't know if I can trust you again."

"I know," she said quietly. "I chose to tell you tonight because of what Skylar shared." He'd said he was falling for her, and she longed to tell him she felt the same, but the words stuck in her throat. He wouldn't believe her now.

Michael stopped pacing before her. "It isn't the best time, Rachel. That would have been the next time I saw you here. Or when we had lunch together."

Rachel lowered her head. He was hurt and angry and nothing else she could say would convince him how difficult it had been to keep this secret, and that there was more to it than just their working relationship. "I'm sorry," she whispered, as her own fears settled around her as the sting of his rejection scorched her.

She left him in the dream, not waiting to see what he would do or say next.

When she woke up, the spots on her ceiling stared back down at her. Her throat ached like someone had raked their fingernails along it. She hugged the other pillow tightly against her frame, waiting for the comfort it usually brought her, but none came. The pain in her throat changed to squeezing, until her mouth and neck ached.

The back of her eyes burned until tears welled up in her eyes, and she expected them to disappear the way they usually did. Instead, they turned to pools and overflowed down her face. A noise she hadn't heard in years burst out of her and she realized she was crying. Her body shook with the strength of the emotions coursing through her. She curled into the fetal position and wept until she was too exhausted to move.

CHAPTER 9

S hock raced through Rachel as Rick's words sank in. *Michael is gone.* She was grateful to be sitting down because her legs might've given way if she wasn't. Gone? How was that possible? *He got on a plane and left.*

Was it because of what happened last night? Or for another reason? The reason didn't matter. He was gone. The ache gnawing at her heart was excruciating. Tears pricked at the back of her eyes, but she held them back with sheer will. *I am not going to cry in the middle of a meeting.*

"Rachel!" Rick practically shouted her name to pull her back to the meeting. The staff's eyes settled on her.

"Yes, Rick?"

"Michael left it to me to continue with the merger until he's able to return, but I'd really like to see that everything is done so there's no need for him to return."

I bet you do. Michael being away gave Rick the opportunity to cover up whatever he was trying to hide. She knew him well enough to know that was the story. What she didn't know was what, but if she had to guess it was an overused expense account with charges that were not all business related.

"I'll help you however I can." *Be damned if I'll help you cover up anything.*

"Thanks, everyone," Rick said.

Rachel stood to leave too, but Rick gestured for her to remain.

"Do you have any idea why Michael left early?"

"No. I thought he spoke with you."

"He only said he had business to take care of with another company and would let me know when he'd return."

Business? Is that the real reason?

Rick's steel eyes pierced her. "You two seemed cozy on more than one occasion over the last two months."

"There was no cozy," Rachel lied. *Sort of.* "We're just work colleagues. Nothing more." At least the last part wasn't a lie. There was nothing more than what they had in the dream world and even that had crashed and burned. His early departure, although soul crushing, was better now than later, after their connection deepened. Breakups had always been easy for her, but last night's cry fest proved otherwise.

"Uh-huh." Rick remained unconvinced.

"Are we done?"

"For now." Rick stood. "But I want to meet with you after lunch today so I can see what Michael had everyone working on."

Rachel rose. *Rick only wants to know if Michael was close to finding out whatever he was trying to hide.* One thing was certain. She'd make sure to find it before he could bury it deeper.

"I'll send you an invite," Rick called after her.

Rachel opened the conference room door and walked back to her office, the heat of Rick's gaze burning the back of her neck.

Arlene was waiting for her when she reached her office. "What are you doing here?"

"Well, you weren't returning my calls, so I had to come and hunt you down." She stretched her plump frame in the office chair.

"You could've stopped by my house."

"So you could ignore my knocks on the door?" Arlene grabbed her purse from the other chair and stood, pushing a stray strand of hair away from her face. "I knew you'd be here and couldn't avoid me."

"I'm not avoiding you."

Arlene snorted. "You're a terrible liar."

"I've been busy."

"Too busy for lunch, or a phone call to say, 'I'm still alive and haven't died at my work desk'?"

Rachel shrugged. "You're the only one who doesn't believe my lies."

"You're going to lunch with me, and I'm not taking no for an answer."

"Perfect timing. I was hungry." Rachel laced her arm in Arlene's, the top of her head just reaching Rachel's shoulder. "But you do know you're paying, right?"

"And you do know this isn't just about feeding you, right?" Arlene pushed the elevator button.

"I know." She offered a smile, but her insides were stone. She hadn't told Arlene much about Michael other than they worked together, and she wasn't sure if she was ready to share details about him with anyone—even Arlene. With him gone, the memory of him and the moments they shared seemed like precious gold she needed to hide away from the world, only to be enjoyed when alone.

Somehow, she knew he wouldn't appear in her dreams. Whether it was because of the distance, or what happened between them last night, the reason didn't matter. He left, and all she had were the moments they shared.

When they reached the restaurant, Arlene didn't press her for answers the way Rachel expected. She just stared at her from across the table as if waiting for her to confess, making Rachel wish she'd just grill her and get it over with. "Fine. What do you want to know?"

Arlene shrugged. "What do you want to tell me?"

The truth was complicated, but somehow Rachel didn't think that would cut it with Arlene, so she decided to start with something less personal. "I think Rick is stealing money from the company and trying to hide it." She probably shouldn't say anything, but she knew Arlene wouldn't share anything she told her in confidence.

"Really?" Arlene didn't probe further.

Not good. Damn! She isn't going to let this go. Her attempt at redirecting the conversation fell flat. Maybe she could hold out until the end of lunch when she had to get back to work? No. Arlene wouldn't let her off so easily.

"Remember the guy I told you about from work?"

A victory grin lit up Arlene's face. "Yes."

"He left without saying goodbye. And I thought there was something special between us."

"Is he coming back?"

"I don't know, but even if he did, I don't think a relationship is possible."

"Why not?"

"I lied to him about something. Something important."

"Can you apologize?"

"I tried, but it was a kind of a big lie. And there's also the issue of distance. He lives in Ireland normally—not exactly close."

"True, but not impossible."

"I don't think he was interested in a long-distance relationship." Rachel swallowed to remove the tightness in her throat forming with every thought of Michael. "Let's talk about something else."

"Tell me about things at work. How is the merger going other than you suspecting Rick is stealing from the company?"

"It's almost finished. Rick's being a bigger jerk than usual to everyone in the office—if that's possible."

Arlene set her glass back on the table after taking a sip. "I don't know why you stayed working with that jackass, especially after what happened between you two."

"Because I love the job and the people that I work with."

"So, start your own business and take the people with you."

Arlene's words were so matter-of-fact, as if starting your own accounting firm was that easy. Rachel chuckled. "You have a million dollars lying around to help me start up?"

"Well, you don't have to take everyone with you. You could start with just you and go from there. I'm sure all your clients love you and would be happy to throw business your way and recommend you to other businesses. All those years should count for something, right?"

The idea sounded simple enough. It had Rachel thinking about the steps she could take until the reality of putting it into action and all that would involve and how her parents would react. The excitement that was starting to bubble to the surface was stamped flat before it had time to grow.

"I couldn't imagine starting a business right now, not to mention my clients and the staff need me. I couldn't leave them at the mercy of Rick."

Arlene didn't try to hide her disappointment. "You can't continue to live your life for other people and their expectations, Rachel."

Those were also Skylar's words about her road ahead, but Rachel was certain Arlene was talking about her parents. They were the only friends who'd been around long enough to understand and witness the strained relationship she shared with her parents. She started to disagree, but stopped and replied instead. "I'll take it into consideration."

Arlene's face lit up. "Yes! I'm going to hold you to that."

"I hope so."

She never thought starting her own business would be a serious consideration, but long after she finished lunch with Arlene, thoughts of being a business owner lingered.

Later that night she dreamed of walking into an office building she'd never seen before and on one of the doors was the name Miller Enterprises. When she walked inside, desk after desk with smiling people filled the space. The only unhappy part of the dream was the dark cloud hovering above everything.

CHAPTER 10

Rachel sat at her desk and stared at the blank screen before her. She glanced at the phone to check the time and to make sure it was working. It was. The days had crept by since Michael left unexpectedly almost two weeks earlier. Even though she left him alone after their last night together, a part of her hoped he'd change his mind and call her. Something. The phone stood silent on her desk, mocking her, and reminding her of the mistake she'd made. She'd kept the truth from him.

What did she expect? He lived thousands of miles away and they barely knew each other. So what if they met in their dreams and were supposed to be soulmates? Big deal! She'd only known Michael for two months.

What it boiled down to for him, she was sure, was that she lied, and her excuses didn't mean anything. Michael was angry and needed time to get over it or decide he couldn't get past it, and they'd never see each other again. Rachel didn't like the thought, but there was nothing she could do but wait to see what would happen. She hated waiting.

"In my office, Rachel." A voice buzzed from her phone.

Here we go. With Michael gone and Rick finalizing the merger, her work life had become more hellish—something she hadn't thought possible. She knew that tone and knew it wasn't good.

"Have a seat." He motioned toward the leather guest chair.

Oh, this is bad. He never asked her to sit. He prefers his victims staff standing while he dished out orders.

"I was disappointed by your involvement in the merger."

Rachel cocked her brow. Seriously? They both knew Michael had chosen her. *Just stay quiet and see what else he has to say.*

"Since I took over and continued with the audit that Michael requested, something troubling has come to my attention."

Troubling? Coldness settled in the pit of her stomach. Suddenly the memories of her dream last night came flooding in. The dark cloud. This was it. Her dreams weren't always clear messages like others and were left to interpretation.

"Turns out funds were being moved to a dummy company."

Tingles tightened her chest. *Does he think it's me?* Despite their turbulent relationship, Rachel was certain Rick knew she wasn't a thief. Her pursed lips loosened as the truth settled around her. That's what Rick had been hiding and why he wanted her to keep such a close eye on Michael. She'd pegged Rick for many things, but being a thief wasn't one of them. However, considering the lack of integrity in other areas of his life, this last one shouldn't surprise her. *How was I ever interested in a man like him?*

"We both know who's behind it and what needs to be done."

Maybe she was wrong. Maybe it wasn't him. Then who? No one in the office came to mind. When his steel gaze held her firmly, her innards did a swift but deadly kick. *He thinks it's me!* The longer their gazes held, the truth descended around her like a slow drizzle, soaking her to the bones. *He's pinning the stolen money on me.* Betrayal gnawed at her heart like a rabid dog before it shifted to rage. *Yeah, his lying, stealing ass needs to be dragged outside and dumped on the sidewalk.* This moment was the dark cloud in her dream. Darkness that threatened her own future and the success of her business.

"If you confess, I'll do everything I can to make sure you're not blacklisted."

Rachel couldn't stop her mouth from falling open, or keeping the rage from her eyes.

"Let me get this straight. You want me to admit to something I didn't do—basically cover for your stealing—and hope that you won't blacklist me on an island where news spreads faster than a wildfire? How much money, Rick?"

He placed his hands on his desk and linked his fingers together. "It's the only way."

"How much money, Rick?" she repeated through gritted teeth, her fisted hands shaking.

"Two million dollars."

Shock rocked her at his gall. Now she understood why he had kept certain accounts from her over the years, claiming they were high-end clients he wanted to pay his own "personal" attention to. He knew if she managed them, she'd spot the discrepancies and dummy company.

"Does this mean Michael found out?" Michael was thorough. A fact she'd noticed while working with him.

"Not exactly."

Meaning he either wasn't sure, or Michael hadn't uncovered everything. "So this is your solution? To pin it on me?"

Rick met her with silence and a steely gaze.

This time he'd gone too far, and she'd had enough. "My confession isn't the only option."

"Oh?"

"I quit," she said quieter than the turmoil inside her.

He snickered. "How convenient for you."

"That's where you're mistaken, Rick." She stood. "I stayed here this long because I liked working for this company, not you. And this isn't convenient for me since I know you'll do everything in your power to pin this on me and have me blacklisted, just to save your own ass, but I have one thing on my side."

A smirk tugged at the corner of his mouth. "What could you possibly have?"

"Integrity and clients who know and love me. And while I might lose some of them because of this. I know I'll get back on my feet. Thanks to you."

"To me?"

"Yes. Your lack of integrity in your life and the vile way you treat the people in this office will shout my innocence to everyone. They'll know it was you and not me who stole that money."

"I'll blacklist you to every accounting firm on the island," he threatened.

She leaned across his desk. "Do your worst, Rick. I'm going to be successful at anything I do, and you know there's nothing you can do to stop it. Just like I know everything in your life from this moment is going to go to hell, and everything bad that you've put out in the world is coming back at you with a vengeance."

Rick flinched but brushed it off with an arrogant laugh. "I'm not sure where all of this confidence is coming from all of a sudden, Rachel, but I have to say, it's sexy on you." He shifted in his chair. "Fine, you can stay, but you help me cover this up."

The man is a moron. "I'm not helping you cover up anything, and my quitting still stands."

His mouth opened to say something else.

"There's nothing you can say to make me to stay. You're an arrogant, nasty man who doesn't deserve the nice employees you have."

"I'll give you more money." Panic itched his face revealing what Rachel had known about him for months. He was a coward and he knew it too.

"Goodbye, Rick."

"I was the one who convinced Michael not to fire you," he called as her hand reached for the doorknob. She turned, failing to hide the shock plastered on her face. *Michael thinks I'm a thief.* Rachel shoved aside the betrayal crawling to the surface to make her cry.

"You were on the short list of people since you handled most of the million-dollar accounts," Rick added, his smug expression returning. "It won't just be me blacklisting you if you walk out that door."

While Michael had more power than Rick, what he didn't have was a reputation on the island and he couldn't stop any clients from deciding to work with her. If the slur came from Rick, she would be safe. Michael might limit her gaining high-end clients, but it wouldn't be the end of the world.

Her face wrinkled in contempt. "You no longer have any say over my life, Rick." She yanked open his office door and slammed it behind her. Rachel walked back to her office, packed the few things in her desk and said polite goodbyes to everyone who all but applauded her for finally leaving. She walked out the glass doors, her head held high even as her throat constricted. This was her only link to Michael. Not that it mattered anymore since he'd planned to fire her, while not even bothering to discuss his suspicions or ask for her help to uncover the truth because he respected her and their working relationship. Rachel choked back a sob as she put the box of her things in the back seat of her car.

They hadn't shared a dream since he left. A fact she accounted to either the distance or his anger at her deceit. Whatever the reason, their link was forever severed. She got into the driver's seat, started the car and drove toward her parents' house, swiping away the tears. She'd cry when she got home.

CHAPTER 11

Rachel glanced out the car window at her parents' house. Not your traditional Caymanian-style house with a wraparound porch, but it wasn't far off. The lawn and lush island landscaping were neatly kept. It was the home she'd grown up in that held beautiful and heartbreaking memories. On the walk up to the house, Rachel couldn't help but notice the beautiful blue house's paint had cracks and wasn't as pristine as it appeared from a distance, much like her parents' relationship.

Technically she didn't need to be here telling her parents she quit her job. Especially since they still treated her like a child who was unable to make her own decisions. Ironic considering the bad ones they made around their relationship with themselves and her and not to mention the embarrassment if they heard about her quitting from someone else. Cayman was too small an island for news not to spread. Who knew how Rick was going to react and what action he'd take to discredit her.

She was an adult, and no matter how desperately she longed for her independence from the constant need for her parents' approval, she respected and loved them. Like most families with deep-seated pain and resentment, theirs was no exception.

She was dreading the conversation, but the fallout would be worse if they found out about her quitting from someone else.

Rachel knocked on the white wooden door. Brian Miller's lean frame filled the doorway when he answered.

"Is everything all right?" His bushy brows narrowed.

The only time she visited them at home was for rare family dinners, or someone's birthday. They usually spoke on the phone or met at a restaurant. "It's better if I tell you and Mom together."

The smell of mothballs and her mother's favorite perfume assaulted her nose as she walked inside and sat on the couch. Karol Miller came out moments later, her usually neat salt-and-pepper hair out of place. She plunked her curvy frame in the rocking chair across from Rachel.

"Are you pregnant?"

The words hung in the air like a bad omen, stabbing Rachel with the level of cruelty in the tone. "No." Rachel's throat tightened, and her eyes already stung from unshed tears.

"That's right. You've been single since Shawn."

Another set of words meant to hurt her. Annoyance sprang up inside her from years of silence. "I quit my job today, and I'm going to start my own accounting firm." The shock and disappointment on both her parents' faces made the revelation worthwhile. She braced herself for the avalanche of questions and responses.

"It was a good job! Why did you quit?" her father asked.

"Do you know how risky it is to start your own business? Where will the money come from? What about your clients?" her mother demanded.

Rachel eased herself into the loveseat while she eyed them both. She let the silence linger because she knew it would annoy them along with the rest of her confession, not to mention the declaration they'd hate more than anything.

"I quit because they were going to pin the disappearance of money on me. And because it was time for me to leave. I've been wanting to start out on my own for a while now—I just didn't know how to tell you." Rachel addressed her father's question first before tackling her mother's. "I've been putting aside an emergency fund that I can use, but I'm leaning toward a loan and using my home as collateral. As for my clients. I'm hoping some of them will transfer with me or recommend me to other businesses."

"It won't be easy."

Brian's shock was now replaced with what Rachel hoped was pride and not disappointment.

"I know."

Karol stood and paced in front of her. "Why would they think you stole money? You've been with the company for years. You were a loyal employee."

"I didn't steal, and they needed someone to be the scapegoat."

"But why don't you fight it?"

"And stay with a company that doesn't trust me?" Not to mention there was no way Rick was letting her anywhere near a computer at the office. "They're not going to press charges because they don't have anything." At least that's what she was banking on. Rick was too much of a coward to take the risk. *How would Michael handle it?* She didn't know or care at this point. Besides, her quitting gave them both the perfect out. And the chance for her to spread her wings. "It's for the best, Mom."

"But won't people think you stole the money?"

"No one knows the truth but my old boss and myself." *And he won't be telling anyone the truth.*

"I know what I'm doing. And if it makes you feel better, I'll get a job with a firm if things don't take off after one year." *The hell I will!* She was enjoying the thought of having her own business. Those words pacified her mother, but the piercing gaze from her father said he didn't believe her. She would cross that bridge in a year. Now came the revelation her parents would hate.

"I dreamed about an office building with the name Miller Enterprises on the door, along with desks filled with people." She left out the part about the dark cloud and held her breath waiting for her parents' response. It'd been years since she mentioned her dreams to them since they sent her to every psychiatrist on the island at the time who tried to reassure them her dreams becoming reality was just a coincidence and her "tendencies" to talk about it would pass once she got older. She learned the hard way to keep them to herself and only share them with Arlene or Skylar since they were the only ones who understood.

Both her parents visibly flinched and looked at each other before glancing back at me.

"I thought you abandoned such ridiculous notions?" her mother admonished.

Rachel flinched internally but kept her expression neutral. "It's a part of who I am, not something to push aside," she finished boldly, even though it was a lie. She'd pushed it aside for them and to be normal to the people around her, even though they never saw her that way.

Brian cleared his throat. "I'm happy for you." It was his way of changing the subject. The way he always did when a difficult topic arose.

He'd been retired for a couple of years now and was likely being driven mad being at home with Karol all day since she'd stopped working two years earlier.

Her mother remained quiet and brooding, clearly still not convinced.

The rest of the afternoon was spent with probing questions from both parents: doubting ones from her mother, and business-related ones from her father, both indicating they didn't believe she could start and run a successful business. Her dream told her as much, and Rachel was determined to prove them wrong.

CHAPTER 12

Michael punched his pillow and adjusted it again. *Four weeks since I returned to Ireland, and I still can't get Rachel out of my head.* He'd tried to reach her through his dreams, the way he had before, but for some reason he couldn't. Maybe it was because of the distance or because he was still angry with her, or that she was blocking him from her dreams somehow. He read everything he could get his hands on about lucid dreams, but nothing was like his experience with Rachel.

As much as he hated to admit it, he missed her. Not just in his dreams, but seeing her face every day. Especially her shy smile and the nervous way she tucked a strand of hair behind her ear when you watched her intently.

Michael rolled onto his back and stared at the crown molding on his ceiling. Rachel had left him in her dreams after giving him the most intimate sexual experience of his life then dropping the bomb she did. The betrayal he felt years ago of a childhood friend ruining Connor's family had crashed around him and he couldn't help but lash out.

With each day that passed, his anger faded. He called himself a fool for just walking away without saying goodbye, but then she did the same to him. Lean fingers raked through his hair. Part of him wished he'd never met her. Then he wouldn't have this wretched feeling in his stomach every time he thought about her.

Her deer-in-the-headlights expression after she confessed tugged at him, but angry words had still spewed from his mouth before he could stop them. What hurt just as much was that she didn't trust him enough to tell him the truth.

The circumstances, good or bad, shouldn't have made a difference, he deserved the truth. Michael kicked the covers off. What was done was done and there was nothing he could do about it—nothing he wanted to do about it. *Liar!* His unwelcomed sister's voice echoed.

Unlike his sister, he didn't make impulsive decisions, especially when it came to his personal life. Their soulmate connection didn't matter. *Damn it!* He punched and adjusted his pillow again trying to convince himself that was true.

Rachel was still on his mind when he got up and left for work. His father's call to deal with a company issue came at a good time, or bad, depending on how he looked at it. It provided the opportunity to avoid Rachel but didn't remove the inevitable fact that he'd see her again when he returned to Cayman. Although he'd asked Rick to move forward with the merger, the decision had been impulsive. Truthfully, Rick was the worst choice since Michael suspected he was stealing money from the company. The sooner he returned to finish his investigations and find the truth, the better. He didn't trust Rick.

"Rick from the Cayman Islands on line two."

Speak of the devil. "Michael here."

"Michael, Rick. Just want to let you know I took care of the problem with the misappropriated funds."

Misappropriated. That is putting it mildly. The person had stolen from the company. Michael had cursed when he got on the plane as he remembered he hadn't dealt with it. He'd planned on delaying his trip home so he could deal with it and spend more time with Rachel. That plan went out the window after his father called and she revealed her secret.

"How did you deal with it?"

"I fired the person who was responsible."

"Oh, you were able to find out who it was?"

"Yes. They were the only person who had access to the files other than me."

"Who was it?" Michael asked even as dread punched him in the gut. From what he remembered Rachel was the only other person who had access to that level of accounts. Rick couldn't mean her. *She is many things, but not a thief, right?* Michael didn't peg her as a liar either, but what did he know?

"Rachel Miller."

Michael's stomach dropped to his toes, but he managed to respond with a steady voice. "How did she take it?"

"As best as can be expected I suppose. It wasn't easy. She's been with the company a long time."

"Longer than you?"

"Yes, she was here when I started."

"Were there suspicions of her before?"

"Not that I'm aware of, but who knows why people do the things they do?"

"Why indeed." *He's lying.* Michael knew it as surely as he knew that Rachel was innocent. He may not know her well, but he always went with his gut when it came to business, and it hadn't failed him yet.

After hanging up, he tried calling Rachel, but realized she only had a company phone, and he now had no way of reaching her.

Trying to contact her through other staff who might alert Rick wasn't an option.

Being fired for stealing in a community as small as Cayman would ruin Rachel's career so he needed to act quickly. Michael called in his assistant and got started on a list of important things to take care of, including getting him on the next plane to Grand Cayman. His father wouldn't be happy, but he'd get over it once he explained the situation regarding the money. Not Rachel. His father wouldn't be open to Rachel for so many reasons—yet another reason why their relationship wouldn't work.

They would see each other when he returned to Cayman and he would fix this issue that Rick created and restore her position with the company, but nothing would come of what happened between them in the dream. The best damn dreams he'd ever had. The best connection he'd ever had with any other woman. *Stop talking shite, Michael. You barely know the woman.* That was true on one level, but on another, it was like they'd known each other for a lifetime.

How many people had those kinds of connections? Not any I know, or at least none that would admit it.

Connor would be the best person to speak to about it. The man read everything and could find you a book on any topic. Michael would stop by his bookstore later. Hopefully, he wouldn't ask him why. *Not likely.* He was an inquisitive bastard, and the status of best friend made it worse. He might be able to offer insight Michael hadn't considered. Something that explained the connection and dreams that he and Rachel shared. Anything that provided insight might make it easier for him when he returned to Cayman and faced her. Thinking about the emotional and physical intimacies they shared almost made him want to blush. It was like having a romantic comedy and porn running in his head at the same time.

Those confidences were another reason he felt so betrayed. They had shared a few private conversations outside their dreams, giving her the opportunity to tell him it was her dream, and he was the man she was dreaming about. Suspicions had circled around them, especially after the tarot reader all but declared they were soulmates. Rachel knew and didn't say anything. Not even in their dreams.

Would another tarot reader be able to tell him? Maybe they could help him understand his connection to Rachel. But where would he find one? Michael didn't have the faintest idea. He certainly couldn't visit one in person. And speaking with Skylar wasn't an option since she was friends with Rachel. A quick search on his computer produced a long list, along with the ones who worked online. He chose one with the most reviews and made an appointment at a time when he'd be at home. *What the hell are ya doing?* jumped into his mind moments after he booked his time.

He needed more data about his connection with Rachel. But the answer he wouldn't get was what to do next, because there wasn't one that would resolve the issues that kept them apart now. *Distance. My family.* The real answer he wanted was what life would be like without her. If it was anything like the past weeks, misery was a word he was going to become familiar with, whether he wanted to or not. Maybe the answer he should look for was how to remove the memories of her from his mind, and their connection from his life so he could live in peace.

Was that even possible? Was that what he wanted? Those were more questions he didn't have the answers to.

CHAPTER 13

Rachel closed her computer screen. *Another two clients signed on.* What she wouldn't give to call Rick and rub it in his smug face—and maybe her parents' a little too. She knew he'd let her resignation stand instead of telling everyone she was fired for stealing even with his threats to ruin her reputation. He couldn't risk anyone digging too deeply into those accounts.

Accounting was a profession she got into because it was what her parents did. It wasn't something she was crazy about, just happened to be good at it. However, one thing she enjoyed was helping clients understand their finances and seeing the relief on their faces when they found out things weren't as bad as they thought, or that she could help them fix the disaster they'd created for their business.

She poured herself another cup of coffee and looked out the apartment window. Three weeks ago, Rachel thought she was where she wanted to be in life. A good, steady, well-paying job. She was single, but that was okay. Never did she imagine someone would invade her dreams and rock her life to the point where she was unhappy with what she had achieved, and wanted more. Remorse the size of Texas weighed on her with each day. She'd wanted Michael to come after her, but she was the one who left him in the dream and should have called him. Something.

Images of his angry face and the hurt expression etched in his eyes reminded her she'd made the right decision. She'd left him to save herself from his rejection. Now she knew how Shawn felt when she broke off their engagement. The difference was, she felt more for Michael in the short time they knew each other than the two years she'd been with Shawn.

Her doorbell rang. Behind the door was Arlene.

"Get dressed. We're going out," she ordered.

"I don't feel like going anywhere."

Arlene put a hand on her plump hip. "Are you gonna get dressed, or do I have to drag you inside and do it for you?"

Rachel knew she meant every word of her threat. It'd been three weeks since losing her job and during that time she had avoided everyone, including Arlene and Skylar. The moment Arlene saw her face, she knew something was wrong, and now Rachel was going to be forced to talk. She was just grateful Skylar wasn't here with her. Rachel could only handle one best friend at a time.

Arlene followed her into the bedroom and sat on the bed while she rummaged through her closet for something to wear.

"Put on something pretty."

Rachel rolled her eyes. "I don't want to meet men."

"Okay, then tell me what's wrong."

Rachel shuffled through a few shirts before coming across a simple, but modest black dress. She pulled it out and held it up. "How's this one?"

"That bad huh?" said Arlene. When Rachel didn't answer she continued. "It is the guy you told me about, because you lost your job, or something you haven't told me—your best friend—about?"

Rachel kept her back turned as she headed toward the bathroom to take a quick shower and get dressed.

Arlene was lounging on Rachel's bed, playing with her phone. "Better. You don't look like death warmed over anymore."

Rachel cracked a smile.

"Wow, he did some number on you if you don't laugh at my jokes." Arlene sat up. "Why haven't I met this guy who's toppled your perfect little life?"

"It's...complicated."

"Oh. I'm liking him already." Her face crinkled. "He's not married, I hope—no, it couldn't be that. Someone you work with? Is that why you got fired? Hot sex in the supply room?" she asked, hopeful.

Rachel shook her head. "Not exactly."

"In your office or..." her voice heightened with excitement, "the staff lunchroom table?"

Rachel gave her a look of horror.

"Okay, I've gone too far. What do you expect if you don't give me any hints?"

Rachel stood before her dresser, picked up the brush and applied a light layer of powder. "He was involved with the merger."

"Ah, a temp?"

"Kind of."

"Would you just tell me already?" Arlene demanded.

Rachel's hand paused in the middle of applying her lipstick. "He's the owner of the company we merged with."

Arlene let out a low whistle. "A brief affair with the boss? That's heavy, for you."

"There's more," she said quietly.

"More than that?"

Rachel fiddled with putting on her earrings. "I met him in my dreams."

She watched Arlene as the words sank in then responded, "Wait. I thought you said he was your boss."

"He was, but I met him in my dreams first."

A long silence followed as Arlene worked through the connection in her mind.

"Let me get this straight. The guy you met in your dreams turned out to be your new boss?"

"Yup."

"Well, at least you saw him coming," Arlene joked. "Did he know it was your dream?"

"What do you think?"

"We're gonna need a lot of drinks for the rest of this story."

Rachel nodded in agreement.

Two hours later, Arlene put down her empty glass of her second drink. "Man!"

Rachel smiled. Arlene had been saying that word a lot after she told her the whole story.

"And you just left him there, alone?" She signaled the bartender to bring them another round of margaritas. "Are you sure he's not still there?"

Rachel laughed. "Yeah, I'm sure."

"And you haven't seen him since? Not even in your dreams?"

Rachel shook her head. "No. I think it was our proximity that made what happened possible. Now that he's back in Ireland, the connection is broken." At least that was her theory.

"Did you consider calling him?"

"Sure, but..."

"But what?"

How could she tell her friend she was terrified of getting rejected by him again, or worse, finding out that he was seeing someone?

"It's complicated."

Arlene stared at her for several moments. "You think what you found comes along every day? If I found something that special, I wouldn't let it get away. And even Skylar's tarot reading said you are soulmates. It doesn't get any clearer than that."

Damn. I hate it when Arlene is right. "I wish it was that easy, Arlene, but he's angry and feels that I betrayed him."

"So, say sorry, kiss, and make up."

Arlene made it sound so simple, but then what? He lived halfway across the world and thought she'd stolen money from his company.

"Can I buy you ladies a drink?"

"You sure can, sweetheart." Arlene spoke with so much sweetness, Rachel had to see what was causing it.

The noise of the club went silent, the people standing around them were motionless—even Arlene when she saw Michael by the bar. Dressed in a burgundy shirt that hugged his shoulders and black pants, he was more gorgeous than she remembered. She devoured him and when their eyes met, he was doing the same. Rachel resisted the urge to jump out of her seat and into his arms. *He's here! Is he here about Rick firing her, and why he isn't pressing charges. Or is he here for me? Is that what she wanted? Wait. How did he know where to find us?*

Everything started moving again when Arlene asked Rachel if she was okay.

"I'm fine."

"You look fine," Michael said with a grin.

She gave him a crooked smile. "Still using those cheesy lines?"

"Didn't want to disappoint you."

"You did a good job."

"You two know each other?" Arlene interrupted. "Wait. Are you the dream guy?"

Michael gave a quick nod.

"Ah man!"

Rachel laughed. That meant she knew the chance of chatting him up was out of the question.

Michael moved to the seat next to Rachel and she turned her chair to face him.

"I didn't think I'd see you again." Rachel reached for her margarita.

"I found out about you being fired."

Was that his reason for being here? Her heart sank to the grungy floor of the bar. "You were misinformed."

"Oh?"

"Rick wanted me to take the blame for his stealing. We disagreed. I quit."

"Hmm. I thought that was the case."

"You did?" *Wait. Rick told me Michael wanted me fired.* Rachel wanted to kick herself. Rick lied. She should've known better.

"Could we get out here and talk?" Michael gestured at the loud noise of the nightclub around them.

"Go for it. I'll be fine." Arlene kissed her cheek and gave her a "I know what you're going to do" wink.

Silence hung in the air like the ending scene of Mrs. Robinson when they rode away on the bus, and now she was wondering "What now" as they walked to Michael's rental and got inside. Music from the radio station kept them company as they drove to her apartment. A million questions raced inside Rachel's mind, and she didn't know which one to start with.

"How would you like your job back?"

Was he serious? Michael thought that's what she wanted from him, her job? Rachel yanked her heart from where it'd fallen at her feet.

"Are you okay?"

"I'm fine," she said through gritted teeth.

"No, you're not."

Maybe he wasn't so stupid after all. "You're right, I'm not fine."

"I fired Rick if you're worried about having to work for him. His position is yours," he offered.

She wanted to smack the smug look from his face that implied he'd solved the problem. "I don't want the job, or any other job you're offering, Michael." She longed to ask him to stop the car so she could get out, but hell if she was going to walk home.

His brows knitted in confusion. "I don't understand."

"Seriously?! I don't see you for over a month and all you have to say to me is a cheesy pickup line and to offer me a job?"

"What do you want me to say? You left me in the dream alone. That said exactly how you felt."

"You were mad. I thought you needed space to cool down," she said quietly, clutching her handbag.

It was only when he shut off the car that she realized they'd reached her house. She got out of the car and tried not to stomp to the front door.

Michael was standing right behind her when she got inside.

"Communication works both ways, Rachel."

The ball was in her court to reach out since she was the one who lied. He didn't say those specific words, but it was implied. He didn't appear angry anymore. *Was that a good thing?*

She turned and stood almost face-to-face with him. The tension was palpable, along with the electricity sparking from their closeness.

Soft blue eyes met hers, and his fingers gently touched her chin. "Do you want to know what I really wanted to say when I saw you?"

Was that a trick question? Her heart raced in anticipation as she nodded.

"The first thing I wanted to do was pull you out of that chair and into my arms. Then I wanted to tell you how much I missed you and couldn't get you out of my mind, no matter how hard I worked to get you out of there."

A lump caught in her throat.

Rachel wanted to throw her arms around him and hug him until no air could escape between them, especially when he stepped closer.

They'd never kissed outside their dreams. Would it be the same or feel different? Delight and dread raced through her as his hands captured her face and then his lips seized hers. Shockwaves rippled through her, making their connection tangible in ways the dreams hadn't. It was exhilarating and terrifying all at once.

Rachel wrapped her arms around his neck as his hand tightened around her waist. He slipped his tongue in her mouth and started a sweet battle that ignited more fire than she expected. Her insides melted and heat waves flashed across every nerve in her body as the kiss deepened. It wasn't like any other kiss she'd experienced before. Soft yet firm, his tongue made love to her mouth. Slow deep strokes assaulted every cell in her body. Rachel gripped the collar of his shirt tightly when his mouth moved from her mouth to her neck, where he made a trail of nibbles to her collar. Moans echoed in her entryway. Was it from him or her? When he captured her mouth again, she realized she didn't give a damn.

"Wow. That was better than our dreams," a breathless Michael said when their lips parted.

"You could say that again," she declared, before realizing she was still clinging to his shirt which was now a wrinkled mess. More than anything she wanted to yank it open and make the buttons fly everywhere, and then throw him down on her couch and kiss every inch of his bare chest.

"Stop looking at me like that or I won't be able to do what I know I need to," his words interrupted her fantasy.

"What do you need to do?" she asked in a teasing tone.

"Leave."

The word was a bucket of ice water on her skin, snatching her from her haze of desire and reminding her of the truth of their situation. A part of her wanted to ignore his sensible suggestion and say she didn't care, just wanted to be with him, but his solemn expression and a knowing deep inside stopped her. He was right. Nothing had changed. He lived in Ireland, and she lived here, and one night of hot passion—really hot passion—wasn't going to change that.

The emotions of when he left crashed into her. If that's how she felt after they'd made love in a dream, how would she feel tomorrow, or the next day, when he went home? It'd be nice to imagine she'd have a beautiful memory to cherish, but she suspected it would have the opposite effect and devastate her instead, leaving a gaping hole that couldn't be replaced, a bigger hole where her heart already was when he left the first time. She should let him leave, but the thought of him leaving without resolving what was left unsaid in the dream weighed on her.

"Would you like a drink? We can talk." Rachel took a step back, putting much-needed space between them, breaking the strong sexual tension binding them moments ago.

A pensive expression lingered on his face before he answered. "Ok." He proceeded to circle the room, looking at all the things in her apartment before he sat on the couch.

Rachel wished she'd cleaned up before she left. Underwear wasn't hanging from anywhere—she was too neat for that—but it could've been better.

Michael dug his hands into his pants pockets as he waited for Rachel to return from the kitchen with their drinks. His heart wanted to explode with the emotions she brought out in him when he first saw her. He didn't want it to end. He loved her, knew that the moment he saw her again. It was crazy, but he didn't care. He felt as if they'd known each other for a lifetime. At times being with her was so easy it was as like they were best friends becoming reacquainted...until their bodies came in close contact. Then it was something else entirely. He didn't quite understand it, but the tarot reader he visited had told him the woman in his life was a soulmate and life partner, confirming what Skylar had said and that they knew each other in another life.

Michael wanted her badly. It took all his strength not to take her to her bedroom and keep her there until she begged him not to leave her again. They had so much to talk about and he knew they wouldn't get to it if he touched her.

He didn't miss her trembling hand when she handed him the glass of wine, making him wonder what was going through her mind.

"I meant what I said about Rick's job. It's yours, if you want it."

Rachel's arms crossed over her chest. *Not a good sign.*

"Are you sure you're not offering it out of guilt?"

"No. You're the best candidate. I could bring in one of my own people, but after talking to the staff, they'd prefer you."

"Is that all you wanted to talk about?"

"You didn't answer my question." He held his breath. According to most of the staff she'd had her eye on that job for a long time. If she still wanted it, it would make his next question a difficult one for her answer.

"If you offered it to me a couple weeks ago, I might have taken it, but now…"

"Now?" he asked a little too eager.

"I'm doing what I really want to."

"What's that?"

"Have my own business. I've got a few clients now, and I landed my first big client this week."

"You could also do consulting."

"Hmm…I hadn't thought about that."

"You could keep your own schedule, work from home."

"I'm doing that now since I can't afford an office just yet," Rachel joked, "but consulting would be nice. A bigger chance of high-end clients."

"It's something you could do from anywhere."

"True."

"Like Ireland."

Her eyes snapped to his. Was that hope in them or fear?

"Are you asking me to move to Ireland with you?"

"Not exactly."

Rachel's eyebrows rose and he wanted to kiss them straight.

"Are you offering me a job?"

He didn't miss the disappointment in her voice.

"Not quite."

Rachel set her wine down on the table next to the couch.

"I'm confused. What exactly are you trying to ask me, Michael?"

He took her hand. "I'm asking you to come with me to Ireland, as my wife." Michael held his breath as he waited for her answer and watched every single emotion he knew move across her face.

"Your wife?"

"Yes. I'm asking you to marry me."

"We hardly know each other."

Michael's hand brushed against her cheek. "We know what we mean to each other."

"True, but marriage?" She rose and paced before him.

This wasn't the response he had expected. He knew it wouldn't be easy, and Rachel didn't strike him as someone who'd rush into things without thinking about them thoroughly first. "Why not marriage?"

"It's a big step."

"Is it because you were engaged before?"

"No. Yes...maybe." She sat back down on the couch next to him. "It's been a little over a year since Shawn and I broke up. I don't want to rush into something new."

"Not even with me?"

"It has nothing to do with you."

"Really? Shouldn't it, considering what we are to each other?"

"I guess, but..."

"You guess?!" He shot off the couch.

It was his turn to pace before her.

"Does what we share mean anything to you?" He raked a hand through his hair, making it a mess.

"Of course it does!"

"I couldn't sleep or eat properly when we were apart. I didn't even want to be with another woman!" *Damn, I hadn't meant to say that last part.*

"Really?"

"Have you been with another man?" Michael asked then wished he hadn't, not wanting to know.

"No," she whispered. "I felt the same way when you weren't here." Rachel stared at her shoes before she finally spoke. "Life without you was painful, Michael, but the truth is, I'm just starting my business and learning to say yes to the things I want for myself instead of what others want or think I should. Getting married would change all that."

A lump caught in Michael's throat at her rejection. "It wouldn't have to be that way. I love that you're doing your own thing. I just want to help you expand."

"True, but you're wanting me to grow it on your terms...and where you live."

Was that her way of asking if he'd give up his life to be here in Cayman? His father would never agree to him running the business here and neglecting other parts of the firm that required frequent traveling.

"I don't want you to give up what you have for me either, Michael." She went to him and placed a hand on his shoulder. "The truth is, we're in two very different places in our lives right now. And honestly, meeting you made me realize I still have a lot to learn about myself—who I want to be, what I want for my life. Until I sort that out, it wouldn't be fair to you, especially when nothing in our lives align right now."

Rachel was right. He knew it, but it didn't stop the ache that squeezed around his heart until it reached his throat. Instead of agreeing with her, he wanted to find the right words to persuade her to marry him and move to Ireland, but then it would only prove what she said. Not to mention selfishly serving his own needs. His father and mother would be upset, as Rachel wasn't their ideal future daughter-in-law. Her own confession about discovering what and who she wanted to be struck a chord. He'd felt the same after returning home, as if how he was living needed to change. He thought it was because Rachel wasn't in it. That was part of it, but the truth was, he'd been living his life for his family too long and needed to discover things he wanted for himself. Michael loved the work he did and even enjoyed traveling, but if he wanted to have a life that included a wife and children, it wasn't ideal. Not if he wanted to be present in his life—unlike his father, who was always gone during his childhood.

"You're right. I'm happy you're trying to build the life you want for yourself, and as much as I want to be a part of it, I don't if that means changing who you are and what you want."

Perplexity crimped her face before she responded. "Thank you for understanding." Rachel took his hands. "Not that I don't wish you'd fight for me a little more." A small smile tugged at her lips.

A warm smile pulled at his lips. "I thought about it."

"What will you do about Rick's position?" she asked, changing the subject.

"I'll need to fill the position before leaving. Any suggestions?"

"None that I can think of, but I can recommend a couple of people who can manage different aspects of the business until you find a replacement."

"I'd appreciate that. I'm in town for a couple of weeks, so you can call me on my cell." He waited until Rachel got her phone before he rattled off the number.

When he left a few minutes later, part of him wished she'd taken him up on his offer, but then what? Give up the business she just started for the unknown? Leave her friends and family behind for a man she barely knew, even with their connection? While it was painful knowing she was letting him go, it was the right thing to do.

CHAPTER 14

Michael smiled at the final candidate before they left the conference room. None of the candidates he interviewed were one hundred percent suitable, but there was one who had potential, with a little support from Rachel's company. He decided before he even started interviewing people that he'd hire her as a consultant to train the new person onboard. He thought about hiring her as a full-time consultant, but that wasn't feasible or sustainable, not to mention he wanted it for the selfish reason of having a connection to her through the company. Not a good enough reason to hire a person or consultant—even if she was the most qualified.

No. The sooner he cut ties with Rachel, the better. Staying connected to her would only make things more difficult if he had to see her, talk to her, and not be able to hold her or kiss her. Michael wished he'd suggested a long-distance relationship, but that was no better than his offer of marriage. He didn't want that kind of relationship with Rachel any more than she did.

This was the best option.

Michael would sign the contract with her company and head back on the first flight to Ireland. They could've had one last dinner or lunch, but what would be the point? Doing so would only draw out the pain of their departure.

He saw pain in her eyes when he shook her hand and caressed it softly with his thumb before pulling away.

His face had displaced his bravest smile as he left her in the conference room, even as his heart felt like it was being ripped from his chest with every step he took. It took strength he didn't know he had not to rush back, hold and kiss her until she promised to marry him, or at least go with him to Ireland to try and make things work.

Instead, he rushed out of the office, jumped into his rental car and drove back to the hotel, hot tears spilling down his face the entire way.

Rachel's shoulders slumped when the conference room door closed behind Michael. She eased herself into one of the chairs and clenched her fists in her lap to keep herself from bursting into tears. He chose to sign the documents at the end of the day so there weren't that many people left in the office, but enough that someone would see her cry and wonder what was wrong. Not the impression she wanted to make with the staff in her new role.

Michael had rushed out with barely a goodbye after caressing her hand. At least one last dinner would've been nice. *Then what?* More time together wasn't going to make his leaving any easier. One more moment wasn't going to ease their pain any more than one more kiss or night together.

Rachel left the conference room and said her goodbyes and see-you-Mondays to everyone who was still in the office and headed to her car as quickly as her heels could take her. It was only when she was on the main road with music blaring that she allowed the tears burning behind her eyes to fall.

As she drove, she realized it was one of the biggest business contracts that had fallen into her lap and instead of being thrilled it was also one of the worst moments of her life. The moment she'd never see Michael again. They might speak on the phone until the transition of the new hire was completed, but Rachel doubted they would speak alone. Emails and conference calls would be their interactions until the end of her contract. That wasn't how she wanted to start her new life.

Then she remembered something Sky told her about during their last session, energy healing. Rachel had only been half listening as Sky talked about it, but she remembered it had something to do with claiming back her energy from others and returning theirs to them. Now, more than ever, she needed her energy to get through everything that lay ahead, and live a happy life without him. She was going to need all the help she could get.

When she pulled into her driveway moments later, she dialed Sky's number and booked a session with her. Taking action toward things she wanted and being free from things that held her back in the past—like fear, the lack of confidence, and a slew of other things she was certain Sky would uncover made her feel lighter. A spark of happiness bloomed inside her.

CHAPTER 15

"You want me to what?" Michael asked Connor, who was on a ladder in his bookstore.

"Meditate. It's done wonders for me, mate."

"Next you'll be telling me to become a monk and live in a monastery."

"You're already a monk," Connor shot back.

He didn't respond as Connor wasn't far from the truth. He'd been with a couple of women in the last month, but being with them didn't stick. Not to mention he felt like an ass for using them just for sex—which is what'd he done. He hoped it would help him to move on from Rachel, but it didn't work. He should've stayed with the tarot reader who was helping him, but they were making him uncover things about himself and his childhood that he wasn't ready to deal with yet. The experience was like therapy—something he avoided.

"It will help to unblock you, man."

"Unblock me? I'm not constipated, ye arse."

Connor started laughing so hard he nearly fell off the ladder. After steadying himself, he grabbed a couple of books off the shelf and handed them to Michael.

"I'm talking about unblocking your energies ye daft fool. Here, read these. They'll explain more of what I'm talking about and help you with your healing."

"Since when did you get into all this spiritual stuff?"

Connor shrugged. "I've been doing a bit of it here and there over the years, but dived in hard the end of last year. Had me own shite to deal with you know."

"What shite?" Michael thought he knew everything about Connor since they'd been friends since grade school, but there was obviously something his friend didn't feel like sharing. *Or maybe you've been a blind man with your head up your arse!* Michael couldn't argue with that logic. He'd been so focused on work and getting over Rachel that he hadn't paid much attention to anything or anyone else around him, including obviously—his friend. "Anything you care to talk about?"

Connor's face raced from pensive to apprehension before he responded with. "Not at the moment, but maybe one day."

"Just know I'm here for you."

"I appreciate that."

"And I promise not to laugh when you tell me."

Connor grinned. "You definitely won't laugh, mate."

Michael thought about pressing him, but it was clear he didn't want to talk about it right now. Connor would tell him when he was ready.

Michael left Connor's bookstore and headed home only to find Shamus Doherty was waiting inside his flat. He didn't bother asking how he got inside. No one told Shamus no—not even the doorman who was supposed to keep everyone who didn't live in the building out.

"What can I do for you, Father?" Michael tried to sound casual even though his insides quaked the way they had when he was a kid and was called into his father's study. Showing up at his flat meant only one thing: serious talk.

"Aren't you going to offer me a drink?"

"You know where I keep the good Scotch. You've already helped yourself to getting inside my flat. Don't go all shy on me now."

Shamus's nose crinkled with annoyance. "You hang around with Connor too much. It causes you to be lax with your manners."

"This from the man who bullied or bribed the doorman to get inside my flat?"

Shamus ignored his comment and headed to the bar where Michael kept his liquor and poured himself a glass of Scotch.

"I came to talk about that woman consultant you hired to onboard Rick's replacement. I heard she was fired from the company." Shamus strolled over to the leather chair next to the couch and sat with a smooth ease that any James Bond would envy.

"You heard wrong." Michael poured his own drink and decided to lean against the matching couch instead of sitting and ignored his father's stern glare that meant he should sit. "She quit because Rick tried to pin the stolen money on her."

"You sure she didn't steal it?"

Michael stared long and hard at his father over the rim of his crystal glass before taking a drink. "I'm certain. Otherwise, I wouldn't have hired her."

"So, you didn't hire her for personal reasons?" Shamus leaned into the chair but still managed to sit ramrod straight.

"She is the best choice because of her familiarity with the company, the clients, and the staff. And she'd worked directly under and with Rick, so she knew his job well enough to train his replacement and offer support to the new hire and newly promoted staff. It was a logical option." *Is my father snooping into my personal life?* Michael had never mentioned his involvement with Rachel to anyone other than the reader and Connor. Connor sure as hell wouldn't tell his father, and he didn't share Rachel's name with the tarot reader, so there was no connection there.

"I see." Shamus set his drink down on the coffee table, making sure to use one of the coasters that were a gift from Michael's mother.

"Her company also gained popularity quickly with a lot of large firms which speaks volumes, too." Michael tried to keep the pride and admiration from his voice but failed miserably.

Shamus picked it up like a dog with a scent. "So, you got to know her quite well then during your visit?"

"As well as you get to know someone during a merger."

"You were there almost two months."

Michael shrugged. "And?"

"You two must have spent some late nights together..." Shamus pressed.

"Are you going to get to the point anytime soon, Father?" *Back off, old man! I'm not telling you anything about Rachel and me.*

"I was curious if anything happened between you because you don't trust people easily, and you trusted her enough to hire her...after what happened."

Shamus's expression gave nothing away, but Michael knew better.

"Your mother mentioned inviting Ciara for lunch on Sunday. I want to let you know, in case your attentions were elsewhere."

Michael was certain his father wouldn't approve of Rachel if he saw and got to know her—no matter how he felt about her. "Even if they were, she's thousands of miles away. Not exactly ideal for a relationship of any kind."

"It worked fine for me and your mother."

If only he knew about the times their mother cried when Shamus missed special family occasions. "Did it?" Michael challenged. His father always insisted family came first, but he was the first one to put them last in his life over the years. *Water under the bridge. But is it really?*

"So, you're fine with Ciara coming over for lunch on Sunday?"

"Do I have a choice?"

"No, but I could relay your unhappiness to your mother." An arrogant smirk twisted Shamus's lips.

His parents and Ciara's parents had been trying to connect them romantically for years. While they did date for a short while, Michael quickly realized she wasn't for him. She was reserved even when she drank—which was a lot—and did nothing but talk about business or her family's charities. Michael couldn't fault her for drinking. Her family put more pressure on her than he and his sister received combined. This was another reason she wasn't for him, her parents. Michael shivered in horror at the thought of them being his in-laws. His were bad enough.

Michael wanted someone warm, funny, and who wasn't afraid to show you inside their heart once you got to know them. Someone like Rachel. She hadn't crossed his mind much today, which was good and bad. Her face was starting to become a distant memory. A memory that shot through his brain painfully when he pictured her face, her smile, her laughter. *Gawd, I miss her.*

"You all right, son?"

"I'm fine," Michael shot back quickly before turning his back to Shamus so he wouldn't see his face and ask questions he didn't want to answer. "I have more work to finish up tonight, so you can see yourself out. Good night." Michael didn't wait for his father to respond but headed straight to his office and shut the door.

When he heard the front door close, he released the breath he was holding in anticipation of Shamus following him. One confrontation with his father was enough. The thought of spending lunch with his parents and Ciara didn't appeal to him. His sister, Regan, would be there, but she wouldn't be much of a buffer because nothing seemed to faze her.

A smile crept onto Michael's face. He'd invite Connor, who had a way of annoying his father in the best way possible. Not to mention it would remove the none-to-obvious hints about he and Ciara being single: "Why don't you spend time together since you made such a great couple before?"

Michael didn't need to spend more time with Ciara to know she wasn't for him. He was looking forward to the lunch on Sunday and the havoc Connor's presence would cause.

CHAPTER 16

Rachel tried to relax into the chair in Sky's room where she did readings, but every muscle in her body was so tense.

"Just relax, Rachel. Deep breaths, the way I showed you. I want you totally relaxed before the sessions starts."

Given that Sky performed tarot readings and did crystal charts, you'd assume her office would look like a mystical shop, but it was completely the opposite. Sure, there were crystals, cards, and other objects she had no clue what they were or did, but it strongly resembled a psychologist's office.

She suspected it was because Sky's father was a widely respected psychiatrist and she couldn't escape those deep roots, no matter how far her practices took her from them.

Rachel took deep breaths in and released short ones as she waited for Skylar to start.

"Thank you, angels, God, and Holy Spirit, for joining us in this session and leading me and guiding me with how to heal the blocks in Rachel's body."

Those words both surprised and soothed Rachel and she relaxed as Sky began the session. At first she felt nothing, but as more time passed a warmth started across her chest and then down her arms and began to heat up, but thankfully not anything uncomfortable. It wasn't a hot heat, but more of the kind you felt in a sauna than outside in the sunshine. The sensation was elating, as if someone was pulling the stress and anxiety she'd been feeling for months slowly from her body and replacing it with a calm and peace she hadn't felt in years. It was a bit like she felt when she was with Michael in their dreams, but different, deeper, more real.

Tears trickled from the corner of her eyes as the session continued and sparks of color flashed behind her eyes in various shades of purple that pulsed. The longer the session continued, the more lightness and happiness radiated from every pore of her body until the sensation was one of floating above her own body. The sensation should've frightened her, but it didn't. It was like between a dream state and being half awake, but much better because her body didn't have the heavy weight trying to pull her back to it. It was no longer physically there—just aware of it below her.

Before long the session was finished, and Sky was helping her to sit up and asking how she felt. Rachel couldn't find the exact words, so she just responded with, "Good." That word didn't begin to describe it, but it was the first one to come to mind.

"Your base, sacral, and solar plexus chakra are all good along with your heart, but your throat and third eye and crown were a bit heavy, so I worked on those the most to help to clear them."

Sky then proceeded to explain about what Rachel could do to help keep them cleared. The block in her throat chakra was obvious to them both. She wasn't telling her parents what they needed to be told. Sky also recommended a book she could read to understand her chakras along with a meditation to help with healing her physically, emotionally, and spiritually. She didn't know exactly how meditation could do that, but if it kept her feeling this amazing, she'd try anything. "I look forward to our next session," Rachel said, picking up her handbag from the couch and heading toward the door.

"I'm glad you found it helpful. The journey isn't always an easy one, but it will be worth it in the long run, Rachel."

She smiled. *If it is anything like today, it is going to be a piece of cake, especially once I get the nerve to speak with my parents.* "I'll pick up the book you recommended."

"And don't forget about the meditation. That's more important than the book."

"Okay." Rachel didn't know the first thing about meditation, but she was certain there was a YouTube video somewhere.

The session with Sky was not what she'd expected. She'd anticipated more questions about her past and her parents, but none of that had come up. Probably because Sky was one of her best friends, and she didn't believe in having friends as patients. Reading and doing energy work was one thing, but being her psychologist was something else entirely. Skylar was a stickler for the rules when it came to her other practice.

This was her first energy session, but certainly not her last. It took a while, but she finally relaxed.

Rachel was happier now that she was running her own business, and it was growing fast. She now had two staff members on her team and was scheduled to hire another if she got the next contract. The journey was amazing, but it came with a mountain of stress, especially with her parents stopping by at least once a week to "inspect" on how things were going.

The large clients she was taking on pacified them, but they still found something to complain about or thought she could improve on. The worst part was when they voiced their opinions in front of her staff before she could usher them into the boardroom.

Rachel hadn't mustered up the strength to tell them she didn't want or need their help, which as Arlene pointed out, was long overdue. It shouldn't have been that hard since she stood her ground when they tried to talk her out of starting her own business, but Rachel didn't have the heart to tell them.

Staying busy kept her mind off Michael, until she was at home alone. Arlene tried to set her up on dates, but she knew she wasn't ready for that step. Maybe one day, but not yet. Arlene had quoted the famous, "Best way to get over a man is to get under another one," but casual relationships were never a phase Rachel had gone through, and it didn't have any appeal for her now.

Rachel sensed she'd only be comparing them to Michael. Not good—even on a first date. No, staying single was the best choice for her now. As Sky said, she needed time to heal and connect with her higher self. She didn't exactly understand what that meant, but she was certain that with Sky's help and guidance, she would learn soon enough. She was strong enough to handle anything that came her way.

Rachel started her car, cranked up the music, wound down the window to let the air inside, and did something she hadn't done since she was a teenager: sang at the top of her lungs.

CHAPTER 17

Michael almost felt guilty about bringing Connor with him to Sunday brunch when he saw the annoyance etched deep into his father's face and the horror on his mother's, although she hid it well. Regan rolled her eyes and turned her attention back to the conversation she was having with Ciara, who was laughing and enjoying whatever Regan had to say. It was probably a joke about Connor. He decided to find out and strolled over, not to mention he didn't particularly want an earful from his parents about bringing Connor.

"What are you ladies discussing?" Michael asked. Connor had followed him, having grabbed a drink first.

"We were talking about bookstores and how they're becoming obsolete," Regan said with a sly grin.

Next to him Connor winced, but quickly replied, "Along with spoiled, rich debutants."

Ciara gasped. Regan's expression remained calm before she broke into a chuckle. "Really Connor? Debutants? We're called socialites now and our charity work helps millions of people around the world."

"And how certain are you the money reaches the people who really need it?"

"I'm certain."

"I see. So you actually go to these places and speak to the people your money supposedly impacts? No, wait. That would require getting your hands dirty. Something Dohertys aren't interested in. But you're happy to throw money at the problem. No offense, lad," Connor said to Michael, but his eyes never left Regan's face.

"None taken."

"My hands get all kinds of dirty, Connor. You'd know that if you bothered to leave your bookstore or lift your head from a book and look around you occasionally. You'd see a lot of things you keep missing out on." Regan locked her arm with Ciara. "If you'll excuse us, we're going to get some fresh air before lunch starts." The young women headed out one of the side balcony doors.

"And another win for Regan," Michael elbowed Connor.

"It would appear so." His friend's brows knotted in annoyance.

Michael laughed. "There's always next time."

Shamus and Moira were waiting for them as they headed to get another drink.

"Nice to see you haven't changed, Connor. Still insulting those who are better than you."

Michael winced at his father's words. Even his mother looked surprised. While she might think it, she was far too polite to let the thought cross her lips.

Connor didn't miss a beat. "Not better. Just richer."

"Isn't that the same?"

"Not even close."

"Class and breeding will always win out, Connor, and you constantly insulting my daughter and my family only confirms that belief."

"You can believe it all you want, Shamus, but that doesn't make it true. It's admirable that your family are generous with your money in ways that others aren't, but until you know the real impact it can make in the lives of the people you send it to, or make sure that it does, you will never know the true meaning of charity and what it means to be a good human being—regardless of all the class and breeding you have." Connor headed outside himself, but on the opposite side of the house from Regan and Ciara.

"Was that really necessary, Father?" Michael asked.

"Of course it was," Shamus responded with enough venom that implied the truth of Connor's words hadn't fazed him. "I can't have him insulting our family every time he comes to my house."

"He's just trying to get you to see another side of things. That's all he's ever tried to do."

"Our charities help people. And because of our class and breeding, we are able to do so. We have the money and the means. What other side is there?"

"That there's more than just giving money. It's about compassion for the people you give that money to, and getting to know their real needs. Not what you think they need."

Shamus snorted. "Don't be preposterous. We know what they need and make sure they have it."

Michael didn't respond, knowing it would be a waste of time to argue. Like every other topic he'd tried to change his father's mind on, nothing changed, and Shamus's opinion remained the same. Nothing and no one was going to change that. In that moment he was grateful Rachel had turned him down and wouldn't have to deal with his father. Regan would love her because he loved her, and his mother would come around, but not his father. He would've made her life a living hell. He wouldn't wish that on anyone, especially the woman he wanted to make his wife.

CHAPTER 18

Rachel took another deep breath the way Sky had taught her when her assistant said her parents had arrived. She purposefully invited them to lunch, and they were supposed to meet her at the restaurant downstairs. Today wasn't going to be easy, but their arrival at her office cemented the fact it was going to be more challenging than she anticipated. *Not a good sign.* She grabbed her handbag from the chair and headed to her office door where her worst nightmare was waiting on the other side.

"Mom. Dad. I thought we were meeting at the restaurant."

"We wanted to stop by and see how things are going and offer our assistance." Karol glanced around the waiting area, her scrunched nose indicating she didn't like the changes Rachel made. "Like this waiting room, it's far too cozy. A more professional look would be better. You want clients to feel they're dealing with a high-end company, not someone's home office, honey."

Rachel gritted her teeth to stop the words trying to come from her mouth. This wasn't a conversation she wanted to have in front of staff, and while her mother had disrespected her by degrading her tastes before an employee, she wouldn't extend the same courtesy to her. Rachel planned to save her "butt out" statements for their lunch to avoid escalating things. Karol would never make a scene in a public place, or so Rachel hoped. She wasn't so sure about her father, who was less predictable when it came to situations like this, but Rachel hoped it wouldn't get out of hand.

"Shall we go to lunch?" Rachel gestured toward the exit and smiled at her assistant, who returned a "good luck" smile.

Rachel refrained from responding to her parents' comments in the elevator, and even after being seated at the restaurant. She planned this luncheon perfectly and she had every intention of sticking to that plan, since it was the only thing saving her sanity. The lunch continued with her parents badgering her about everything in her business, from the décor to allowing them to see her systems to make sure they were set up correctly, to reviewing the staff to make sure they were a good fit. They didn't ask about client files, as they understood and respected those were confidential. If only they'd respect that this was her business and not theirs, and only offer their assistance if she required it. On and on they continued during the meal, and Rachel was grateful for her meditation breathing to keep her sane and calm the entire time until the perfect time came.

Rachel placed her fork down with determination after she took the final bite of her meal. "Mom, Dad. You know that I value your opinion and respect that between you, there's more than forty years of experience in this industry, but you need to stop."

"Stop what?" Karol asked in surprise. Her father's expression remained stoic, as if he suspected what she meant and knew there was more to come.

"Stop undermining me in front of my staff whenever you visit my office."

"I don't—" Karol started, but Rachel's raised hand stopped her as displeasure shot across her face. Rachel continued.

"Stop telling me how I should run my business. I'll ask for your help if I want it." Rachel rested her elbow on the table, a gesture to annoy her mother, before she continued. "Remember that I have over fifteen years of experience myself. Not only did I start this company on my own, but I've grown it exponentially in a short time, all without your help and doing it my way. That should indicate to you that I know what I'm doing."

Rachel paused when the waiter came over to ask if they needed anything else. Everyone shook their heads. Sensing the tension, he mumbled, "Let me know when you're ready for the check," and left quickly.

"I love you both, but you raised me to handle this." That statement was a stretch, since they'd never encouraged her to own her own business, but she hoped it would act as an olive branch.

"As you said, we have forty years of experience and we're simply trying to help," her father stated.

"I appreciate it, and if I ever need help, I know I can come to you. For now, I just need you to stay out of my business. Figuratively and literally."

Rachel watched her parents as they digested her words. Recently she'd defied pretty much everything they'd taught her, from leaving the company she was with to starting her own business. If she were married, she was certain she'd be telling them to get out of her marriage as well. It was a lot for them, since she'd always been amiable to their advice. *More like a pushover, people pleaser.*

"But owning a business is a huge risk, and we want to make sure you're not going to regret it, or put yourself in financial straits."

"My business is doing well, and I'm being careful to plan for the long-term for myself and my business, so I'm prepared for anything that comes my way. If I fail, then I know I tried, and I can do something different."

"But we don't want you to fail, honey. That's the point." Brian stated.

Rachel smiled, and realized for the first time what their hovering was all about. "Failure is a part of life, Dad." She placed her hands on the table, palms up in a welcome for theirs. Rachel squeezed their hands. "It's how we learn and grow and go on to bigger and better things. Failure isn't a bad thing. Giving up is."

Brian and Karol glanced at each other, then then her. "Since when did you get so wise?" Her father inquired.

"I've always been wise. I've just been keeping it to myself." Rachel let out the breath she was holding, relieved the conversation was going better than she imagined. Perhaps her parents were starting to mellow in their old age. Whatever the reason, she was grateful.

They all laughed for a moment. Brian asked, "So do you need a silent partner who's willing to invest in your business to get some of the profit you're bragging about, but who promises to stay out of your daily business affairs?"

Rachel chuckled. "I'll see what I can do for you."

"Maybe we can use the money to take that world cruise we've been wanting to take for years," Karol voiced with enthusiasm.

Brian rolled his eyes. "We haven't even made the money yet and you're keen to spend it."

"What? I have faith in my daughter's remarkably successful business, and maybe it's time for us to spend some quality time together again. Especially now that we're both retired." The words were firm and confident, but a hint of fear in Karol's eyes said otherwise.

This was the first time Rachel had heard her mother extend a hand to repair their relationship, although that might've happened before without her there. Rachel held her breath, along with her mother's.

Brian reached for his wife's hand, brought it to his lips, and smiled brightly before saying, "I think that's a brilliant idea!" He waved the waiter over. "I think this calls for a celebration. Bring us the biggest piece of cheesecake you can find, and three spoons." The waiter nodded and scurried off.

"What exactly are we celebrating?" Rachel asked. They'd covered so many things today, she wasn't sure.

"We're celebrating our successful daughter, and new beginnings." Brian lifted his water glass and gestured for them to do the same. Their glasses clinked and the waiter returned with the dessert and three spoons. They all dug in.

Laughter and talk of the future and happy memories filled out the rest of the lunch with her parents, and Rachel quickly messaged her assistant to have her reschedule her afternoon meetings so she could stay in this moment with her parents. While she hoped and prayed it really was the start of something new, she wanted to savor it...just in case.

When Rachel returned to the office, a smile was plastered to her face that wouldn't stop. Today was the most she'd truly smiled in a long time, and not just with her parents. The sessions with Sky and the regular meditations seemed like they were taking her on a rollercoaster ride. Her emotions, along with memories from her childhood that she thought she'd forgotten, were branded not only on her mind but as a part of her life in ways she hadn't realized. She had stopped speaking up for herself and was doing things to please others instead of doing what she wanted. She'd been taught it was the right way—the nice way—when in truth it was chipping away at her soul and stealing her joy. Especially when pleasing others resulted in the detriment of things that were important to her, or things she didn't want for herself.

The journey that Michael and Sky had set her on was helping her to recover parts of herself she locked away because they weren't welcomed, wanted, or appreciated. She also discovered she'd become another person to please her parents, teachers, and bosses who had their expectations of who they thought she should be, act, and become.

Rachel spent many meditations crying as she realized the years she wasted, the dreams she never explored, and the times she remained silent when she should've spoken up to protect herself from those who hurt her on an emotional and spiritual level.

In those times, she was like a little girl watching from the corner with duct tape on her mouth as others chastised everything she said and did. Tearing up the papers with drawings of the dreams and desires she wanted and shoved their own images of what she should want for her life. With each day that passed, that child became a crumpled heap in the corner, curled up into a ball, her face covered and eyes closed.

In recent months that little girl had lifted her head to look around, her eyes filled with hope one moment and fear the next. Her hands tugged at the tape on her mouth gently pulling at the edges as her eyes darted about frantically.

Today, Rachel imagined her ripping off the tape and smiling. Her eyes were shining with hope instead of fear, doubt, or emotions that had stopped her from being happy in the past or kept her hidden in the corner. Rachel imagined her standing proudly, fearless as she walked toward the window where the sun was peeking through. She sat down at the table that contained crayons, markers, papers, and other materials and drew new pictures with her dreams. They were the ones shredded years earlier, or new ones she'd kept hidden when she was curled up in the corner alone.

Rachel wasn't ready to peek over her shoulder and see the new pictures she was drawing, but she would soon. That filled her with excitement.

Her dreams at night were like her spiritual journey. Some days she didn't remember them five minutes after waking up, but felt light and happy, while other days the dreams kept her puzzled for hours, contemplating what they could mean. Sky had been urging her to listen more to her intuition and be open to what her subconscious was telling her with her dreams, but sometimes they were just a confusing mess that either made no sense, or she couldn't remember.

Whenever she felt overwhelmed, she reminded herself of the journey she was on, and that it wasn't one where she'd reach her destination in a day, or maybe even ever. It was a journey of her life to become a happier and whole version of herself, and best of all she'd be at peace.

Michael was the only variable in her journey. They settled into comfortable communication with each other whenever they met to discuss his business. There were always other people on the call at both ends, never speaking to each other alone. That made it easy to keep the conversations professional. While they hadn't planned it that way intentionally, it worked. Neither wanted to open a wound that had never fully healed and might not anytime soon. The deep treble of his voice on the other end of the phone, along with his rich Irish accent, still made her smile and sent a ripple through her on the occasions she indulged in remembering his mouth close to her ear, or the warmth of his lips on her neck and shoulders. Those were memories she gradually let go of so she wouldn't recall them during inappropriate times, or even when she was alone. Rachel was grateful she didn't have to see his face. She didn't know if an image would let her forget, or if she could stop from reacting to him if she had to encounter him on a regular basis.

Only a couple more weeks remained on her contract, and Rachel knew there was no need to renew it. The replacement was making great strides, and everyone who was promoted was more than ready to make the transition. That contract was the only thing tying her to Michael. Once it ended, her business relationship with him would be severed for good.

Like a broken record, her mind relived the scene in her apartment when he asked her to marry him and move to Ireland. Her mind filled with endless questions: Would they have been married by now, or still planning the wedding? Would Michael's family like her? What did Michael's apartment look like? What would their everyday life together be like? Did Michael cook? What kind of wife would he expect her to be? She'd Googled his family—not only were they old money, but they also supported several charities. Would his family expect her to participate in them? What was life like in Ireland? Would she fit in with his friends? Did he have friends?

The endless questions regurgitated in her mind until it gave her headaches and heartaches as she remembered she'd said no and Michael was not in her life. That she was still in Cayman and he was across the world in Ireland and that wouldn't change unless she decided to give up the company she was building and loved and leave behind her friends and family for a man she barely knew.

Sure, she acknowledged the connection between them, but there was more to building a life together, and the experiences they shared in their dreams and their talks over lunches and the occasional dinners did not provide that. It would only be enough to start a relationship and see if things could grow into the seed of promise it showed, but not give up your life completely.

The joy from lunch with her parents was quickly evaporating. *This is why I need to stop focusing on Michael and what could have been and focus on myself. Every time I start thinking about Michael, I spiral out of control into unhappiness.* That direction wasn't going to give her the peace she needed in order to move forward. She didn't want to leave Michael behind. The desire to have him in her life was a strong feeling deep in her soul. He was meant to be in her life. Knowing how much he meant and the deep connection they shared made it harder to let go and truly separate from him. But it was a step she had to take and sever—if that was a thing—herself and their connection. She longed to be in a place where she could remember him and their time together as a happy memory, and not be dragged down into pain, hurt, and a crippling sense of loss. She would get there with the help of Sky and continuing her own personal journey. She'd get to that place of peace.

That night, she dreamed of Michael.

CHAPTER 19

Rachel glanced across the room at Michael. *He's here. He's really here.* She never doubted he'd return to Cayman, since he owned a company here, but she never imagined he'd reach out to her. Between the time passing and the fact he'd never tried to reach out before now convinced her that he'd moved on. Or so she'd thought.

Then, out of the blue, she dreamed about him. The dream was nothing like the ones they shared, but it was vivid and powerful. Meaning she'd see him again. What she didn't know was when and how they'd react and feel when they saw each other. Each day that passed and he didn't show up in her life, she rationalized it was her way of letting him go. That theory went out the window when she got his message with a request to meet her for dinner.

When she'd walked into the crowded restaurant and saw him sitting at the table, her heart jumped in her chest when he smiled. Her reaction to him was the same, but she chalked it up to the shock of the moment.

The noise of people talking and laughing around her went silent. So did the clinking of glasses and silverware against plates. Every sound and person around her disappeared as she walked toward him. For her, they were the only two people in the room.

He'd changed. Hints of gray peeked through his hair, which he wore a little longer. He hadn't aged much, but it had only been a year, although in some ways it seemed so much longer. She was a completely different person than the one he met and got to know. Had he changed too, or was he still the same?

Michael rose and greeted her with a polite kiss on the cheek before pulling out a chair for her. The kiss surprised her, sending a wave of warmth down to her toes and back through her body and out through the top of her head. *Oh oh!*

The clatters and clinks resumed with a vengeance, drawing her back to her body and the restaurant, reminding her they weren't alone.

"Nice to see you, Rachel." His voice was calm, as if he hadn't experienced the same sensation. Michael motioned for the waiter. "Would you like a glass of red wine or water to start?"

He remembered what I like to drink. "Red wine, please." *I'm going to need it.* Rachel watched Michael peruse the menu and order their drinks. He then continued to glance at the menu.

"Do you know what you want to order?"

The last thing on her mind was food. She hadn't even glanced at the menu. Not that she needed to. She'd eaten at this restaurant more times than she could count, and they hadn't even heard the specials. Wanting to provide him with an answer, she picked up the menu and flipped through the pages for her favorite dishes to see which one jumped out at her for tonight. None of them did, her mind and eyes wandering to Michael, curious as to why he arranged this meeting. *Deep breaths, Rachel!* She hadn't had to say to herself in a long time, as deep breathing throughout her day now came naturally and she did it unconsciously. A wave of calm and peace came over her once she breathed deeply behind the menu. This encounter with Michael was a wonderful opportunity for her to enjoy his company and maybe tie up any loose ends with their connection—if any presented themselves. She was out to dinner with a nice-looking and charming man, and that was something to be present for and appreciate. It was the words she used to convince herself.

She told him her meal choice. "What are you having?"

His eyes remained on the menu. "I haven't decided yet."

She rattled off a few of her favorites as recommendations and waited for him to glance at her, but he didn't. "How's business?"

"Busy, but good."

A generic response, and still no glance away from the menu. He was different, for sure. The old Michael would've chosen and been plying her with questions by now. Rachel did a mental shrug. Whatever the reason for this meeting, it would present itself soon enough. "How is your family?"

Those words got his attention and he finally pried himself away from the menu and set it down on the table. She'd hit a nerve, obviously. Was he about to tell her about an engagement, or some big family announcement? Thinking of him engaged pricked at her heart. *I'd be happy for him, right?* Rachel honestly didn't know how she'd feel.

"They're well. Thanks for asking. How are yours?"

"Very well, traveling around the world." Rachel laughed. "Actually, they've been at it for some time now, and loving every minute of it. They became silent partners in my business, and we're both enjoying that new arrangement."

Michael smiled. "Sounds like your relationship with them has improved."

"It has. A lot—and for the better. We're planning to meet up for the holidays, although I'm not sure where it's going to be yet.

Celebrating Christmas somewhere different will feel strange, but I'm really looking forward to it."

"Have you done any traveling yourself?" Michael asked after the waiter set down their drinks and left.

"No. I've been too busy with the business, but I take a spa day once a month to destress and reset myself." Rachel sipped her wine. *And a crap load of meditation and sessions with Sky.*

"I'm glad to hear you're taking care of yourself and not getting burned out with work. I've been trying to do the same. I took up golfing, but I plan on trying something else because I really suck at it, and I'm not getting any better."

They laughed.

"Do you enjoy it?"

He nodded.

"Then that's all that matters. And if it helps you to relax…"

"It does for the most part, but I also go for a massage once a week and I'm training for a marathon."

"Wow! That sounds like a lot of time away from work for you. How's your father taking it?"

Michael chuckled. "He wasn't thrilled at first, but he's settled into an unhappy grudge. I've promoted other people within the company to handle more of the workload."

"He'll come around," Rachel offered. Anything was possible. Look at how things had changed with her parents' relationship and so quickly too.

"Perhaps," Michael answered just as a waiter came to take their food order.

Their food arrived and the conversation took twists and turns, and Michael still hadn't said why he asked to meet with her. She was enjoying herself so much that she didn't care. If they'd been on a date, she would've rated it as the best one in a long time. The conversation flowed easily, along with the laughter and Rachel felt more at ease with him than other times they were together, and that said a lot. Being in Michael's company was always inexplicable. She felt at ease, as if they'd known each other for years, but the sexual tension was so poignant it could make things uncomfortable. But maybe that's because their relationship had been different before. Their in-person meetings were confusing because of the dream connections. They'd never shared a physical connection in real life, but the one in their dreams made it clear it would be amazing no matter where it was.

Being around each other now was different, but in a good way. The attraction wasn't overpowering or uncomfortable and everything felt easier. Rachel smiled. This was why they'd needed to connect at this dinner, to close out any possible "what-ifs" about their relationship. Now there'd be no wondering when she thought about him in the future. Their connection was meant to happen, to wake her up, heal her—and things in her life that needed to heal—and she'd be forever grateful to him for that. Their relationship had to happen the way it did. It was okay that they'd moved on. Their strong connection didn't have to become more, and they'd both be just fine to go about the rest of their lives, trying to find love that would better fit them and their lives. The lessons she learned from her relationship with Michael were some of the best, and she'd cherish their shared experiences.

Michael surprised her, reaching for her hand on the table. "I appreciate you agreeing to have dinner with me. I wasn't certain you'd accept my invitation."

"Why wouldn't I?" Their last meeting didn't end as badly as the last time they were in a dream together, and they'd been civil to each other on the phone when they talked business.

"I thought maybe you'd shut the door on me after your contract ended, and wouldn't want to think about or remember me."

Not remember you? I couldn't forget you if I tried. "I didn't want to forget you, Michael. Even with everything that happened between us, you changed my life in a way no one else has."

He squeezed her hand. "I'm happy to hear that, because I feel the same way too. Knowing you has changed me, and my life, and I'll be forever grateful to you for that."

The longer they held hands, the more the emotions and energy between them grew and expanded, making Rachel realize that what had happened between them wasn't truly over in the way she thought or hoped. She removed her hand from his. A long dead fear rippled through her, piercing her heart like a small chard of ice, spreading to every cell in her body. *Not good.*

"Are you okay?"

The words "I'm fine," almost slipped out. She didn't want to speak that lie, as it betrayed who she was now. She never wanted to go back to that person, filled with fear, doubt, and self-loathing, and knowing she was pretending to be someone she wasn't. Someone she didn't want to be.

"No." Rachel tucked a strand of hair behind her ear and stared into his sea-blue eyes, hoping the emotions were fleeting, but when she felt the ice chard twist, she understood they weren't going anywhere. "I agreed to meet with you because I wanted to see if I'd still feel the same way. I didn't realize that was the real reason, and not the one I convinced myself of: that you were someone I used to care for, but things didn't work out because we were in different places in our lives."

"And what did you discover?"

"That things are different between us. We've changed in some ways and are the same in others. I'm a stronger person now than when I first met you, both inside and outside our dreams. I know exactly what I want for my life now, even though I'm still navigating my way and enjoying each moment to the fullest. I discovered that while I not only survived while we were apart, I thrived, both professionally and personally. I healed parts of myself that I didn't realize needed healing, and I'm complete and fully happy for the first time in my life."

"But?" Michael voice was lined with question and anticipation.

"But I also discovered how much I missed spending time with you like this. Missed how easy it is to talk and connect with you in ways I haven't with other men. I missed your smile, your jokes, and laughing with you. Missed the way you look at me like I'm the most beautiful woman in the room, and it's only me you want to be with. The way I want to run my fingers through your hair and touch your face while I listen to you speak."

The words flew from her mouth. He needed to hear them as much as she needed to purge them from her mind and heart. She was ripping the bandage that covered her heart and showing it to the person who hurt her the most, hoping he wouldn't tear it out but cover it with something more substantial. The moment was excruciating and exhilarating at the same time. Rachel finally gazed up at Michael to see his reaction.

"Rachel, I—" His words were interrupted by the waiter who came over to ask if they needed anything else. "Just the check."

Rachel heart sank to her high heels. His asking for the check was a death sentence to their conversation. It meant he had moved on—maybe even found someone. *Stop making assumptions!* The truth was, she didn't know what he was thinking or going to say, only that he asked for the check, and she had to be patient and see how the rest of the night would unfold. Spilling her heart to Michael wasn't part of her plan. In fact, she was certain in her original thoughts that their time together was complete with this meeting. But each time she looked at him, part of that thought was chipped away to the truth: She still loved him deeply and wanted to be in his life. The realization made her feel stupid, with a lesson she was doomed to repeat. Nothing of their reality had changed.

Rachel stood when the check was paid and walked to the exit with Michael. No words were said as they headed toward the parking lot. He followed her to her car. "Thank you for dinner."

"You're more than welcome." He took her hand. "We should finish our talk. How about I follow you home?"

Rachel nodded, got inside her car, and watched him in the rearview mirror, waiting for him to get in and follow her.

CHAPTER 20

Tonight was not turning out the way he planned. Michael got into his rental and followed Rachel's car as it pulled out of the parking lot and headed to her house. The scene felt familiar, because this is exactly what happened the last time he returned to Cayman. That visit had ended with heartbreak, even though it was the right decision. Rachel's declaration at dinner were not the words he expected, given how easy and casual their interaction was. He was shaken. He'd expected the evening to end with polite smiles and maybe a friendly hug in memory of what they'd shared and meant to each other. Their encounter was supposed to be the start of a growing friendship—something he'd hoped for.

Rachel's declaration complicated what he planned, and he hadn't decided if it was a good thing or if he should reconsider his trip's purpose. Their connection was still strong, but it was different, and Michael was grateful because it ached less to be near her.

He had been looking forward to seeing her, and that excitement overflowed when she walked into the restaurant looking as beautiful as he remembered. But he noticed immediately there was something different about her as confidence exuded. She glowed with something he couldn't name, and her smile was like sunshine lighting up the room. She was happy. At first Michael thought it was because she was in a new relationship, but there was no ring on her finger, and she didn't mention anyone during their talk. He chalked it up to her improved relationship with her parents and a successful business. Her personal relationships were none of his business, and in a small way, he really didn't want to know. Her company was the reason he was here, but he suddenly felt awkward discussing his plans after her words at dinner.

A combination of shock, terror, and sheer joy had pierced him as she shared what he meant to her. With each word, he realized the words reflected his own emotions. The same feelings he thought about when he was alone at night, remembering his time with her and fantasizing about what their life might be like. They were fantasies he didn't indulge in often because the joy he felt from the memories often turned to sadness and pulled him to a place he didn't want to return from.

The past few weeks were different. That joy remained as he embraced the memories fully and absorbed every emotion, instead of trying to push them aside or stuff them down because he was sure his visions would never happen. Happy couples no longer made him sad or regretful, but brought a smile to his face and spread a warmth throughout him, thinking he could have the same.

He parked his car next to Rachel's and followed her inside her apartment. He'd hoped the drive would give him time to decide how to respond to her declaration of feelings, but no solution came.

"Can I get you a drink?"

Michael expected her to avoid his direct gaze, but she met his boldly. She really was different. The old Rachel would've been blushing and unable to meet his gaze, especially with her declaration, one she would've never made so boldly. "Water, please."

Rachel left and returned with two glasses of water. She handed him one and headed toward the couch and sat. Michael gazed at the space next to her and then at the single chair before deciding to take the seat next to her. *I'm a grown man and can handle this!*

Rachel spoke first. "Just so you know, I didn't intend to say those words." She laughed nervously. "They came out all on their own, so I guess they needed saying." She sipped her water. "I know nothing's changed between us, and it's possible you have someone, and I have no idea what your life is like now, but I just wanted to let you know how I felt. I didn't want to wish, after you returned to Ireland, that I'd said something. The feelings were unexpected for me. I thought the evening was going well and that we'd end as friends saying a pleasant farewell and remembering each other fondly in the future." Rachel smiled. "But surprise, surprise."

"Your words were unexpected. For me, the evening was intended to be a business proposal, but I found myself forgetting all about that and enjoying your company and our talk immensely."

"Business?" Rachel inquired. Surprised etched into her face before it formed into embarrassment. "I didn't realize..." she stammered.

"You couldn't have known," he assured her. "I didn't mention it when I asked for a meeting. Maybe I should've."

"I doubt I would've said what I did if I'd known." Rachel chuckled. "That explains your terrified look while I spoke."

"Terrified? That's how I looked?" Michael hadn't realized. "I assumed it was shock. I didn't mean for you to feel more embarrassed or make things more awkward than they already were." Her laughter said she was taking the uncomfortable situation in stride—another difference from the Rachel he remembered.

"I figured I was already at the entrance of the rabbit hole, so I might as well jump in and make things even more uncomfortable."

She leaned back onto the couch and ran a hand through her hair. The color was the same, but it was considerably longer from the last time he'd seen her. It suited her.

"I'm glad you did." *I mean it.* Her confession broke open the dam of emotions he hadn't realized he was holding back from the moment she walked into the restaurant.

Their interaction stirred a place deep inside him that had been sleeping, and while his reaction to her wasn't the same as when they first met, it was just as strong and meaningful. The way he felt about her hadn't changed. In fact, it had evolved into something quite wonderful and easy and comfortable. Maybe it was because they were different from when they first met. It was obvious Rachel had gone through her own spiritual journey and come out healed on the other side.

Her glow was magnetic and pulled him to her in ways no other woman did, not even the ones he tried to have a relationship with. There was always something missing, but not just the spark; it was Rachel. He wanted her in his life now as much as the last time he was here in this apartment, and while some things had changed, a lot of it was the same. It all hinged on how Rachel responded to his proposal.

"You're glad?" Rachel asked hopeful.

"Yes. I still feel the same about you."

"But—"

"But we're still in the same place we were before as far as living on the other side of the world, and neither wanting a long-distance relationship."

"True." Rachel's face was crestfallen.

"But, I do have a proposal for you. The one I'd intended to make tonight."

"Yes...business."

"I came here to offer you a consulting job. One that means managing a division of our businesses, like what you did for the company here, but on a much larger scale. I know you've grown your business and I feel you're ready for expansion—if you're interested."

"What division of the business?" Rachel asked, her interest piqued.

"The Irish one."

Surprise created waves on Rachel's face as she digested his words. "You want me to oversee your financial business in Ireland? Surely there are other companies there who are a much better choice."

"Just as good, yes, but not better, and not ones that I trust as fully as you. And not ones that would not be easily controlled by my father's objections." While he knew Rachel was more than competent, he was worried if she'd be able to handle the pressure her father and the board would apply. Rachel stood up to Rick who was a nasty piece of work, and managed to work for him for years, left the company with dignity, and cared deeply about the people the company was responsible for. That made her an ideal candidate, and seeing how she'd grown stronger and more determined personally and professionally while retaining her compassion is exactly what he wanted for his business in Ireland. It wouldn't be an easy transition, but he was confident Rachel could handle it.

"I'm honored."

"I hear a 'but' coming."

"I have my business here to manage. While I was looking to expand, it was in the Caribbean not halfway around the world." She shifted her position on the couch. "It's a huge step. I'd have to promote someone to manage this branch as flying back regularly wouldn't be practical—I'd have to rent or sell my apartment."

"The position comes with a flat...apartment," Michael added.

Rachel's silence told him the wheels in her head were turning, and he hoped they were in his favor.

"The opportunity sounds amazing, but there is one major problem with it."

Michael searched his mind to see if he missed any details, but he'd told her all the great parts, and even the not-so-great ones. Her being in Ireland meant they'd be in the same country, which was better than being so far away. Their relationship would have a chance to develop and grow. "What problem?" he asked finally.

"You'll be my boss again and having a relationship is out of the question."

That was one angle he hadn't thought through carefully. While he wouldn't be her boss in the traditional sense, it could complicate things. "You won't work for me directly. You'll be a consultant so it's slightly different."

Rachel gave him a sideways glance. "It's almost the same. Besides, what will your father and the board think if they know we're together? They'll think you gave me this job because of our relationship. That's not how I want to be seen."

"So, you admit we'd have a relationship?" Michael touched her cheek. The reaction of skin to skin was instant, and she felt it too as evidence from the sharp intake of her breath. He longed to kiss her, but they'd been apart for a long time. Rushing into a relationship wasn't the best idea, especially when they hadn't established the status of their "relationship" yet.

Michael removed his hand. "I honestly don't care what my father or others are going to think or say." *Not a complete lie.* "They'll just have to get used to the idea of us together."

"How nice for you. But how is that going to affect my relationship with them?"

Michael hadn't thought beyond having Rachel back in his life and that she still cared about him. His mind had quickly shifted from his business proposal to reconnecting with her, and solely focused on that. He had not had much thought about what it would mean for her working relationship with everyone else. They would question her abilities and assume Michael hired her for personal reasons. While that was true on a lot of levels, her authority, and any hope of her building a solid business relationship with his father, coworkers, and the board would be tainted. "Damn!"

"I couldn't agree more," Rachel responded. "We'll have to keep our relationship professional."

"I don't want just a professional relationship with you."

"I don't either, but what choice do we have?"

"We could keep our relationship a secret?" Michael suggested. *Not a good idea.* That's the last thing he wanted, but it was the first thing that jumped into his mind.

"I don't want to be a dirty secret you keep hidden away, Michael." The hurt in her voice was clear.

He ran a hand through his hair in frustration. "I don't want that either. I want to shout to the world that I'm crazy about you. I want to introduce you to my friends and family, and have them come to know and love you."

Rachel touched his arm. "I want that too, but that's not possible if I take this job, and if I don't take the job, we'll still be miles away. It's a no-win situation."

"I don't like no-win situations." He stood up and paced before her. "Maybe we could ease everyone into the idea of us being a couple? We'll have them get to know you in a business capacity and on a personal level, not as my girlfriend, but a business associate. Once you win them over with your sweetness, charm, and business savviness, then we can start seeing each other for real. No one will blame me. I'll just be another victim of your loveliness," Michael teased.

"Seriously? That's your plan?"

"Why not?"

"There are SO many things wrong with it."

"Like what?"

"Like I won't be able to hold your hand or touch your face when I want to."

"Or kiss me." Michael added.

She smiled. "Yes, or kiss you whenever I want."

He plunked down on the couch next to her. "It won't be easy, but we've waited this long to be together. What's another few months before we're open about our relationship? In the meantime, we can spend time together, getting to know each other again. Sacrificing a few months of keeping our hands to ourselves will be worth it. Don't you think?"

Rachel studied him for several moments before standing up. He held his breath as he waited for her answer. A part of him was certain he'd made his case and there was no reason for her to say no. Another part was filled with fear because he was asking her to give up a lot even if she was getting more in return. Her parents were traveling so they were already no longer part of her everyday life. Michael knew what her business meant to her, but he also knew she was ready to expand, even if it wasn't as far as Ireland. It also meant delaying having the kind of relationship she longed for. Michael sensed she was ready for this move in a way she wasn't the last time, but was she really ready to make such a huge change both on a professional and personal level? The decision was not easy.

"I'll still need to work through some details from the business end of things with one of my managers and speak with my parents, since they're part owners of the business. And of course, I'll want to see the contract with the job you're proposing, and go through it with my lawyer before I sign anything...but my answer is yes. Yes, to everything."

Michael jumped off the couch and lifted her in the air as he shouted, "Yes!"

"Our relationship wouldn't be put on hold, just slowed down to a crawl, but we'll still see each other, spend time together. We'll have to put off kissing, and other physical activities, but maybe that's a good thing because it'll give us time to get to know the people we are now," said Michael.

Rachel laughed and hugged him when he finally set her feet on the ground. "I like that idea for the most part. But is there any chance I could get an advance on a kiss? To seal the deal?" she suggested with a mischievous grin.

A smirk pulled at the edges of his lips. "I think that could be arranged."

He cupped her face in his hands and pressed his lips against hers, soft and slow so he could savor her feel and taste. A surge of energy sparked between them, shooting from their mouths to every pore on the surface of his skin. It was the most delightful feeling he'd had in the longest time. The urge to intensify the kiss was strong, but he resisted, since they'd just agreed to take things slow. Rachel must've sensed the same, because she didn't open her mouth or try to put her tongue in his. Michael was grateful. Resisting her would've been difficult.

"Better than I remembered."

He laughed. "Happy to please." Rachel was right. Their kiss was better than he remembered or had dreamed about during their time apart. He caressed her cheek before kissing her on the forehead. "I should go. I've got a contract to send to you and you've got your own work to do."

She frowned. "I thought you'd stay a little longer."

"Sweetheart, if I stay near you too long, I might not be able to control myself." Michael wiggled his eyebrows.

Rachel laughed, a beautiful sound to his ears and heart. Michael hoped to hear it more often in the future.

"You're probably right. I am pretty irresistible."

"Hey! Me too."

She shrugged her shoulders. Michael grabbed her and started tickling her until they fell on the couch and tears streamed down her face. Michael gazed down and brushed the tears from her eyes. This was a side of their relationship they'd been unable to explore, and he was eager to share more moments like this with her. Michael kissed the tip of her nose before standing and helping her up.

They walked hand in hand to the door.

"Night, mo chroí." Michael's lips lingered on hers.

"What does that mean?"

"It's an endearment."

Rachel cupped his face with her hands. "Oh. Okay. Good night."

"I'll call you tomorrow."

Rachel nodded before closing the door behind him.

The space around him seemed to float as Michael walked to his car. Coming back to Cayman and offering the job to Rachel was the best decision he'd made in a long time. Everything turned out better than he could have imagined, and while he knew there'd be complications ahead for them on both business and professional levels, he was confident they'd handle them and finally be able to be together the way they were meant to be. Before the trip, Michael resolved that his relationship with Rachel would be no more than professional, content she'd be in his life in any capacity. He was grateful that things had gone better than he anticipated. Michael whistled all the way to his car, and on the drive back to the hotel. Life was good and about to get better.

CHAPTER 21

Rachel called her parents two days later. She needed to speak with them before talking to the staff. Her parents would be the hardest to convince of her decision, at least she hoped so. The last thing she needed was to lose any of her people.

"You're what?" Brian Miller asked.

"I'm taking a consulting job in Ireland."

"But why? I thought you were expanding your business in the Caribbean?" Karol asked, poking her head into their video call before sitting next to her husband.

"I was offered this amazing opportunity, and I don't want to pass it up. I'll send you the contract so you can see for yourself, but I'm calling you about the structural changes I'll need to make to the business here to make it work. Since you're part owners, you can let me know what you think, and if it sounds feasible to you."

"I'm going to reserve saying more until I see the contract, but I must admit I'm both skeptical and excited for you. It's an opportunity to take your business—our business—further than we dreamed. I'm so proud of you, honey," Brian admonished. He nudged his wife.

"We're thrilled," Karol mumbled, her voice thick with uncertainty.

Her mother was the pragmatic one and wouldn't be convinced until she saw in writing how fabulous an opportunity the offer was. She couldn't blame her. After Michael left, her mind raced with questions and doubts about the decision, but she calmed herself by remembering no official documents were signed, and she still had the option to back out or to make changes that better suited her and her business if she desired. She trusted Michael—thanks to the time they'd spent working together—and knew he'd never take advantage of her, or her business. The only thing left was to sort out all the details so she could feel confident about leaving her company and starting a new personal and professional adventure in another country.

"No official documents have been signed, so there's still an opportunity to negotiate everything." Rachel smiled as her mother's face lit up. While she knew Karol was thinking she had time to talk Rachel out of the decision, she also knew it was time for her mother to see what an amazing option this was for her, and their business. Hours of phone time and back-and-forth were ahead of her, but in the end, she was confident her parents would come to the same conclusion she had: Michael's offer was an amazing opportunity.

"We trust your judgment, honey, and if you feel this is a good opportunity for you and the business, we'll reserve saying more until we've seen the contract and your proposed changes to the company to make it happen. I'll be happy if I don't have to come out of retirement," Brian joked. "Besides, it'll give us an opportunity to visit you on that side of the world. Ireland and Scotland are on my bucket list, so I'll take that as a good sign."

"What kind of sign is that?" Karol rolled her eyes.

"The best kind," Brian assured her. "Everything happens for a reason. Scotland and Ireland are on our list and then we get an opportunity to expand our business to Ireland? If that's not a sign, I'm not sure what is."

"It's just a coincidence," Karol stated firmly.

"There are no coincidences," Brian replied.

Rachel could tell where the direction of the conversation was going and decided to get out before she was dragged in. "I'll send you the contract and company changes in a couple of days, once I've had a chance to speak with the management team."

"All right, honey. I look forward to it. Speak to you soon." Brian waved and held up his wife's hand, and waved again before the video ended.

Later that day Rachel glanced across the table at her team, whose expressions were a combination of speechless and excitement.

"Any chance I could come with you?" Angela asked.

Rachel and the other staff laughed. "No, but there's an opportunity for you to be promoted if you're interested." Angela had proven herself on more than one occasion and would make an excellent addition to the management team.

"Does this mean we aren't branching into the Caribbean?" Sloane asked with disappointment, as she'd shown the most enthusiasm about the expansion.

"Not at all. I think you're more than capable of handling the expansion with a little guidance. And we'll take smaller steps, so we don't expand too quickly."

Sloane's eyes widened and a huge smile lit up her face.

"This offer is an opportunity for everyone in the company to handle more responsibilities and gain promotions—and more money of course," Rachel added in case there was any doubt. Because of her own experience with Rick, she made sure her own staff were always clear where they stood with her and within the organization, and that they were treated with respect and paid well.

Rachel clicked to the organizational chart for the presentation. "These are the changes I'm proposing, however I'm open to hearing from anyone who wants a different position or responsibilities. If more than one person wants the same position, then we'll sit down and figure out who's the best candidate and go from there. I'll fly down once a quarter to assess the business overall and meet with the management team once a month by video call to ensure as smooth a transition as possible. If changes are needed because certain areas aren't working, then we'll tackle them as they come. I have complete faith in all of you."

The meeting ended on a high note, with only two people wanting the same position, for which Rachel was grateful. Having a team of only five people has its advantages. Time had passed so quickly she didn't realize it was past lunchtime until she checked her phone. There were also two missed calls from Michael. Rachel dialed his number.

"Hello beautiful."

Rachel smiled. "Hi yourself. You called?"

"Yes. If you haven't eaten, would you like to have lunch with me?"

"I'd love to." They agreed on a place and Rachel walked over, her stomach growling, an indication she'd skipped breakfast for another cup of coffee.

Michael kissed her on the cheek when she arrived.

"How are things going?" he asked, waving a waiter over.

"They're going well for the most part." She gave him a quick update of the meetings with her team and parents, leaving out the business parts he didn't need to know about.

"Happy to hear it. Have you decided if you're going to rent or sell your apartment?"

"Probably rent. I know a realtor who handles rentals, so everything is taken care of from this end."

"Excellent."

"I still need to show your contract to my lawyer, but from what I've seen, everything looks good. Although I am going to propose a couple of changes."

"Changes? Anything dire I should know about?"

"Nothing serious. Just about relocation costs and the time you want me to start in Ireland."

"Minor indeed, but I hope you're not going to make me wait too long to see you again." Michael touched her face.

"You're going to have to get used to not being so familiar with me if we're going to convince everyone we don't have a personal relationship."

Michael dropped his hand. "You're right, but it won't be easy."

"It'll be easier when we're surrounded by your friends and family, not to mention business associates."

"I hope you're right. The last thing I want is to jeopardize your relationship with the team you'll be responsible for before they have a chance to know you."

"You could just remove yourself from the scenario completely. Don't you have other staff who can interact with me on a regular basis?"

"Honestly, we won't have to interact with each other often from a business standpoint, once you get settled it, but it's the initial start that's going to be a problem. Lots of late nights, and luncheons."

"We'll make sure they're well-lit and very public places, so you won't be tempted," Rachel teased.

"Me? I'm certain it's you who won't be able to keep your eyes from adoring me and your hands from wanting to touch me."

Rachel laughed. "I can control myself."

"Are you sure you can resist all of this?" Michael ran his hands along the length of his torso.

She rolled her eyes. "It'll be difficult, but I'm certain. It's you I'm worried about. I am adorable and highly irresistible—you said so yourself a couple nights ago."

Michael chuckled. "I did say that and meant every word. We can manage and when it's all said and done, you can have me to your heart's content."

Rachel giggled. "I can't wait." She rested a hand on his shoulder. "The most important thing is that I'll know you're all mine, even if I can't show it. I can claim it where it matters. In here." She pointed to her heart and his.

He kissed her hand. "That's right, baby."

"Baby?" Rachel wrinkled her nose. "Not sure I like that one."

"Honey? Sweetheart?" Michael offered.

"I preferred the name you used the other night."

His eyebrow quirked. "Ah. Mo chroí."

"How about just calling me Rachel for now to be on the safe side. The last thing you need is to call me an endearment in the middle of an important meeting." Rachel grinned.

"You're right. Besides, we'll have lots of time to come up with cute names for each other."

"Yes, we will."

The rest of lunch was spent laughing and sharing silly stories of things they'd say and do with each other once their relationship became public. Rachel was certain it wouldn't be as easy or comical as they were making it, but they'd have each other and be there for each other no matter how rocky the road. The chance for them to have an amazing love story was worth it.

In that moment she realized she hadn't told Arlene or Skylar about the move. She was so focused on the business side of things, she didn't give a thought about telling them...or maybe subconsciously she was blocking telling them because they wouldn't be happy about her leaving. They were the only people who she'd really miss when she left. And while they could video chat regularly and visit, the move would change the dynamics of their relationship forever. That realization was something she wasn't ready to face or admit out loud. Skylar was another matter. Rachel expected her phone to ring the moment Michael left her apartment. Like Arlene, her relationship with Skylar was going to change, but Skylar would no doubt have something enlightening to say like, *Life is full of changes you must embrace.*

Rachel kissed Michael goodbye in front of the elevator and returned to her office. He left in two days and then their relationship would be different. His fingers entangled with hers just before the elevator doors closed. Like her, Rachel knew he wanted every moment before Ireland to last.

Rachel dialed Arlene's number as she exited the hallway. She kept her voice neutral as she invited her friend for dinner that evening to her house, which would be a safer bet than in a public place, as Arlene was likely to make a scene. Although, there was a chance she'd kill her in apartment if they were alone together, Rachel thought with a grin. The conversation wasn't going to be an easy one, but necessary for the sake of their friendship. Her phone rang and she grinned when Skylar's name popped up on the screen. "Be at my house tonight at seven."

"I was trying to give you space, but the wait is killing me!"

"I'm surprised you restrained yourself."

"Me too." Skylar laughed. "Especially with news as big as this. Did you dream about it?"

"Not exactly. Just about Michael."

"Hmm."

"Save your analysis until tonight, Sky."

"What?" The thick sarcasm of her tone came through their call.

"You know what! Let me enjoy this moment."

"For once you listened to me." A chuckle came through the phone.

"I always listen to you."

Sky snorted. "We'll see. Do I need to bring anything?"

"What? You mean you don't know?" Rachel teased.

Sky grunted. "I don't know everything."

They both laughed before hanging up.

CHAPTER 22

Rachel jumped when the doorbell went off. She'd been deep in thought about how she'd tell Arlene the news, but all the words she chose landed flat, even to her. There was no easy way to say she was moving to another country, no matter how wonderful an opportunity it was.

Arlene and Sklyar stood in the doorway, each with two bottles of wine. They all hugged and stepped inside, placing the bottles of wine on the kitchen table before Arlene rummaged through the drawers for an opener. She found one and proceeded to open one bottle of white and one of red and poured a glass for each of them in the glasses Rachel put out earlier.

"You set the table? Must be big news." Arlene observed, since they usually ate on the couch.

"It is," Skylar said, sipping her wine.

Arlene rolled her eyes, but her face lit up with excitement. "You met someone!"

"Sort of." That wasn't far from the truth.

Arlene squealed and hugged her friend. "I knew it was only a matter of time."

"Wait for it..." Sklyar added.

"Will you stop?!" She glared at Skylar. "Tell us who."

"It's Michael."

Arlene's brows knotted. "The dream guy? I thought he was in Ireland..."

"He came back a couple of days ago."

"That's fabulous! That means you two can finally be together. What a relief! Although you seemed happier lately, I knew you were still pining for him."

"That's not exactly the whole story," Rachel stated.

Arlene shot a warning glance at Skylar.

"He offered my company a consulting job."

The glass of wine paused at Arlene's lips. "So, no relationship then?" She shrugged. "That's disappointing for your personal life but good for your business. Who knows? Maybe working together will rekindle your relationship."

Rachel froze. She couldn't find the words to say what her friend needed to hear.

Arlene strolled into the kitchen and glanced around. "We're having takeout? When you said dinner at your place, I thought you were going to cook." Arlene glanced at Rachel who stood in the living room with her drink. "What's wrong?"

For once Arlene looked to Skylar for a hint. Her face was directed at her drink.

"There's more to the story, isn't there?" Arlene walked to Rachel. "You have to move, don't you?"

She nodded.

"Shit! Shit! Shit! Why didn't you warn me?" she shrieked, pointing at Skylar.

"You always get annoyed when I do."

"This is different!" Arlene said as harshly as only a friend who was about to lose one of her best friends, confidantes, and partners in crime could say. "How soon do you have to leave?"

"There's no firm date yet, but I imagine within the next month or so."

"Tell me this opportunity is totally worth uprooting your life for. It won't make me feel better, but it will soften the blow—a bit."

"It means expanding my business in Ireland, as well as the Caribbean."

"Wow, so you're still going ahead with your expansion on this side of the world?"

Rachel nodded and brought her friends up to speed, everything that had happened from the day Michael made the offer until she met with her staff. They listened intently and the more Rachel's voice escalated with excitement, the more deflated Arlene's expression became.

The food arrived and they sat at the table to eat.

Skylar put an arm around Arlene. "This is an opportunity for us to become better friends."

"Any better friends and you'll be taking up space in my head."

Skylar grinned. "Maybe now you'll take my hints about where to find the man of your dreams."

Rachel laughed. It was a running joke between them.

"I already told you, if he wants me, he'll have to find me. I'm not chasing after anyone. Besides, I'm happy with my single life."

"Whatever you say," Sky retorted.

"So, this is really happening." Arlene's voice was lined with disbelief and a heap of sorrow. "I'm SO happy for you, I am," she assured Rachel. "Who's going to keep me out of trouble with you gone?"

She pointed to Skylar. "Don't answer that!"

"Maybe that dream man will finally make an honest woman out of you," Rachel teased.

"Bite your tongue!" Arlene was happy to help the people in her life find love or a relationship, but she had no interest in anything long-term for herself. Rachel doubted there was a man out there who was a perfect fit (despite what Skylar thought) and always joked about Arlene being the queen of the nursing home when she grew old.

"You can come with me. We'll take Ireland by storm," Rachel joked, knowing Arlene wouldn't leave her family behind, especially her aging mother.

"I'll come visit as often as I can, and we'll keep in touch on a regular basis. We won't become those friends who promise to keep in touch but never do. We've been best friends forever and we won't lose you!"

Rachel reached across the table, extending each hand to them. "You won't lose me. I'll be back four times a year to check on my business and we can catch up then. Add that to your visit and that's at least five times a year we'll see each other, not to mention the Facetime calls and the booty calls when you're drinking," Rachel lips curled into a teasing smirk.

Tears pooled in Arlene's eyes. "Five times a year isn't enough!"

It wasn't, but Rachel couldn't say the word out loud without a lump blocking her throat and an ache filling her chest. Rachel was losing the two most important people in her life and no amount of joking or thrill from the opportunity would ease the vacant spot. Leaving them and Cayman was a new chapter in her personal and professional life, but an old one was closing, one that might never return. Bittersweet feelings surrounded her as she realized she was losing more of what she loved, but unlike the other chapters, where she released and lost things that no longer served her, she'd be leaving behind dear friends. Rachel knew that although she would meet new people and make friends, these relationships would never be the same.

They hugged for a long time before Arlene spoke. "Now it's just getting awkward." They broke apart and wiped their tears while roaring with laughter.

"I'm going to miss your humor the least." Rachel shifted to a comfortable sitting position. "Your jokes are worse than my father's dad jokes."

Arlene snorted. "You love my jokes." She glared at Skylar, daring her to argue.

Rachel smiled into her glass of wine before taking a sip.

"So, what is the horrible movie you have picked out for us to watch?"

Rachel scoffed. "My taste in movies is better than yours. Remember the last disaster of a movie you picked? We didn't make it halfway through before having to choose another one."

"What? It wasn't that bad!" Arlene gave Rachel and Skylar a sideways glance.

"You're right. It wasn't bad—it was horrible." Skylar insisted as Rachel scrolled through the rows of movies on the screen before making her selection.

"You've got to be kidding," Arlene voiced when she saw the cover image of a sci-fi movie. She hated sci-fi movies.

Rachel knew her taste was more toward thrillers but was happy to meet them in the middle with rom-coms, but only so she could debunk the ridiculousness of the scenes. Skylar happily watched them argue every time.

"What? It's a good one, I promise," Rachel assured her, although she was certain Arlene still wouldn't like it. She thought sci-fi movies were a waste of time since nothing in them was feasible or believable, no matter how adamantly Rachel assured her that a lot of old sci-fi movies were inspiration for technology today.

"I won't fight you because you're leaving soon."

"And it's my turn to choose the movie," Rachel countered, grinning at the disgruntlement etched on Arlene's face.

Rachel started the movie, and the night was filled with bad jokes, snorting, lots more wine, and a few tears before Arlene dozed off. Rachel covered her friend with the blanket that decorated the couch.

"You were quiet," Rachel said to Skylar, who was helping her clear the coffee table of their wine glasses and empty bottles.

"Arlene wasn't going to like what I have to say."

"Is this a bad decision?" Rachel asked. She hadn't dreamed of anything negative, but her insights weren't nearly as powerful as Skylar's.

"I'm happy for you."

"I hear a 'but' in there."

"No buts. Just a word of caution."

"About Michael?"

"Yes and no," Skylar said cryptically.

"Spit it out, Sky!"

"His family. The road with them will be difficult."

Rachel's heart sank.

"Will they ever come around?"

"His sister will love you, but everyone else will take...time."

"Anything else?" Rachel asked, sensing there was more.

"Yes, but it's difficult to say."

Rachel gritted her teeth. "Okay, Yoda."

Skylar grinned at the nickname they used whenever she said anything was "difficult to see."

142

"You're strong now, so I know you can handle it. And if things get rough, I'll sic Arlene on them."

They both laughed at the childhood term they used for sending Arlene to attack anyone who messed with them because of their weirdness. They hugged and Rachel headed to bed while Sklyar left quietly out the front door.

As Rachel tried to sleep, her emotions teetered between the excitement of starting a new adventure with Michael and her business, and the sadness of leaving her old life, including her friends, behind.

CHAPTER 23

Rachel glanced out the window from her aisle seat on the plane. The window seat usually made her nauseous, but she wanted to catch a glimpse of the country she was about to call her new home. The view was better than she imagined, but she stopped staring when her stomach protested. She turned the cool air above her to the maximum level and took deep breaths. She loved traveling, but flying was not her favorite choice. Thankfully, she'd outgrown having painful ears, and the nausea had never turned to vomiting, like she'd seen happen with other passengers over the years. Once she sat in the aisle seat and concentrated on her breathing, she was fine.

Every bad effect from flying melted away by the time she reached customs. Michael promised to pick her up from the airport, so she was excited to see him for the first time in almost a month. Alone time with Michael was going to be just what the doctor ordered, and something she was looking forward to before their relationship had to return to being professional when she started work next week. Maybe they could sneak in a private dinner at her new place, although it'd have to be takeout since she wasn't likely to have groceries. *Who cares what we eat?* Rachel was certain Michael wouldn't care either—only that they'd be together.

He was waiting for her in the crowd of people. She spotted him immediately, towering over most of the people standing next to him. Rachel was about to rush up and wrap her arms around him and plant a hot kiss on his mouth when she noticed his solemn expression. Either something was wrong, or something bad had happened. Rachel's brows knitted in question and followed his eyes to the slim brunette standing next to him. Was she one of the partners? Family? Why was she at the airport? Jealousy stabbed her. Before she had time for fears and doubts to fill her mind, the woman stepped forward.

"Hi, Rachel. I'm Regan, Michael's sister," she blurted excitedly as she extended a hand. Rachel had the urge to hug her but knew it wouldn't be appropriate.

"Nice to meet you, Regan." Rachel shook her hand firmly and met her penetrating gaze with one of her own. Michael hadn't told her much about Regan, but he had said she was sweet, nice, and a bit of a rebel. *Much like Arlene.*

Regan smiled, making her already youthful face appear younger. "Lovely to meet you too. I suspect we're going to be the best of friends."

Rachel didn't have the heart to tell her she already had best friends, but she knew Regan would be an ally since she was more down-to-earth and friendly than the rest of the family, or so Michael had told her. It was a small step through the door, but she was taking it. "I look forward to getting to know you, too."

"You mean Michael hasn't told you everything about me already?"

Rachel grinned. "Not everything." She was relieved that his parents weren't there. That might've been awkward.

"You've been invited to a party my parents are hosting tomorrow night. Father wants to suss you out."

So much for avoiding uncomfortable encounters with Michael's family. "Is it normal for your family to invite consultants to your house?"

"Not really, but it's not unheard of," Regan stated, glancing around Rachel. "Is that all the luggage you brought?"

"No. I have a couple of boxes that should arrive here in a couple of weeks. I gave most of my stuff away or left it with my apartment for the renters. I figured I could buy anything I needed here."

"Smart and generous of you," Regan commented before gesturing at Michael to carry the largest suitcase. "I'm glad we brought my car and not yours. Mine has more trunk space. When do you get a car?"

Rachel glanced at Michael. "My assistant will contact you with the details, but I've arranged a car service to take you anywhere you need to go."

"That's awful generous of you to pick her up from the airport instead of using the car service," Regan observed, glancing between them as if trying to read their minds.

"We got to know each other during the merger in Cayman—I thought it would be nice for her to see a friendly face after traveling so far."

Rachel nodded in agreement.

Regan smiled knowingly as if she'd discovered some deep dark secret. "I see. And now you've hired her consulting company to manage one of the largest divisions of the business here in Ireland. You've must've gotten to know each other very well."

Rachel gritted her teeth. And here she thought Regan was an ally. Michael wasn't lying when he said people were going to make assumptions. She just never expected them to start with his family. "Actually, he had the opportunity to see me and my company in action as I handled the transition after the director was fired and knows I'm not only trustworthy, but good at what I do. He also knew I wanted to expand my business into other countries, so it was advantageous for both of us." Rachel's tone implied she would put Regan in her place if she even hinted that Michael hired her for any other reason than her abilities and integrity.

Regan laughed. "Bravo! That's just the kind of fight you're going to need if you're going to handle the board and a lot of people in the company who are going to be skeptical about why Michael hired a company outside of Ireland. Why he hired you."

"Is this why you came with Michael to pick me up?"

"Partly. And I wanted to see the woman who lights up my brother's face whenever he mentions you." Regan smiled warmly.

Rachel blushed and avoided their gazes as she pushed her suitcase behind them through the airport parking garage. Her heart fluttered with a combination of excitement and dread. If Regan picked up on Michael's feelings, would other people? If they did, it would make her transition incredibly difficult and delay their relationship even more. *Shit!* Rachel took a deep calming breath to silence the rampant thoughts that threatened to escape. Regan was Michael's sister and knew him better than other people. There was a risk of his father knowing, but surely he wouldn't expose his son's feelings. *He might call for my termination, but nothing more*, Rachel thought. Thankfully, the contract was signed, so she had that going for her if the shit really did hit the fan.

Everything's going to be fine. Rachel hadn't yet met a person she couldn't get along with, and if she could work with Rick and his volatile and nasty attitude, she could work with anyone in any situation. Rachel's spirits lifted, pushing out the seed of fear that had reared its ugly head. "So, what can I expect at dinner tomorrow night?" she asked Regan as she handed Michael her suitcase to put in the back of Regan's SUV.

Regan gave her a rundown of attendees and whether they'd confirmed to be there or not. Some were board members while others were just business associates or friends of the family. "So, this is a dinner party?" Rachel asked, relieved it wasn't going to be just Michael's family.

They glanced at each other before their gaze settled on Rachel. "Yes, but my parents were adamant you attend."

"I'm assuming the attire isn't casual?"

Regan laughed, giving Rachel the answer. "Don't worry, I'll text you the location of a dress shop close to you that'll have what you need. I can come with you if you'd like."

"Thank you, but I'll be fine." Rachel hadn't purchased a formal dress in years and didn't think she would be needing one so soon.

As they drove from the airport to downtown Dublin, Rachel took in the mixture of old and new roads, bridges, and buildings made of stone, brick, and very few glass. The combination was beautiful, especially with the golden shades of the setting sun casting shadows in the background. She longed to open the windows and smell the air, but suspected she'd get strange looks, even from Michael. Sometime later, they pulled up to an enormous glass building. Michael handed the keys to a man by the door along with a tip to take the bags to the top floor.

Rachel glanced at the building that could only be described as a beautiful tower of glass and steel that seemed to hold the sunlight captive. When Michael said her apartment was nice, she didn't suspect anything like this. Her heart raced with excitement as they rode up the elevator to the top floor. It opened to the apartment and Rachel realized it was the penthouse. She glanced at Michael. "It's too much! I don't need a penthouse!"

Michael laughed. "It's company owned and comes with the position so..."

"But it's so big!" Rachel argued.

"It's only two bedrooms, with an office. It's large to entertain staff, and possibly host occasional meetings with your highly demanding boss," Michael declared.

"Only two bedrooms?" Rachel glanced around. The apartment was spacious and tastefully decorated, although not to her taste, but she didn't care. It was elegant and fancier than any hotel she'd ever stayed in. The office space wasn't as large as she expected, but almost the size of her office in Cayman. The bedrooms were large with walk-in closets. The kitchen was enormous, and Rachel felt guilty it would go to waste.

As if reading her mind, Michael said, "A large kitchen works well for catered parties."

"That makes sense," Rachel replied, although she didn't have a clue. Her assistant usually handled all the company events, as they were small enough that she didn't have to be that involved. "The apartment is stunning. I especially love the views. I hope I get to enjoy them," she joked, but suspected she'd be spending more time at the office than the apartment, at least for the first few months.

"The kitchen has been stocked with a few items, so you don't starve before you get to the supermarket, but there are a lot of nice restaurants in the area if you get hungry later."

"I'm too tired to eat, but maybe I'll check out one of the restaurants for breakfast tomorrow," Rachel replied.

"Well, we'll leave so you can settle in." Michael glanced at his sister and then Rachel.

"Thanks. I'm pretty jet-lagged and I'm headed straight to bed. Apparently, I have a dinner party to attend tomorrow and need to prepare for." She tried to hide the longing in her eyes when she gazed at Michael, wishing they'd had a moment alone.

"I'll wait for you downstairs," Regan stammered, "to give you a minute to talk...business...in private."

"Thank you, Regan. I'll just be a minute."

"Lovely to meet you, Rachel." Regan kissed her on the cheek. Not as personal as a hug, but it was warm and felt welcoming. Rachel was grateful for it.

"Nice meeting you too, Regan, and I'll call you if I run into any problems getting ready for tomorrow night."

"Please do," Regan assured her before pressing the button on the elevator.

Because they were on the top floor, it took a minute for it to arrive, and Michael chatted about the projects he wanted her to focus on when she started. He stopped talking the moment the elevator door closed leaving them alone and hugged her. "I missed you so bloody much." They'd talked on the phone almost every day before she arrived, discussing details of the contract, and getting to know each other, but it was nothing like being in the same room with him, or touching him. His hands were in her hair then cupped her face while he kissed her.

Rachel sensed he was holding back since his kisses only went as far as her lips. "I missed you too." She hugged him back just as tightly before running her fingers through his hair until they locked at the back of his neck. "I wish you didn't have to leave so soon, but I wasn't kidding about the jetlag. I'm beat," Rachel said before laughing.

"I wish I could stay longer too. I was going to offer to come back but you need your rest. So, I'll say good night and sweet dreams for now."

"Night." Rachel kissed him again, locking their lips tightly, wanting to make the moment last a little longer.

Michael squeezed her frame and then broke their kiss and headed to the elevator. "Night, love." He blew her a kiss right before the door closed.

Now that she was alone, the silence of her new home echoed loudly. She took her time walking through each room to see what was there and if there was anything she might need to pick up tomorrow. With each room she looked at, her body grew heavier. Rachel longed for a shower but doubted she could muster up the strength.

After checking out both bedrooms, she decided to choose the one with the nicest view. She undressed and crawled into bed, too exhausted to rummage through her suitcase to find pajamas, her toothbrush, or anything else that was part of her nighttime routine. *I'll worry about everything else once I've had a good night's rest.*

Rachel smiled, remembering Michael's kiss and the feeling of him pressed against her. She was in Ireland with Michael and no longer talking about the new adventure that would change her life and business forever. From this moment she was living it, and she was going to relish every moment, even the challenges of maneuvering her complex relationship with Michael. From now on, things were only going to get better.

"Does Father know about you and Rachel?" Regan asked when Michael got into her SUV.

"Not exactly. He knows about her in a business capacity and that we connected on a personal level but doesn't know we had a relationship."

"You won't be able to keep it a secret for long."

Michael watched the street and lights from the buildings move across his window. "I don't know what you're talking about." Michael didn't waste time trying to deny his feelings for Rachel. He trusted his sister not to say anything, but he didn't want to burden her with such a big secret. Thankfully, she took the hint.

"What did you think of her?" He knew Regan liked her. She would never hide true disdain behind niceties, but he needed to know that Rachel had someone in her corner.

"I like her, a lot, despite not knowing much about her, but I can tell she's important to you, so I'll make an extra effort to get to know her."

"Good. She's going to need all the friends she can get."

That was an understatement. Rachel was in for the ride of her life, and although he suspected she realized that, Michael didn't know exactly how bad things would turn, how long it would last or if people really would come around to the idea of their relationship. He didn't care much about others. The people he cared about liking Rachel were his parents, Regan, and Connor. Everyone else could go to hell, including the board members since they didn't control his personal life. He longed for the days when he could stay the night without wondering if someone would find out. That seemed like a lifetime away. He couldn't wait, and knew Rachel was eager for it too.

Michael went straight to bed after Regan dropped him home. He sat, crossed-legged on his bed, and turned on his meditation music. When Connor told him about the practice, he hadn't given it much thought, thinking it was too out there for him. But, when the reader made the same suggestion, he couldn't help but consider trying, especially when Connor and the tarot reader explained the science behind meditation, which made him feel less like a hippy—the term his father would use if he ever found out.

After meditating, Michael stared at the ceiling, his mind drifting to Rachel. He wished they could meet in their dreams, like they did during his first visit to Cayman. Those times must've been a fluke, ones he was grateful for since they brought them together. He picked up the phone and dialed her number. Rachel picked up after the third ring.

"Miss me already?" Rachel answered with a chuckle.

"Actually, I was calling to talk about work stuff."

"Liar." A scuffling noise echoed through the phone. "You miss me."

Michael laughed. "What's that noise?"

"I was just adjusting my pillows. There's so many on the bed, I'm drowning in them."

Michael grinned. "You find what you needed for tonight?"

"Honestly, I just crawled into bed. I didn't unpack anything."

"You're in bed, clothes and all?" Michael adjusted his position so holding the phone was more comfortable.

"Actually, I just took them off. I couldn't be bothered to look for pajamas." Rachel laughed.

A vision of Rachel, naked in her flat and in a gigantic bed covered in pillows, and heat rushed through him, making him wish he'd stayed there with her and told his sister to leave without him.

"Michael? Are you still there?"

"Yes...I'm still here." he mumbled. "But now I'm going to need a cold shower before I can sleep."

"Why would you need a cold sho..." Rachel trailed off.

Silence hung between them for several seconds before Michael spoke. "You can skip the party tomorrow night, or leave early, if you're still struggling with jet lag."

"That won't gain me any fans. Besides, it might be nice meeting everyone in an informal environment before we start working together. Take some of the pressure off."

"True, but don't feel you have to stay longer than you need. I don't want you burned out before you even start working."

"All right, boss. I'll keep that in mind."

Michael groaned. "Please don't call me that."

"What should I call you? Michael might be a little too personal at first."

"That's what you called me in Cayman, and most people know we have a past working relationship."

"How about I call you Mike? Mikey? Mr. Doherty?" Rachel offered.

"Call me Mike or Mikey and I'll fire you!" Michael warned.

Rachel giggled. "Mr. Doherty is it, then."

"Mr. Doherty implies you don't know me, and that's far from true." Michael's voice was soft and low. They did know each other too well to not go by first names, whether it was because of their working relationship or the intimacies they shared. Michael remembered every inch of her body from memory and knew every crease on her face when she smiled, and the one adorable, crooked tooth.

"I know." The silence on the phone stretched out. "The truth is, I'm nervous our history is going to complicate the situation."

"It will, but I have every faith you'll handle it with grace and professionalism."

They said their good nights, knowing the road ahead could only be taken one day at a time. What mattered was they'd be together.

CHAPTER 24

Rachel glanced in the mirror, barely recognizing herself with more makeup than she'd worn in years. One good thing was her hair, which had needed a makeover more than her face did. The length was still the same, but with more wavy curls. Rachel couldn't deny she looked nice, but just not herself. *Will anyone recognize me when I start work?* she joked to herself. Regan had been more than happy to help her. Rachel wasn't planning on reaching out to her, but she was determined to make a good first impression on his family. Regan had been sweet and helpful and saved her tons of time searching for shops. Based on what Michael had told her about the social events, they leaned more toward the formal side, and Rachel didn't want to arrive in the wrong attire.

She longed to remove some of the makeup, but knew she'd end up messing it up if she did. The phone rang and the doorman announced a car was waiting for her downstairs. She grabbed a clutch and headed to the elevator, taking deep breaths to calm her nerves. She'd managed to unpack a few of her things, but not a lot since she spent most of the day shopping and preparing for tonight. She was grateful for coffee and the sleep she got last night to help with the jet lag and made sure to drink tons of water.

The driver was waiting at the front of the building with the door open when she strode outside. Rachel smiled and stepped in carefully. She made idle conversation with the driver, whose name turned out to be Liam and who was obviously not used to the people he drove speaking to him other than to tell him where they needed to go. Her heartbeat was pounding in her ears so loudly when they arrived that she barely heard Liam wish her luck and give her a warm smile. Somehow Rachel sensed she was going to need something more than that tonight, but she'd take whatever anyone offered. She thanked him and told him what time to come and collect her. She didn't plan on staying at the party too long. Jet lag was going to be her excuse, one no one could deny given she just flew into Ireland.

When the elevator doors opened, the splendor of the hallway took Rachel by surprise. Between the elegant décor of pastel-colored flower arrangements that lined the wall to the old-world beauty of the interior, she couldn't help but stop and admire her surroundings as she waited behind the line of people entering what she assumed was the main room where the event was hosted. She was so lost in her observation that she didn't notice someone come up behind her.

"You must be Rachel," a thick Irish brogue asked.

Rachel turned to find a gorgeous man with stunning blue-gray eyes and a head of sandy-blond hair with streaks of dark red. She smiled. "You must be Connor."

"I am," he replied with a smile. If she weren't already crazy about Michael, he would have made her melt to her knees. He appeared slightly taller than Michael, but she couldn't be certain because of her heels. Rachel took his extended arm. "It's lovely to finally meet you. I've heard so much about you."

Michael told Connor about me? She had the urge to learn exactly what Michael said but stopped. While Connor might know about them because of their friendship, this was certainly not the time or place to discuss it. "I've heard a lot about you too."

"Only the good things, I hope," he said with a cheeky wink.

Rachel laughed. "Of course."

They made small talk on the way inside the room, as Rachel brought Connor up to speed with his questions about her business and the trip here. She grilled him about his bookstore, and they exchanged numbers so she could visit and have a personal tour and order some books. "Are ye sure you'll have time to read?" he teased.

"There's always time to read." Rachel assured him.

Connor smiled brilliantly. "Yes, there is. I think this is the beginning of a beautiful friendship."

"I couldn't agree more." Rachel squeezed his arm affectionately.

"A word of advice: Don't let anyone intimidate you. They'll try just because you're an outsider, Michael's family included. It won't matter how qualified you are to handle the job or how highly Michael thinks of you. They're a tough bunch, but he must've thought you could handle it if he bought you here."

"I'd like to think so, but I appreciate the advice." Rachel glanced around the room, shocked by the number of people. "W-w-what about Regan?" she stammered, suddenly growing nervous. "She seemed genuinely friendly."

Connor was visibly relieved. "That's good. You'd know it if she didn't like you."

"I figured Michael's father and my coworkers are going to be the most difficult." Rachel glanced around the room, trying to figure out who was who, but there was no way of knowing until she was introduced. She searched for Michael in the crowd but couldn't find him. Not surprising given the number of people.

"You're right. Moira won't be easy either—Michael's mother," Connor offered.

"Are these parties always this busy, with this many people?"

Connor glanced at her sideways. "This is a small affair. Wait until you attend one of their charity events. You won't run into the same person twice."

Rachel's eyes widened. *What the hell have I gotten myself into?* She was still wondering when she caught sight of Michael across the room. She resisted the urge to wave like an idiot and tapered her expression to a polite look. She took the glass of champagne Connor offered, knowing it would calm her nerves for whatever came during the rest of the night. Rachel watched the trays of food passing. Her watering mouth was an indicator she had forgotten to eat dinner. She hadn't thought about it since she'd had a late breakfast and lunch. She made a mental note to grab something when the next tray passed. Turning her attention back to Connor, she asked. "Why didn't you bring a date tonight?"

Connor surprised her by blushing. "The person is already here, sort of."

"I'm intrigued."

"It's complicated," Connor responded as his gaze moved over the room.

Rachel laughed. "It usually is." Was it an employee of Michael's? Whatever the reason, Rachel couldn't help but sympathize because of her own situation.

"Connor. I didn't realize you were invited."

They both turned at the sharp tone. A tall man with a full head of gray hair and piercing blue eyes raked over her before settling on Connor. *Does everyone in this country have blue eyes?* Rachel wondered, surprised by his tone.

"I'm always invited. I don't always attend," Connor replied.

Has to be a board member, Rachel assessed, trying to size him up. She knew she had to be polite despite the man's obvious snobbishness. "I'm Rachel Miller." She extended her hand.

The man glanced at her hand, then her face as if trying to place either the name or her face, or perhaps both.

"Ms. Miller. You look different from your photographs," he responded, not taking her hand, but continuing to glare at her with displeasure.

Rachel waited for him to introduce himself, but he didn't offer a name.

"Rachel, meet Shamus Doherty. Michael's father," Connor offered.

She tried to hide her surprise. "Mr. Doherty," she said with a slight nod. The words, nice to meet you, would be wasted on him.

"Ms. Miller. I presume you'll be ready for our meeting on Monday?"

"Absolutely, sir. Michael has briefed me on what projects he wants me to focus on."

"We'll see," Shamus stated and left, not bothering with common niceties.

Rachel watched him weave through the crowd, smiling at the people he passed, and she wished she'd gotten one of them. "Did I detect a little hostility between you two?" *And for me too*, making her wonder if he knew her and Michael's secret.

She turned her attention to Connor, grabbing a napkin and selecting one of each of the four hors d'oeuvres on the tray the waiter held before her. She longed to take more, but would wait until the next tray passed so she wasn't caught stuffing her face. The encounter with Shamus was no doubt an indicator of what meeting the board of directors would be like, along with the other people she'd be working with. *One day at a time, Rachel.*

"You could say that. I always seem to rub Shamus the wrong way. He thinks I'm a bad influence on Michael."

"Are you a bad influence?" Rachel asked, although she couldn't see anyone influencing Michael more than he personally allowed.

Connor grinned wickedly. "I used to be, but I enjoy rubbing Shamus the wrong way. It keeps the boredom at bay."

"Maybe you need to find another hobby," Rachel suggested. In that moment, she noticed his gaze narrowed onto someone. She looked in the same direction, but there were too many people around to tell which person he was focused on. Then Regan broke through the crowd around her and headed toward them. Dressed in an elegant blue silk dress, she sashayed in their direction with a brilliant smile on her face when she saw Rachel. The smile wavered for a microsecond when she caught sight of Connor. Rachel glanced past her hoping to get a glimpse of Michael, but he was nowhere in sight.

"Rachel. Lovely to see you again," Regan greeted her warmly. She held out Rachel's arms as she openly perused her attire and appearance. "Beautiful. I never had a doubt."

"Liar," Rachel shot back with a grin.

Regan laughed. "I did have a doubt or two, but I'm happy to see you've proved me wrong." Her attention turned to Connor. "I didn't think you'd be here tonight. You hate these events."

Connor took a sip of his champagne. "I do, but I thought tonight would be worth attending, and I wanted to meet the woman Michael talks so much about."

He was talking about her, but his eyes never left Regan's face. His gaze raked over her in a way that made her wonder and wish if that's the way Michael glanced at her. The heat and tension were palpable. *Is it like this between Michael and me?* Rachel hoped not, otherwise their attempt at hiding a relationship was doomed. The situation was a nice reminder to be aware of her attention while around Michael, especially when other people were with them. *Are they a couple? Is this the complicated relationship he spoke of?* That was an understatement, given the tension between Connor and Shamus. Somehow Rachel couldn't imagine Shamus being okay with Connor dating his daughter.

"You look lovely by the way." Connor attempted the compliment with a casual tone.

"I know," Regan fired back confidently. Rachel half expected her to flip her hair over her shoulders.

"Nice to see you're as modest as ever." Connor returned, as if he'd just accepted a challenge.

"You cleaned up nicely tonight. At least you didn't show up in shorts."

"They would've stopped me at the door if I had."

"Yes. I made sure of it after the last time. Black tie includes the pants, Connor, and not just the top half," Regan said coolly, trying to suppress a grin.

"I know, but the look on your parents' faces made it worth it."

"Mother threatened to ban you from all future events if you stepped out of line again."

"She did, but I know you'd change her mind."

"Me? I think you mean Michael. He's the one who pulls you from the fire each time."

"Ouch. And here I thought you were on my side."

"When have I ever been on your side?" Regan asked.

"Point taken. A fella can dream, can't he?" Connor said, flashing a charming smile.

Regan didn't answer, merely shook her head. She linked an arm with Rachel. "So, who have you met so far? Anyone interesting?"

"Your father is the only person."

Regan winced. "I hope he wasn't too harsh, but I assume Michael warned you?"

Rachel shrugged. "I knew without Michael that the transition would be challenging."

"That's an understatement," Connor mumbled.

"Shh! You don't want to scare her off."

Rachel laughed. "I don't scare easily."

"I hope for your and Michael's sakes that's true." Her glance shot to Connor, who gave her a knowing look, as if they both knew about her and Michael's secret relationship and promised to keep it between them.

Rachel didn't know either of them well, but she was certain they cared enough about Michael not to say anything. "Where is Michael?" she asked casually.

"He is mingling his way over to us." Regan gestured with a tip of her head to a cluster of people in front of them.

Sure enough, he was in the middle. A woman stood next to him, her arm linked in his and jealousy shot through her like a bullet. Rachel took a long sip of champagne and a slow deep breath. Michael had never given her reason not to trust him, but she couldn't keep her eyes from watching the woman. She was stunning in a full-length burgundy dress with a sweeping bare back and midnight black hair that flowed in waves down her back. She threw her head back as she laughed at whatever Michael said to the crowd of people around them. As if sensing her eyes on him, he glanced at her and smiled when their gazes met. He excused himself, unlocking the woman's arm from his. The crowd around them melted away as he strolled toward her. He was a handsome man on any given day but dressed in a tux that hugged his muscular frame, he was devastating her senses.

The tug of Regan's arm reminded her of the surroundings, and she managed to taper her expression to one of polite interest by the time he reached them.

"Rachel. I'm thrilled to see you could attend."

Michael kissed her hand and then her wrist before she yanked it away, even as chills raced across her skin. If the eyes of Connor and Regan and other people around them weren't watching them, she would've glared at him.

"I thought it was a wonderful opportunity to get to know everyone in a casual setting before meeting them officially next week," Rachel replied in a professional tone. "Perhaps you could introduce me to the relevant people."

Michael cleared his throat as if catching himself and nodded casually. "Of course." He offered his arm, but Rachel pretended not to see it, directing her attention to Regan and Connor. "Nice seeing you again, Regan. Connor, it's been interesting and I'm sure we'll see each other again soon."

Rachel followed Michael to a cluster of people, and she took a deep calming breath to raise her vibration, the way Sky showed her, so she could protect her energy, and keep her emotions balanced when interacting with a lot of people who had negative energies. Rachel had a feeling she would need it, and when she came face-to-face with many sour expressions, she wished she'd taken Sky's advice and purchased energy-blocking jewelry. Rachel wasn't convinced it would work, but she was willing to try anything if it meant dealing with all the negative energies she felt bombarding her. Each person in the circle assessed her and shot either daggers at her, or fake smiles. Rachel prayed she was wrong, instead hoping the sour and dour expressions were friendships waiting to be formed, or at the very least respectful professional relationships.

"Who is this lovely creature?" a man with dark hair and a jaw sharp enough to cut glass, asked.

"That's the new consultant Michael hired from that tiny island," said the woman who was standing with Michael earlier.

"My name is Rachel Miller." She extended her hand, ignoring the quip about her home.

"I'm Declan Kelly," he declared proudly, as if it should mean something to her.

He caressed her hand in a way that made her skin crawl, along with the way he glared at her. She pulled her hand away as politely and quickly as she could, resisting the urge to wipe it clean.

"Declan is one of the company's top solicitors," Michael said.

"Oh. Nice to meet you. I'm certain we'll be working together."

"I sure hope so." His blue gaze assessed her from top to bottom, lingering on her breasts that were more exposed in her dress.

Creep was the first word that came to mind. Rachel didn't bother with a smile or fake niceties. The last thing this guy needed was any hint of encouragement.

"I'm his sister, Ciara. Our families have been friends and business associates for many years. We're very close." She glanced at Michael and smiled for good measure.

"That's nice," Rachel managed, although she wanted to punch her in the face. "And what is it that you do?"

"I host charities to help the less fortunate."

"How wonderful that you have a charitable heart. It must be rewarding to get out in the community and help those in need."

"Heavens no! I don't go into the communities. I just raise money for them."

"Oh. But how do you know what they need if you don't connect with them?"

Ciara scoffed. "Of course we know what they need."

Rachel dropped the topic, not wanting to create a scene, but knew Ciara didn't have one charitable bone in her body. For her it was all about appearances and no doubt the tax breaks that came with it.

An hour later, Rachel was ready to use her jet lag excuse to escape meeting one more person whose name she was certain she'd forget. Even after sneaking more food from passing trays, she couldn't ignore her growling stomach and aching feet that weren't used to wearing heels for so long.

Michael must've sensed her fatigue because he pulled her to a quiet corner. "I just have two more people for you to meet, and then I'll take you home."

Rachel shook her head. "I'll call the driver. As much as I'd love for you to drive me home and rub my feet, our leaving together is bound to raise a few eyebrows and start the rumor mill."

"You're right, but how about I stop by tomorrow morning? We'll have breakfast together—I'll bring it with me, and I'll even rub your feet."

"That sounds delightful." Rachel wished she could touch his face or put fingers through his hair, but it would have to wait until tomorrow. The temptation to invite him over tonight was strong, but she suspected she'd fall asleep the moment she got home. "Who are the two people you want me to meet?" Rachel asked.

"My parents."

"Oh. Well, I've already met your dad. An interesting interaction for sure." Rachel grinned.

"Why didn't you tell me sooner? I hope he wasn't too brash..."

"No more than I expected," Rachel assured him. "I want to know your parents and I can't do that if I'm avoiding them."

"I was hoping you'd meet them together. He's usually on his best behavior with my mother around."

"That's sweet, but it's better for me to know the real him. The good, the bad, and the ugly, so I know how to deal with him and your mom. Especially if we're going to have a relationship."

"You're right. The sooner you know all sides of my family and vice versa, the better. I just don't want them to scare you off."

"I'm not going anywhere, Michael," Rachel assured him.

His gaze softened. "I wish I could touch you."

"I wish you could too," Rachel replied, though she kept a solemn face for anyone who might be watching them. "I hope you know I'm touching you like crazy tomorrow." Rachel blushed when she realized how her words sounded.

Michael laughed. "I look forward to it."

"And I can't wait for that foot massage."

"Massage. I thought it was just a foot rub. I might have to rethink my offer."

"Sorry. No backies!"

Michael laughed harder and Rachel joined him. "Let's go meet your parents so I can get home and sleep." Rachel tugged on his arm.

Michael's expression turned solemn when his gaze met the two people he was taking her to meet. "Mother, Father."

The formal manner in which Michael addressed them surprised her. *Is it because of the public setting?* "Lovely to meet you, Mrs. Doherty," Rachel extended her hand and wasn't disappointed when Michael's mother shook it firmly. Her gaze moved over Rachel methodically, as if searching for something wrong in her appearance that could be pointed out. Rachel waited breathlessly, but no words came. *Is that a good thing or bad?* "Mr. Doherty." She gave him a curt nod, figuring he wouldn't take her hand and she wasn't about to make a fool of herself again.

Shamus grunted. So much for good behavior in front of his wife. Moira pursed her lips and nudged him lightly with her elbow. "Good to see you again," he mumbled.

Rachel wasn't sure exactly why Mr. Doherty didn't like her, but she was certain she'd get an earful during their meeting next week. Whatever the reason, she planned to make it work. It needed to work if she and Michael were going to be together.

Michael's parents were an attractive couple who had obviously passed down those traits to their children. *Don't say it, Rachel. They'll think you're trying to suck up to the boss.* Shamus was taller than his wife, but thicker overall, unlike Moira, who appeared to have kept her slim figure. The possessive way Shamus's hand rested on his wife's waist told other men to stay away, although Rachel was certain he could maintain the same effect with one of his intimidating glares. Rachel didn't sense their closeness was just for the crowd, the affection between them seemed genuine. That gave her hope.

"How is the flat?" Moira asked.

"It's wonderful, thank you. I especially love the views. The city is quite beautiful."

"I didn't think you'd like living in such a modern or crowded space."

Because I grew up on an island? Rachel was curious how she knew so much about her. "I don't mind crowded, as long as I have a view of the sky."

"Rachel's offices in Cayman are quite modern, Mother." Michael added. Thankfully, he didn't mention that her apartment was also. That might raise questions.

"I prefer modern styles, Mrs. Doherty. The sleek, clean lines are simple and organized to me." Rachel relaxed the tension coiled inside her when Michael's mother appeared to like her response.

"Please, call me Moira. Tell me, Rachel, how did you end up in the financial industry?" Moira unhooked her arm from her husband, which caused him to frown.

"Both my parents are accountants, although my father specialized in fund management. They pushed me into it at a young age and I happen to be good at it."

"Was there another profession you thought about pursuing instead?"

Rachel laughed. "I wanted to be a romance writer, but my parents quickly squashed that dream. Thankfully, my other dream was to work for myself and own my business, so everything worked out for the better."

"What makes you think a company your size is capable of handling one as large as Doherty's?" Shamus interjected. Michael started to answer, but she shook her head. While she appreciated the gesture, the sooner Shamus understood her, the better, and Michael rescuing her wasn't going to speed things along.

"My company manages many companies. While not as large as yours, more financially lucrative. I've been in the industry for over fifteen years, and during that time, I managed billion-dollar companies' finances and their financial staff. My company is also in the process of expanding into the Caribbean, and we share similar company values regarding our staff. We make sure they're provided for and treated with respect. This arrangement is on a contract basis, Mr. Doherty, which provides both Doherty Industries and me the opportunity to explore if it's a good fit."

She finished in a tone a bit firmer than she intended, but for some reason Shamus rubbed her the wrong way. She'd need a rock the size of her hand to keep his energy at bay. "Besides, your son is a smart man, whom I'm sure you trust, and he wouldn't have offered me this contract if he didn't think I could handle it."

Shamus remained silent, but a vein pulsed at his temple. "We shall see." He stormed off, leaving his wife behind.

"It was a pleasure meeting you, Rachel." Moira held her hand and squeezed it before she gave Michael a kiss on the cheek and a charming smile that reflected his own.

After she left, Michael spoke. "My mother likes you. So do a couple of people you'll be working with. A good start." The pride in his voice was obvious.

"You really think your mother likes me?" Rachel wasn't entirely sure, although she was hopeful. Moira appeared as open and friendly as Regan, but she didn't know them well. "I'm glad a couple people from the company liked me. While I'm not here to make friends, getting along with people you work with does make this kind of transition easier."

"My father will come around once you dazzle him with your brains. The look on his face was priceless. Regan will be sorry she missed it." Michael chuckled.

"I hope you're right. Having your father like me is important."

"It would make things easier," Michael added. He linked her arm in his. "Let me walk you outside and wait for the driver. It'll give us time away from prying eyes. Maybe I can steal a kiss?" Michael teased.

Rachel's expression remained neutral. "You do realize there are no cameras in the elevator..."

Michael laughed and Rachel grinned when they were in the hallway. They practically sprinted to the elevator and crossed their fingers that no one else would be inside.

They hoorayed when an empty elevator greeted them and rushed inside. Michael's lips were pressed against hers, and her fingers were in his hair the moment the doors closed. Rachel slipped her tongue in his mouth, longing for any form of intimacy in that moment. He moaned and pressed her against the side of the elevator, cupping her face with his hands and turning his head so he could deepen the kiss. Rachel melted at the slowness and softness of the kiss. It showed his patience and that despite his excitement, he would take his time. Sparks shot through her body, and she wished this was the elevator to her apartment, where after the ding they would be alone and able to do more than just kiss hotly.

The elevator slowed, indicating it was stopping, and Michael released her abruptly. He strolled them casually from the elevator while her legs still trembled, remembering the feel of his tongue against hers. Michael led them through the main area of the hotel where people gathered, laughing, talking, and waiting to be checked in, totally oblivious to them, a glorious feeling after being under a microscope for the last couple of hours. She longed to rest her head on his shoulder but squeezed his arm instead as they headed outside. The night air held a chill, making her realize she needed to buy winter clothes soon.

"Cold?" Michael asked as he led her to a bench where they could sit and wait.

"A little." Rachel sat and rubbed her shoulders.

Michael removed his jacket and placed it around her shoulders before taking a seat next to her. The smell of his cologne and his warmth engulfed her like the material of the jacket around her.

"Not a bad night," Michael observed.

"Could've been worse," Rachel chuckled. "I suspect it would've been if people knew about us."

Michael laughed. "Yes. Much worse. For you mostly, and it's why they need time to adjust to you and then us together."

"Your mother was nice."

"She is."

Rachel didn't mention Shamus, as they both knew he was going to be the last person to come around. "So, what time are you coming over to rub my feet?" Rachel stretched her feet until her shoes stuck out from beneath her long dress. "I'm totally holding you to that promise."

Michael chuckled. "I'm a man of my word. What would you like for breakfast?" He placed his fingers to his temples as if attempting to read her mind. "Belgium waffles with a mountain of fruit and whipped cream?"

Rachel grinned. That was what she always ordered whenever they had a working breakfast. Michael never ceased to amaze her with the details he remembered during their short time together. "Of course," she responded with a warm smile.

There was no one nearby from the party, as far as she could tell, and it was nice having a moment alone, even if it was only until the driver arrived. The lights from the area outside the hotel cast shadows before and around them, and large trees stretched out their branches, creating an inviting and calming canopy. It was a moment to savor, the first of many, now that they lived in the same country.

The ping of her phone startled her. A message from the driver stating he'd arrived. Michael stood with her, offering her his arm. She took it as they headed toward where the driver was parked.

The driver stood by the car with the door open. "Good night, Mr. Doherty." Rachel addressed him formally, handing him back his jacket. "Thank you for escorting me down."

Michael raised an eyebrow but played along. "Good night, Ms. Miller. It was my pleasure." He held her hand to help her ease into the back seat of the car and gave it a squeeze.

The drive to her apartment was quiet, with the driver only asking if she enjoyed her evening. Rachel was grateful. She was exhausted and not really in the mood for a regular conversation, much less an idle one.

Rachel thanked the driver and wished him a good night before dragging her tired body to the elevator. When the elevator door opened, she staggered to the bedroom, stripped down to her underwear, and flopped into bed. Before she could close her eyes, her phone rang. She thought about ignoring it, but realized it was probably Michael calling to make sure she made it home, or at least she hoped so, given it was almost one o'clock in the morning. She didn't have the strength to handle an emergency.

Michael's name flashed on the screen. "Yes, I made it home in one piece."

"I know because I asked the driver to text me after he dropped you off. I just wanted to tell you good night one last time."

The gesture was so sickeningly sweet she wanted to hurl, but loved every minute of it. "Good night. I can't wait to see you in the morning," she purred.

"You're just saying that because you want waffles and a foot rub."

"Is there any other reason?"

"Hmm. Maybe because you're crazy about me?"

Rachel met him with a long silence before responding with, "I might be."

CHAPTER 25

The silence and discomfort of everyone in the room was deafening. Rachel had hoped that after meeting everyone in a social setting, this transition would be easy. Not so much. Thankfully Michael was beside her, but Shamus challenged every statement she made, which only added tension to the already tense room. Rachel assured everyone that she was there to help and support them, and that her first order of business was to get a feel for their department and how they and their staff fit into the company overall. She explained that she'd seen how the company worked on paper, along with their roles, but it was important for her to get to know them on a personal level, so she understood the best way to support them and their staff.

Shamus had reacted like a disgruntled child, to the point that Rachel was tempted to call security and have them remove him from the room. Michael's attempts to defuse him worked for the most part but it was obvious that the staff were painfully conflicted.

"I look forward to connecting with you in the next few weeks. Thank you for your time." Rachel smiled, giving the five heads of departments direct eye contact as they stood to leave, one of them taking a muffin she'd brought for the meeting. Rachel knew the way to a staff member's heart was making them feel noticed and appreciated. The muffins and good coffee were the first step. Thankfully Shamus remained silent as the staff left, but what could he say at this point? He'd completely highjacked the meeting. Rachel didn't want to ruffle his feathers in front of the staff; however, she had no intention of allowing him to disrespect her, either. She appreciated Michael stepping in, but she needed to handle Shamus herself if this transition was going to be successful and if she were to gain the respect of the staff...and her own peace of mind.

The last employee left the boardroom, and Rachel closed the door behind them. "Shamus. If this is going to work, I'd appreciate if you'd share your opinions with me privately instead of disrespecting me in front of the rest of the staff. I intend and plan to continue to extend that courtesy to you, and I'd appreciate if you reciprocated."

Shamus's face turned red, and his mouth opened and closed like a giant human puffer fish.

"She's right, Father." Michael added.

"And you need to stop fighting my battles," she said to Michael. "While I appreciate your support in a business capacity, the staff need to see and know that I can handle my own confrontations. It's necessary if I'm going to earn their respect."

Michael's mouth opened and closed like Shamus's before his gaze turned to admiration and he nodded in agreement.

"This is my company," Shamus blustered.

"Actually, it's Michael's company. He's the one who hired me and the person I report to. You were invited as a courtesy since you're on the board; however, your daily input is not necessary or a requirement, unless you feel I'm jeopardizing the company in any way, which I haven't had the chance to do since this is my first day. I'm sure you want what's in the best interests of the business, I do and so does Michael. That's why he hired me." Rachel finished firmly, holding Shamus's glance until he was the first to look away. Rachel gave herself a mental high five and Michael and his father friendly smiles. "Wonderful. Now, let's get down to business." Rachel sat and finished the meeting, encouraging Shamus to remain but only to listen unless he had something constructive and valuable to add to the discussion. He left.

Michael and Rachel chuckled after the door closed behind him. "You handled that brilliantly, as I knew you would."

"Thank you."

"You're most welcome."

They continued their meeting even after Ashley, Rachel's new personal assistant, came in to refill the water in the room and bring the completed minutes. Rachel thanked her and asked her to schedule the upcoming department head meetings to fit everyone's schedules. Ashley nodded and a strand of black hair fell into her heavily made-up face. "Shall I order you lunch?"

Rachel glanced at her watch and then at Michael. It was almost one o'clock. "Lunch?" she asked with a smile, remembering all the lunches they shared when they worked together before.

Michael checked his phone. "I have another meeting in an hour. How about we have lunch delivered here so we can finish our meeting?"

They gave Ashley their lunch orders.

It arrived thirty minutes later just as they finished, for which Rachel was happy. That left thirty minutes for them to chat about something other than work.

"Thanks again for yesterday, and for being such a gentleman." Rachel bit into her roast beef sandwich.

"It wasn't easy after you answered the door in a robe, and forced me to rub your feet. And let's not forget the way you shoveled those waffles into your mouth," he teased.

She kicked him under the table. "Hey, you took forever to come over. I was starving. You said breakfast, not brunch."

"I was being considerate and letting you sleep."

"I don't generally sleep after six unless I'm truly exhausted. I was tired last night and didn't get to bed until late."

Michael set his sandwich down. "I'm not in a rush. We have lots of time to get reacquainted." He winked. "Besides, I technically know it'll be amazing between us."

Rachel's gaze was quizzical, and then she blushed remembering their dreams. He was right. There was no rush.

"My next meeting is about to start." He stood and kissed her on the cheek. "We'll catch up later this evening."

"Okay." She finished up her sandwich and glanced around the boardroom, still a little in awe of where life had taken her. She was in Ireland. Her business was expanding into other countries, and she'd reconnected with the man of her dreams—technically from her dreams. How many people could say those words out loud?

Rachel had the urge to call Sky and tell her everything that happened. They had a weekly call coming up, and Rachel was looking forward to it. Sky seemed distracted on their last call, and Rachel sensed something in her life was causing havoc.

Ashley knocked on the door with questions and items to go over.

Rachel threw away the garbage and headed back to her office. Today was her first day, and the first of many long days and nights ahead. She smiled with excitement. Time to change the world, or rather, this company.

CHAPTER 26

Rachel studied Michael across the boardroom table. No matter how often she watched him speak to his team, she was always amazed by how firm yet respectful he was. It wasn't all that difficult without Shamus in the room. Thankfully, he wasn't present so often these days, and Rachel wasn't sure if it was because of Michael's insistence or because Shamus was happy with the changes they were making to handle the expansion. Whatever the reason for his absence, Rachel was grateful.

The past three months flew by in a haze of meetings with the board, staff members, and everyone in between. The hours were long, and most nights she fell into bed with some piece of clothing still on because she was too exhausted to remove it. Rachel knew she couldn't keep up with this pace if she wanted to make it out of her thirties, but they were necessary for now. The only relief were her late dinner meetings with Michael, and kissing him good night before the car took her home. His dropping her home every night wasn't possible, although he tried to at least once a week so they could have time alone, and give the driver a night off.

Rachel looked forward to those nights when, after their meeting and dinner, they spent time on the couch talking about anything but work, snuggling and kissing. Michael was always a gentleman, which Rachel appreciated, but some nights she wished he'd take her, either there on the couch, or to her bedroom. She would've been happy with the coffee table or the floor at this point! She knew Michael wanted her as badly as she wanted him, and although they agreed to take it slowly, she had no idea he meant a snail's pace. It wasn't as though they were strangers. They knew each other before getting involved, not to mention been intimate, even if it was in a dream. Now was not the time! If Michael needed her input, she had to be alert. Otherwise it would appear that she wasn't paying attention to the boss.

That wouldn't be good, since half the company was still torn. The journey wasn't an easy one, especially with management and the board, but some of the staff were also skeptical about her involvement. Most were nice enough and she'd managed to win over a few, but it wasn't effortless, especially when they noticed how close she and Michael were. Some staff knew about their past working relationship and why Michael hired her, but not everyone. She could feel their judging eyes whenever she and Michael spoke, or had a lunch meeting.

Rachel was thankful when their meeting finished a few minutes later and watched as everyone left her and Michael alone. Everyone except for Declan.

She cringed internally when he approached her.

"Rachel, lovely to see you again," his smarmy gaze swept over her. "I thought we could have lunch and get to know each other better."

She gulped to stop herself from vomiting in her mouth. This wasn't the first time he'd asked her to lunch. At least once a week, he was in her office, offering to take her out to lunch or dinner. His attempt at making it sound business related was beyond pathetic. The idea of being alone with him did not entice her in any way. Today was the first time he asked her with Michael in the room.

Michael's jaw visibly twitched before saying, "We already have a lunch meeting."

If they were alone, she would've kissed him. Instead, she couldn't resist giving Declan a glare.

Declan tipped his head in acceptance, but he couldn't hide the flash of fury from his eyes as he left them alone.

"Is he a problem for you?" Michael asked with furrowed brows.

"Not at the moment."

"Let me know if it becomes one. I don't want him anywhere near you," his voice laced with distain.

"I thought you were friends?"

"Friends is a strong word. We're more like rivals. Delan takes competitiveness to a whole other level." He grasped her hand. "Promise you'll tell me if he becomes inappropriate."

She squeezed his hand. "I will." She assumed they were friends and suddenly wanted to know the story behind their rivalry.

The door burst open, and Ashley popped in her head to ask if they wanted her to order lunch.

"How about we head out to lunch today?"

Rachel's eyes lit up. "Outside? In the sunshine?" she teased. Most days they didn't leave the office until it was dark.

Michael laughed. "Yes, outside."

Ashley was smiling when she nodded and closed the door behind her.

"I think we could use a break. Don't you?"

"Yes. Some alone time wouldn't hurt either."

Michael pushed his chair away from the table and strolled to where she sat. He pulled her out of her chair and kissed her—something he'd never done in the office. Rachel didn't resist because the boardroom door was closed and no one could see them, but she didn't let the kiss linger because she also knew the door wasn't locked and anyone could come in at any moment.

"Chicken," Michael teased when she pulled away.

"Just being cautious."

"Most of them probably think we're sleeping together anyways so why don't we prove them right?" Michael nuzzled her neck.

"That works great for you, but not so great for me." Rachel gave him a firm shove.

"You're right, but all this sneaking around is driving me crazy."

She couldn't agree more, but it was still too soon. It might always be too soon. *Perhaps we should wait until after my contract is over.*

"Me too, but you know it's better this way. Even if we told everyone, we'd still have to remain professional at the office." Rachel walked through the door he held open and toward the elevator in silence until the mechanical door closed. "Making our relationship public now would only add to an already strained situation."

"You're right," Michael ran his hand through his hair. "But I'm tired of not holding your hand when we're out to dinner or touching you when I want."

"Maybe we should wait until my contract ends."

The silence was deafening, but before it could be broken, the elevator door opened and people poured inside, pushing them further apart. Rachel couldn't see his face clearly, but she saw the tension in his jawline and that his gaze remained fixed on one spot of the elevator wall. There was easily another nine months on her contract, and if he wanted to reveal their relationship at this stage, there was no way he'd be happy waiting much longer. *Could I?*

If she were honest, the only reason she wanted to wait was because of how it would affect the people they worked with. She was serious that as Michael was a Doherty, he wouldn't be impacted as harshly.

The door opened at the ground level, and they poured out with everyone and headed toward the main doors leading them outside. "Where do you want to eat?" Rachel asked.

"Doesn't matter," Michael mumbled.

She led them to one of her favorite spots from which they usually got delivery, but chose a seat outside, wanting to feel the sun on her face. There was a chill in the air that wasn't just from the small gusts of wind that rushed past.

"You're obviously not happy about what I said, so let's talk about it," Rachel said after the waiter seated them.

"I thought I made how I feel clear in the boardroom when I said I hate the sneaking around."

"You did, but I don't think you fully understand how it will affect the smooth transition we're trying to make. It'll only complicate my already strained relationship with staff, your father, and the board members I have yet to charm." Rachel tried to joke but it fell flat.

"You don't know that for sure."

Rachel glanced at him.

"I hate to admit it, but you're right. It's still too soon, but there's no way in hell I'm waiting until the end of your contract to make our relationship public," he said firmly, taking her hand in his.

Rachel didn't try to remove her hand the way she usually did. "Maybe we could start by telling your family and Connor."

Michael's smile nearly blinded her. Getting Shamus used to their relationship first might be an easier route. *Not likely, Rachel.* Shamus might take the longest to accept their relationship, but Michael's family was the one she cared about the most in the long term. She didn't know what her plans would be when the contract ended, but unless things went horribly wrong with Michael, she didn't see herself leaving Ireland anytime soon. She could travel back to Cayman when she needed and work on expanding her business on this side of the world. The connection with Michael was deepening, even with the challenges of keeping their relationship secret. She wanted nothing more than to take the steps that normal relationships took like meeting friends and family and sharing special moments together. Well, the last one might be a challenge out in public, but she'd take what she could for now.

"Actually, my sister already knows and so does Connor."

"No surprise, but I'm glad they haven't spilled the beans—especially your sister."

"Regan understands our situation and agrees that keeping it a secret is a good idea."

"Does she still feel that way?"

Michael shrugged. "Not sure, but it doesn't matter. I like the idea of taking this first step. You've been here for three months already, and I know most of the staff already suspects. While some might not like it, if we continue to be professional, they'll come around when we share the truth with them."

His words sounded good in theory, but Rachel knew from how her relationship with Rick crashed and burned that office romances always created friction. *Michael isn't Rick...* They were vastly different people, but the work situation was much more complicated.

"You're right. We should continue to be professional at the office regardless of whether the staff knows we're dating or not."

"Does that mean I can't kiss you behind closed doors?"

"And smudge my lipstick?" Rachel feigned shock.

Michael laughed. "All right I'll save it until I drop you home."

"I have no objections when we're out of the office." Rachel leaned closer to Michael in invitation.

The waiter returned with their drinks before their lips met and they burst into laughter when he left. "I hope that's not a sign."

Michael lips tipped into a smirk. "Maybe the universe is trying to tell us that we should get a room."

Rachel slapped his arm playfully but laughed. "We have been taking it very slowly."

"Maybe a little too slow." The words held a hint of question, as if he were asking how she felt.

"Maybe. You've been a complete gentleman, which I appreciate, but I must admit it has been annoying at times."

His eyes twinkled mischievously. "I can be annoying."

"You can, but I did appreciate it."

"We both needed the time." His answer surprised her. Most guys didn't need time and were happy to jump in with both feet, but he wasn't like the men she knew—something she was grateful for.

She touched his arm. "Agreed, but it would be nice to spend some alone time together longer than a couple of hours at my apartment."

Michael raised an eyebrow, and a mischievous glint lit his eyes. "Is that your way of saying you're ready to jump my bones?"

She roared, catching the attention of people seated around them. "Not quite so crass, but something like that." She caressed his arm resting on the table. His hand covered hers and they leaned in and kissed. As much as they'd kissed in the past, Rachel was always amazed at how easily her heart raced and her insides melted at the feel of his lips. The gentleness of his kisses filled her with a sense of peace and safety she'd never experienced with anyone. In her heart she knew she never would. Michael was it for her.

He broke the kiss. They were in a public place, and close to their office. Anyone passing could see them kissing.

"Come with me to my parents' home this Sunday."

Sundays with his parents was an event she had understood and respected wasn't meant for anyone outside of the family. Even though Connor attended occasionally, he was much closer to being family because of his friendship with Michael.

"Are you sure?" The last thing Rachel wanted was Shamus and Moira thinking she was ambushing their family time.

"Yes. It's the perfect opportunity, and it'll be easier for them to accept," Michael clarified, answering her question without knowing it.

"In that case, I'd love to."

"Make sure to dress appropriately," he said casually, as if she'd know what that meant.

Rachel made a mental note to call Regan and ask her. The last thing she wanted was to show up at the Doherty house inappropriately dressed. Excitement and dread swirled in her stomach. Their relationship was about to take a huge step. Rather than let her mind create scenarios, she planned to enjoy it and remain present in every moment presented.

The rest of their lunch was spent laughing and talking about childhood troubles they got into, but no work or plans for their future.

CHAPTER 27

R achel longed to stab the food on the plate before her in frustration, but she reached for her mimosa instead. It had only been two hours and Shamus had managed to get under her skin in ways no one else could. Tonight's meditation session was going to be a long one to uncover where these triggers were coming from. *How the heck is he going to react when he finds out about our relationship? Does he suspect, and that's why he's giving me such a hard time?* Rachel's gaze shifted from one end of the table to the other, wishing Connor were there and she wasn't the only outsider.

"Tell us about your family, Rachel," Moira interrupted Shamus from another cutting comment.

Rachel gave her a look of thanks before answering. "My parents are both from the Cayman Islands and recently retired, although they are partners in my business."

"So, your parents were the ones who helped you get started?" Shamus interjected.

"Actually, they asked for an opportunity to invest once they saw how successful my company was," Rachel retorted. "Accountants themselves, they were ready to retire and wanted somewhere to invest some of their money. They're currently traveling around the world; however, they do like to check in once in a while to make sure their investment is still lucrative, but mostly they trust me to take care of the business." *Digest that for a while, Shamus!*

"You come from a family of accountants?" Regan asked. "And I thought my family gatherings were boring."

Michael hid his laughter with a cough after his mother shot him a stern gaze.

"Our conversations were much more enlightening once I told them what I wanted for my life was not what they wanted for my life. It was challenging at first, but they warmed up to the idea once they saw I was happier."

"How long did it take them to come around?" Regan asked quickly.

"There were weeks of lectures and guilt trips, but they eventually warmed up. I didn't let them get to me." Rachel smiled. "I was determined to live the life I wanted."

Regan nodded and smiled, as if understanding.

"Children always think they know better than their parents," Shamus' stare bore into Regan. "But history usually proves them wrong."

"I think it's history that proves adults are happier when they aren't trying to live the lives others want for them. Sometimes they line up, but when they don't you have unhappy children and adults who go through their entire life experiencing one they don't want."

Shamus's face turned red.

You went too far, Rachel. She'd just made things harder for Michael to share the news about their relationship. *Nice going!*

"Speaking of living one's own life," Michael interjected. "I have news." His gaze shifted between his parents and sister.

Rachel closed her eyes to calm her nerves and said a silent prayer that Shamus wouldn't have the butler drag her out of the house.

Not that Moira would allow such a scene, but Rachel wouldn't put it past him.

"Rachel and I are seeing each other."

The silence was thicker than butter just removed from the freezer—there was no cutting through it, even with a hot knife.

Regan sent them a smile and a "you're very brave" gaze as Shamus's face became so red Rachel thought he would explode. Moira's face returned to a solemn expression after her brief expression of shock passed.

Everyone's gaze eventually landed on Shamus, as if waiting for his response. Rachel eyed the door, wondering if she could rush out without anyone noticing. Not likely.

The silence dragged on. Shamus looked down at his food, up at them, took a drink of whatever brown liquid was in his glass, and set the glass down. Sweat coated Rachel's palms and her armpits, while her stomach and heart couldn't decide if they should stay in place, drop to her feet, or pop out of her mouth and run from the room screaming.

"What do your staff think about your relationship?" Regan asked when Shamus remained silent.

Rachel and Michael looked at each other. "We plan to keep it to ourselves for now."

"Yes," Rachel agreed. "Remaining professional in the office is crucial for our working relationship."

"How long has this been going on?" Regan asked, even though Rachel suspected she knew.

"After Rachel moved," Michael offered, since it wasn't a straightforward answer.

"So, you hired her because of your relationship?"

Rachel winced at Shamus's snide tone.

"No!" Michael and Rachel answered in unison.

"I had to convince her to start a relationship with me, and to take the job. Rachel wanted to keep the relationship secret until her contract ended, but I didn't want to wait that long."

"Sounds like that would've been a good option," Moira said with a grim stare as she placed her napkin on the table.

"Not for me, Mother. I want to go out in public and hold Rachel's hand without worrying someone we know will see us."

"You could just continue to dip your wick in private," Shamus stated harshly.

"Shamus!" Moira admonished, and Regan gasped. Michael's jawline twitched and even Rachel had the urge to fly across the table and tackle him. She clenched her fists underneath the table instead.

"We care about each other, Father. Our relationship is more than just physical. We have a connection that goes deeper than that."

Shamus snorted. "How deep could it be? You barely know each other."

"We've known each other for almost two years, Shamus. How many years does it take to know you care about someone?" Rachel asked, getting fed up with his rude responses.

"I still think it's better for you to keep your relationship a secret for the sake of your working relationship," Moira stated. "You won't feel the brunt of your decision, Michael, but Rachel will, and I suspect it's the reason she didn't want to move forward with your relationship in the beginning."

Rachel nodded, feeling better that someone understood, and that it wasn't because she didn't care about Michael.

"It won't be the first time coworkers have started a relationship, or even boss and worker, for that matter," Regan added.

"No, but people will question the validity of my integrity and company because of our relationship and wonder if I really earned it. Or is my business growing because of my connection and relationship with Michael? Not the kind of questions I want associated with my business, especially since I want to grow it in this part of the world when my contract ends."

"So, you do plan to stay on this side of the world?" Regan said with a smile.

"Yes."

"I'm happy to hear that," Moira added. "Especially if you plan to pursue a relationship with my son."

Shamus rolled his eyes. "Who cares about all that. The impact from their relationship going public is not only going to affect our business, but social standing as well. Think about the charities and events we host."

"How will it affect your social standing?" Rachel asked, although she suspected the meaning behind his comment. She hadn't given it much thought since Moira and Regan hadn't so much as hinted at it, but she had gotten looks and occasional comments from others at work. Comments she either shut down or brushed aside.

"Let's be honest. You're not one of us!"

"Irish?" Rachel pressed, wanting him to say it out loud. That's when people usually came to the realization about their prejudices.

"You know damn well what I mean," Shamus blustered.

"I want to hear you say it," Rachel pressed, the tone of her voice growing as irate as Shamus's. She could feel Michael's and everyone else's eyes on her and Shamus, as if they were watching an accident happen but there was nothing they could do to stop it.

Shamus's face turned red as he glared at her. "I would feel the same if you were someone uneducated, and white, with no social standing."

Rachel snorted. "I'm sure you'd be fine if I looked the part. Nothing but arm candy for people to admire. A brainless bimbo." She pushed the chair away from the table, knowing that if she didn't leave now, words would be said that couldn't be taken back. The last thing she wanted was to ruin the already tense relationship she had with Shamus.

"I love your son, Shamus. And I'm sorry it doesn't come in the package you want, but I happen to like who I am. If that's not good enough for you, then there's nothing I can say or do that will change your mind. Thank you for the lovely meal and company, Moira. Regan."

"I'll walk you out." Michael was already out of his seat and walking toward her as she headed for the exit.

Michael walked alongside her in silence as they traveled through his family home and to the parking lot. "I'm sorry about my father, Rachel." Michael spoke when they were outside, and away from prying eyes and ears of staff.

"Thank you." She appreciated his apology and wouldn't dismiss it with an "it's okay" comment like she would've in the past because it wasn't okay.

"He just needs time," Michael said, but she heard the doubt beneath the surface.

She remained silent, not wanting to add to it.

"I'll drive you home." He led her toward his car. They arrived together, but after the scene they just walked away from, Rachel expected the driver to take her home so Michael could put out the fires their announcement caused.

"Are you sure? I'm fine with using the driver."

Michael paused from opening the door for her and placed his arms around her waist. "You just declared you love me in front of my entire family. The least I can do is drive you home." His soft gaze held her captive.

Rachel blushed, remembering. She hadn't even told him she loved him and certainly never intended to say it for the first time in front of his family.

Michael lifted her chin. "I love you, too, by the way."

There was no need to wonder if he meant it. They'd both felt the emotion even if they hadn't said it out loud before. Love seemed to surround them whenever they were alone.

Rachel put her arms around his neck and kissed him with every emotion she'd felt from the moment she first met him until the moment she realized she loved him. His lips pressed against hers, soft and slow, once, twice before their tongues joined the kiss, heating her up from deep inside to every inch of her skin until it ached with longing for more contact.

Michael broke their kiss and opened the door and Rachel got in. As they drove to her apartment, her mind raced with clever statements she could use to invite him to stay the night, but her heart thundering in her ears drowned out all her other thoughts until the words she wanted to say were nothing more than a garble of nonsense. By the time he pulled into her parking garage, she had decided to let him make the move, and keep her mouth shut for fear of what might come out.

The conversation was made up of idle chatter in the elevator, making Rachel wonder if he was struggling with finding the right words too. That helped her relax. While she was certainly ready for their relationship to become physical, she wanted to make sure the moment was right, and not rushed or assumed because they declared they loved each other.

The elevator door opened into her apartment and Rachel stepped out, feeling Michael's eyes watching her. When she turned, he was still watching her as if he were trying to read her mind. "Are you as nervous as I am?"

Michael laughed. "Yes. I was trying to figure out what to do and say when we got here. I still haven't decided what to do or say."

"Me either." Rachel wrapped her arms around his waist and rested her head on his shoulder. "How about we start with a movie and some dinner?" Michael offered.

"Agreed. I hardly ate anything at lunch. I was terrified food would be stuck in my teeth or I'd make a mess of the food on my plate." Rachel buried her face in his chest.

Michael's laughter shook them both. "I figured, since your appetite is quite healthy when you're around me."

Rachel slapped him playfully. "Is that your way of saying I eat like a pig?"

"No! I meant, you're not afraid to eat more than a salad."

"Good answer."

Michael called the restaurant after they decided what to eat while she fired up the TV and chose the movie.

They ate when the food arrived and snuggled while they watched the movie. Michael rose to leave the way he usually did, and Rachel made no move to stop him as she walked with him to the elevator. She sensed they had all the time in the world to have a physical relationship, and wanted to savor moments like these and the ones they'd create now that their relationship was closer to being public. Michael's kiss was long and slow until the elevator doors opened.

"Good night, mo chroí," he said just before the elevator doors closed.

Rachel blew him a kiss. "Night."

As she headed to bed, she couldn't help but do a little jig and grin. The man she loved, loved her in return. That was more than any person could ask for, but she was also content, and had a thriving company. What more could a woman ask for?

Shamus invaded her happy thoughts with his sour, disapproving face. His approval of their relationship was a hurdle, but Rachel was grateful it wasn't one that she needed to be happy with Michael, and she prayed he wouldn't either.

Rachel fell into bed, the memory of Michael's sweet words and the feel of his kiss on her lips.

CHAPTER 28

Rachel sat on her balcony, a glass of red wine in her hand. It had been a long week, and she was grateful it was over. She was looking forward to a little peace and quiet, and time away from work. There was work she could do, but her last session with Sky pointed out she needed to take more breaks for downtime and to rejuvenate if she didn't want to burn out physically and emotionally. Sky was right. Whenever she took time to meditate, catch up with her and Arlene, go for a walk or exercise, her vibration elevated, and she felt better. Happier.

After the stress of work, and telling Michael's family about their relationship, she could use a week's vacation. A week wasn't possible, but right now she'd settle for a weekend. As much as she loved hanging out with Michael, she was ready for a little alone time.

She needed to reflect on everything that had happened, along with what was going to happen at the end of her contract. Although she'd been confident with her declaration to Shamus, the truth was she didn't know if she wanted to build her business on this side of the world as well as back in the Caribbean. *Maybe I needed a consultant,* she joked. *One to help me figure out how to make it happen without adding tons of stress to my already stressful life.* And what about her relationship with Michael? How would their relationship make it if she were traveling around the world, and the same for him? They'd never see each other, and that's not what either of them wanted. Selling her company was an option, but what would that mean? Was she ready to give up her business?

This time was supposed to be about relaxation and enjoying the peace and quiet of the moment, and being away from work.

Rachel started the meditation app on her phone and was in the middle of deep breaths when her doorbell rang. She tried to ignore it, but whoever wanted to come up the elevator was persistent and rang several times.

Annoyed, Rachel pushed herself up from her seated position and headed to the elevator, stifling a series of curses.

When the elevator reached her floor, Michael stood inside, roses in one hand and a picnic basket in another. "I'm hijacking you for the weekend."

So much for alone time. The boyish tip of his lips and mischievous glint in his eye made Rachel's heartbeat jump. Who could resist him? Not her.

"Don't worry, there are lots of surprises, including moments for you and me, together and alone," Michael responded as if reading her mind.

She loved how attuned he was to her thoughts and needs. "Let me get dressed first and pack a quick bag." She stood on her tiptoes to place a noisy kiss on his cheek.

Michael bowed. "I'll wait for you here, m'lady."

She laughed and rushed off to get ready. After shoving toiletries and a few outfits into an overnight bag, she returned to where he was waiting. He handed her the flowers and took her bag. When they reached downstairs, Liam was waiting for them with a smile and an open door.

"Where are we going?" she asked once they were in the car and settled.

"It's a surprise." Michael winked.

Rachel's pulse raced. She loved surprises, and while she wasn't the most spontaneous person, she did enjoy activities outside the norm. This was the first time she and Michael had gone somewhere that wasn't her apartment, the office, or a restaurant. Were they just going for a drive in the country, or were they getting on an airplane? Michael's family owned a jet, so anything was possible. Her question was answered when the driver dropped them at the train station. Not what she was expecting.

Once they found their seats, Rachel expected him to tell her where they were headed, but he was a vault. The announcements on the train didn't help because it was making more than one stop. With every name called out, Rachel's eyes darted to him, waiting for him to stand, but with each time he stayed seated, reading a book as if he didn't have a care in the world. Rachel was growing more annoyed with each stop, having difficulty concentrating on her own book and reading more than one page several times.

"Are you sure it's okay for us to leave?"

Michael grinned. "I'm the boss so I get to make the rules. Besides, it's the weekend."

Those words meant nothing since they had worked many weekends before.

The announcer stated this was their last stop and Rachel stood to reach for her bag, but Michael remained seated. "Aren't we getting off? It's the last stop."

"We are, but what's the rush?"

Rachel ground her teeth in frustration.

Michael laughed and stood. "And here I thought you were the patient one."

"I am! I'm just eager to see what you have planned for us."

Someone was holding a sign with their names on it outside the train.

As they drove down the long driveway toward a resort, Rachel couldn't help but gasp. The view was stunning. She hadn't seen nature in an exceedingly long time, other than the trees along the pathways she walked, and most times she hadn't noticed them, too busy talking with Michael or another staff member she was having a work lunch with.

At the end of the driveway was a stunning old-world castle with minor modern upgrades to the entrance. Most of the grounds consisted of a golf course that apparently went on for miles, a large pond, and lush landscaping comprised of thick shrubbery starting close to the castle and diminished to huge trees.

Rachel resisted the urge to wind down the window and hang her head outside so she could take in the smells she was certain were outside. The driver opened the door for them and informed them their bags would be delivered to their rooms.

Her neck craned up, glancing at the tall entrance to the front door. Inside, the lobby boasted high ceilings, stone walls, and a large fireplace.

The front desk checked them in, and they strolled down the hallway to their room. Their suite had two separate bedrooms, but shared a kitchen and living space—not that Rachel thought they'd be there long enough to use the kitchen. The views from the room were even more beautiful than when they walked inside, with rolling hills in the distance seen through giant windows that let in an amazing amount of natural light.

Rachel jumped when she heard someone speak, too busy gawking at the scenery to notice someone else in the room.

"There are several restaurants at the resort, along with a spa, and scheduled events that include outdoor and indoor activities. The list is here," he lifted a binder before setting it back down on the counter. "I'm Gunther, your butler. Please feel free to call on me with anything you need."

"Thank you, Gunther," Michael said.

She gestured for Michael to tip him, but he shook his head.

"You tip at the end of your stay," he clarified after the butler left.

"Aww. Like on a cruise."

"Yes, but a bigger tip."

"Thank you for getting two rooms," Rachel said, wrapping her arms around his waist.

"I didn't want you to feel pressured."

Rachel kissed him. "I know, and I appreciate it." They had lots of time.

"What's on the agenda for today?" she asked.

"Well for one, removing agenda from our vocabulary while we're here." Michael strolled over to the kitchen and picked up the folder and flipped through the pages. "There's a hike this afternoon, karaoke tonight, and dinner specials at the restaurants, and of course, there's the spa."

Rachel's eyes lit up. "Ooh, spa. Maybe we can do a couples massage, or sit in a tub of mud together?"

His nose crinkled with displeasure.

She gave him the best puppy eyes she could muster. "Come on. It'll be fun, and much better than just a manicure. Your skin will be as smooth as silk."

"Because that's what every man wants." Michael rolled his eyes. "How about you visit the spa and I'll go golfing and we meet for an early dinner?"

She pouted but agreed because she was ecstatic about visiting the spa. She hadn't been in years, and her tense back and shoulders screamed she needed it. "All right! But after dinner tonight, you're doing karaoke."

Terror erupted on his face.

"Just kidding. You go play your bad game of golf," Rachel teased, kissing him quickly on the cheek. He swatted her on the ass playfully before she headed out the door.

An hour later, Rachel's body was a pile of mush after the masseuse finished with her. She poured into her robe and took the glass of cucumber water he held for her outside the door. She strolled to the lounge area where other clients sat and in the corner was a table full of fruit, healthy snacks, and more fruit and herb-infused water. She took a free chair with a view of the rolling hills. *I could get used to this.* Arlene came to mind, and Rachel wished she was there with her enjoying this moment, and so she could talk with her about the visit to Michael's parents. Guilt racked Rachel as she realized she hadn't chatted with her in a couple of weeks. She and Sky spoke during their occasional sessions, and took time at the end to catch up. Arlene had called and left a message, but Rachel was so busy she forgot to call her back—like her parents.

As excited as she was about her relationship with Michael, she was starting to feel a bit stretched, and while she enjoyed the challenges of the job, she had no intention of continuing at this pace. She needed a change, perhaps delegating more of her work to someone else. Ashley was ambitious, so she'd have a talk with her when she returned. Rachel relaxed further into her lounge chair and took a long drink of the cucumber water. Delicious wasn't the word she'd use to describe it, but it was refreshing. She took a few deep breaths to help release the toxins the massage had started along with the water. Her breathing was interrupted when a woman sat in the chair next to her.

"You're Rachel Miller, aren't you?"

She focused on a woman who was stunning, with her jet-black hair and piercing blue eyes. Her gaze was the kind that could either make you feel admired or cut you to shreds in seconds. She looked familiar but Rachel couldn't quite place her.

"I'm Ciara. We met when you first arrived."

Rachel smiled even though her heart dropped to her feet. She was the woman who Michael's parents were always going on about and pushing him to rekindle a relationship with. Who could blame them? They were perfect for each other—they came from the same social status, and their families knew each other. "Nice to see you again."

"Are you here alone?"

Straight for the jugular, just like her brother, Declan. But unlike her brother, she didn't try to corner her at every moment. "I'm here with you." Rachel sidestepped the question. "What about you?"

Ciara's gaze sliced through her as if trying to detect her mood and how hard she should press for an answer. Rachel was relieved when she didn't push, and side stepped her question too. "I love this place. We come here all the time."

"It's lovely. My first time, but I'm enjoying myself so far."

"I didn't think someone like you could afford a place like this?"

Rachel cringed inwardly at the words, "someone like you," knowing it had a double meaning. She sipped her cucumber water. "Me and my mother used to go to places like this once a month back home." It wasn't as nice, but Ciara didn't know that. "The perks of owning a successful business." She didn't know a lot about Ciara, but she was certain the woman never worked a day in her life. "How long are you staying for?"

"Just the weekend. And you?"

"Same. I needed a relaxing weekend."

"Perhaps we could meet later for dinner, or one of the events?" Ciara inquired.

"I'm here to relax, so I'll either be in my room reading, going for long nature walks, or here."

Ciara crinkled her nose. "Sounds dreadful, except for being here, of course."

"Well, then, I guess that works out for both of us." Rachel stood to leave. "Enjoy your weekend."

Ciara nodded but was clearly annoyed.

Rachel dressed and returned to the room to wait for Michael, checking behind her to make sure she wasn't being followed.

She didn't mention running into Ciara when he returned, but recommended they have dinner in the room. Michael didn't object and headed for the shower, sweaty from golf. When he came out, they ordered food and relaxed with a glass of the wine Michael brought with them.

"This was a great idea." Rachel glanced out their room window at the sun setting in the distance.

"I agree." He reached over and caressed her face.

She closed her eyes and rested her cheek in his palm, enjoying the feel of his touch. "How was golf?" she asked when she opened her eyes.

"Bad, as usual." Michael grinned, his eyes never leaving hers as he stroked her cheek. He was leaning in to kiss her when someone knocked at the door and called out, "Room service."

Michael stood and let them in, directing them where to set up the food. "Are you hungry?"

"Famished," Rachel whispered. She was alone in a beautiful hotel with the man she loved.

His intense gaze matched hers as she moved to sit at the table where their dinner was laid out.

She sat in the chair next to him, and as her butt hit the cushion, he dragged her chair flush against his so their bodies were touching. "Much better," he winked with a playful smirk.

They usually sat close to each other when alone, but this felt different. Her skin felt uncomfortable beneath her clothes and the atmosphere in the room grew tense with an energy they knew all too well, but had never explored.

His arm brushed against hers as he placed a napkin in his lap and picked up his silverware. He started eating and she joined him after gulping down half of her wine to cool her heated insides.

He shared funny stories about his golf game, and she finally told him about running into Ciara, but he didn't seem to care. Their elbows bumped against each other, sometimes by accident and other times with playful nudges between bites of their food.

When he finished eating, his hand moved to caress the back of her neck. Rachel froze, goosebumps racing across her skin. She put down her fork, afraid it might fall and clatter against her plate. His hand moved from the back of her neck to the flesh of her bare shoulder blades, and up the side of her neck. When she turned to face him, his eyes were smoldering and heat shot straight to her toes and throughout the rest of her body. Michael had watched her hotly before, but nothing like he did now. *Oh my God!*

"Are you finished eating?"

Rachel nodded. Her tongue felt like lead in her mouth and her insides quivered in anticipation. Although he removed the pressure by getting a suite with two rooms, the last thing she wanted was to sleep alone.

"Did you want dessert?"

You bet your ass I do. Oh wait. Is he talking about actual dessert?
"No. You?"

"Yes, but not the kind you order off a menu," he said huskily.

Oh my! I've never seen this side of him before. I like it! He was usually so reserved and knew his limit, so their make-out sessions never went too far. Even when they kissed on the couch while watching TV, he always maintained control. It was something she admired about him, even if it did drive her crazy sometimes.

Michael stood and headed to the kitchen area, leaning casually against the counter, as if he didn't have a care in the world and was giving her time to make her decision.

The choice was an easy one. She wanted Michael more than she'd ever wanted another man. He stirred emotions in her she didn't realize were possible. The desire to touch him whenever he was near and not just sexually, as if being connected to him in some way would soothe her physically and emotionally, even spiritually.

When they touched, the sensations were like sparks zipping across her skin, and inside her body burned with a heat that started as a small flicker and spread into a firestorm the longer they stayed connected. The feelings he evoked were thrilling, terrifying, and strangely calming as well. Being around Michael was maddening and yet made her feel safe all at the same time.

His eyes slid slowly up and down the length of her body. "So, mo chroí, are ye ready to join me in the bedroom?" His deep voice, laced with a thicker accent than usual, raced across her skin, vibrating right to her core.

Rachel eased herself from the chair and nodded slowly, because no words formed in her mind. Her legs remained immobile, frozen with excitement and anticipation.

Michael pushed away from the counter, strode toward her like a lion stalking his prey.

Her fingers clutched at the edges of her dress as she watched him.

Then in a flash, Michael swooped her off her feet and carried her into his room, bridal style. She giggled like a little schoolgirl with her crush, after the shock of his action passed. "Why Mr. Doherty, who knew you were such as a romantic?"

His darkened eyes raked over her face and down her body. "Believe me, Ms. Miller. I'm all about the romance."

Shivers danced across her skin. *This man is going to be the death of me. I can't wait!*

CHAPTER 29

M ichael put her back on her feet when they reached his room, and disappointment pinched at the loss of his warmth and arms around her.

Shadows that had danced across the surfaces of the room rushed out of sight and only crept back when Michael adjusted the lighting to a soft glow.

With each step he took toward her, her heartbeat increased, and her chest tightened. The sheer look of him unnerved her the way it did the first time he walked through the boardroom in Cayman and whenever he'd watched her intently while she spoke or in her dreams. She thought by now she'd get used to how gorgeous he was, but he still took her by surprise and knocked the breath from her body.

She wanted this weekend, and this moment, to go slowly so they could live in it as long as possible. A weekend without someone walking into the office whenever they wanted to gaze at each other, touch each other, or kiss. Time to kiss him for hours or run her fingertips along every inch of his naked skin without the interruptions of people or calls. Their phones on silent since dinner.

Her hands touched the front of his shirt and then moved slowly up his chest until they reached his neck, and her fingers slipped into his hair. Rachel stepped closer as a warm, soft glow spread across her body. His arms locked around her waist and pulled her against him, and then he lowered his face to kiss her. His kiss was sweet, his lips tasting hers again and again before sliding his tongue in her mouth. The soft, slow feel of his tongue against hers was exquisite, as if they hadn't done so several times before. Her hands moved from his hair to the sides of his cheeks, longing for the feel of his skin against her fingertips. They stood there for what seemed an eternity kissing, holding each other before Rachel pulled away, breathless and knees shaking.

Rachel unbuttoned Michael's shirt, expecting him to start undressing, but he stood still, just watching her. He wanted this moment to last. The way she did.

Her hands trembled as she thought about their time together in her dream and the intensity and realness of it. Would this time be the same or different? In her dreams she'd been able to feel his skin and his body against her as if they were in the room together physically. This time they were in the same room, touching, connecting in person. Knowing it thrilled and terrified her at the same time.

The sound of Michael's pant zipper along with the whoosh of them landing on the bedroom floor, pulled her from her thoughts. He pushed down his underwear and stood naked before her. She'd seen him naked in her dreams, but the man before her was another story. Hard, and lean and powerful, with beautiful skin.

Rachel reached out to touch it with her fingertips the way she'd thought about earlier. *Electric.* She ran her hands over his chest and shoulders. She stepped closer so she could taste it with her lips and tongue. Michael's sharp intake of breath made her smile, along with his moan with the addition of her hands moving over his skin, moving from his shoulders to his neck and back, making a full circle until she faced him again.

Michael's grip on her tightened as he pulled her against him and kissed her hotly. "You're not making it easy to go slow," he rasped in her ear, and then proceeded to nibble his way from her neck to her shoulders. At the same time, his hands pushed the straps of her dress from her shoulders until it slid to the ground next to his own clothes. His fingers unhooked her bra and dug into her back, making their way down so he could lower her underwear.

When he stood, they faced each other, naked and exposed in ways they hadn't been in her dream. It was frightening, exhilarating, and highly erotic. Their eyes roamed over each inch of their bodies hotly before their gazes returned to stare at each other. Michael touched her cheek. "More beautiful in real life," he declared, as if reading her mind.

"I couldn't agree more." Rachel linked her fingers with his. The warmth of his hand spread up her arm and rushed across the rest of her body. Michael linked the fingers of his other hand with hers as if closing the circle around them until it felt as if they were vibrating.

A rush of emotions she couldn't describe pulsed within and around her. As she gazed into Michael's eyes, the realization there was only one emotion it could be descended on her: Love. True it came with other feelings, joy, peace, and hope, but at the core of all those emotions was only one. Love.

Linked hands turned into a long hug before their hands started exploring each other's bodies again. Rachel started to tremble with each long stroke of Michael's fingers over her shoulders, down her arms and hips, and up her back. "I need to sit, otherwise you're going to have to hold me up," Rachel rasped.

Michael chuckled and swept her up in his arms and carried her. He tried to set her down easily, but they ended up flopping on the bed together. "Well, that certainly didn't work the way I thought it would."

Rachel laughed. "It never does."

"I was trying to make this night perfect," he said, touching her cheek.

"I'm with you. That's all I need to make it perfect."

His eyes held her captive before he kissed her, running his hand along every inch of skin he could reach. His lips moved to her neck, and he kissed a trail to her breast, sucking and licking each one.

She moaned and arched her back to get closer to his mouth.

He chuckled and ran his hand along her back, lifting her closer to him before easing himself lower down her body. His other hand joined, grasping both her hips, and bringing her core right up to his mouth.

"Oh shit!" Rachel whimpered when she realized his intension, and when his tongue licked the length of her center. She bit her lips to keep from crying out loudly.

"Eyes on me, sweetheart." His voice rumbled.

She glanced down at him, heat rushing to her face.

"I want to hear every moan, every grasp. And I want your eyes on me when you come. I don't want to miss a second of you," his tone rough, and his eyes dark before he continued his torture.

His powerful stare and bold words shot through her like a fast pulse, taking her closer to the edge. She gripped his hair with one hand and reached for the sheets with the other, clutching both for dear life as her thighs quivered, and her heartbeat rushed to her ears as her orgasm barreled down on her.

"Michael!" she screamed, her body bowing.

"Beautiful," he whispered, crawling up her body to kiss her mouth. "So much better than our dream."

Rachel giggled and reached out and stoked his cheek. "Definitely!"

His fingers brushed her hair from her face. "And we're just getting started," his brows jumped suggestively.

"Really? I think I'm good."

"What?" he asked in disbelief, before realizing she was teasing him.

"Oh, you'll pay for that." He placed his legs on either side of her body, trapping her beneath him and tickled her.

"Michael. No!" she shrieked and bucked her body to stop him. It brought their bodies together, so his erection pressed against her core.

Her hand shifted so they ran along his back down to his ass and pushed them closer and rubbed against him harder.

Michael's moan rumbled in his chest, deep and long. "Geez, woman. You're killing me."

Her tongue licked his lips. "Then what are you waiting for?"

His sea-blue eyes focused intently on her face before claiming her mouth roughly, his tongue delving into her mouth with possession that stole her breath.

The kiss stopped abruptly, and he reached into the nightstand and pulled out a condom. He tore it quickly with his teeth.

Rachel gazed up at him hotly. "Let me do it."

Michael nodded and watched her, pulling her into another kiss when she finished. "You're so sexy, Rachel. You make it difficult to remain in control," he whispered, his voice thick with an edge she'd never heard before.

"I don't want your control. I want you. All of you. However you want to give yourself to me," her voice cracked with emotion and heat.

"God, Rachel. You will be the death of me," he groaned. Wrapping her legs around his waist, he gripped her hips tightly.

"Eyes on me," Michael rasped as he inched his way inside her.

Their collective moans echoed off the walls of the room.

"So good. Hot. Tight," he growled as he thrust into her.

"Harder," she cried, arching and pushed against the headboard.

"Tell me you're close, cause I'm not going to last long." He ground his teeth.

She nodded, no wording coming from her mouth but gasps and whimpers as her legs trembled and heat rushed over her body.

"Don't close your eyes, Rachel," he barked. His shifted his position, the angle thrusting him even deeper.

"Michael," she screamed as hot sparks shot behind her eyes and down her body.

"That's it, baby," Michael roared, gripping her hips as he chased his own release.

His movements slowed as they came down from their high, and their pulses returned to normal.

Michael went to the bathroom and when he returned, he crawled into bed next to her and pulled her against his body. She snuggled into his neck, inhaling his scent of sandalwood, pine, and another smell that was only him, a smell she loved.

"That was..."

"Better than any dream," he answered.

"I couldn't agree more."

He kissed her forehead and gripped her chin and tilted her face to his. "The night's not over yet, mo chroí," his voice laced with hunger as his hand ran along her back.

A glimmer of laughter came into her eyes. "Aren't you full of surprises, Mr. Doherty."

He rolled them over, so she was on her back. "You have no idea, Ms. Miller."

Michael watched Rachel sleep. She had given so much of herself during their connection. She hadn't held back, sharing every inch of her mind, body, and spirit. He'd never experienced anything like it in his life. This was stronger, deeper, and scarier. *And hot as hell.* He'd taken everything she shared with him when their bodies were joined and given her more of himself than to any other woman...but part of him had held back out of fear, just enjoying everything she was giving him. There was so much to their relationship where she always gave more than he did, and he wanted to change that. He never wanted her to feel underappreciated, because he loved her with emotions he didn't know how to express or communicate, especially what her being a part of his life meant to him. Rachel brought him happiness he never imagined, a calm that soothed his soul and a passion for life he didn't know existed inside him. As he brushed a stray hair from her face, he decided he didn't want a life without her.

The decision was one he made before she moved to Ireland after they reconnected, and it grew stronger with each moment they spent together. She was a part of his soul and had dug herself deeper into every crevice of his life and he wanted it to remain that way. A life without Rachel in any capacity wasn't a life. He realized that when they were apart, even as he'd made the choice to move on with his life. The moment he was near her and with her, the idea of being away from her was a torture he didn't want to live through.

He loved her more deeply than he thought it was possible to love someone.

This step would wreak havoc on his family, his business, and every part of his life because of the rushed time frame, but he didn't care. She had brought sunshine and love into his life, and while it would take time for everyone else to adjust to the idea, he didn't want to wait another minute. *I want Rachel as my wife.*

The hardest part would be convincing her. Rachel loved him, and under normal circumstances, a quick engagement and marriage would be nothing but a blip. But their personal and business lives complicated things.

Doubt washed over him. People had gotten married knowing each other in less time. *But they didn't have the family and business entanglements I have.* Michael rolled onto his back on stared at the high ceilings. *You don't even have a ring. Rachel wouldn't care about that,* he shot back.

He groaned. He was having an argument with himself.

Deciding to marry Rachel should be a happy and easy decision, but he was beginning to realize that while the idea itself was a good one, executing it was something else entirely.

CHAPTER 30

"What did you say?" Rachel blinked as she stared at him, certain she'd heard different words. *No, you misunderstood, Rachel.*

"I said, will you marry me." Michael knelt at the side of the bed, stroking her hair.

Her heart raced and plummeted in unison, rushing to her feet and then through her brain until it rattled around.

"I—I—" Rachel stammered. The first word that came to her mind was *Yes*, but then the faces of Michael's family paraded before her, along with all the people at work. They'd just told his parents about their relationship and this huge step felt like they were skipping the one hundred other ones that were supposed to happen before they were here. Rachel longed to tell him yes and start their new life together, but it wasn't that straight forward.

Michael's excited expression fell, and Rachel's heart ached with the words she needed to say but wished she didn't.

"I know it's fast, and there are about a million steps we should be taking before this one, but the truth is, Rachel, I love you. And I'm tired of putting off starting our lives. I know you're the woman I want to spend the rest of my life with. I know the hurdles we face are horrendous, with both our personal and professional lives, but

I know that between the two of us, we can figure things out if we take it one step at a time."

Tears streamed down Rachel's face, and her heart was bursting. The man she loved was asking her to share his life, and she was more worried about what others would think and how it would affect them. She forgot the most important thing to consider, what she wanted. She wanted exactly what he did. To share her life with him now, tomorrow, and every day after. Other people wouldn't be living their life, they would, and they deserved to be happy.

Rachel took Michael's face in her hands and kissed him as tears streamed down his face. "Yes. I'll marry you."

The pained expression on Michael's face melted and he kissed her deeply before crawling into bed to hold her. His hands stroked her hair and then down the length of her back before squeezing her tightly.

Rachel squealed.

He chuckled before rolling them over so he was above her. He kissed her softly. "It won't be easy."

She stroked his cheek. "I know, but you're worth it." She pushed down the fear bubbling below the surface.

"We're worth it," Michael clarified. "Do you want to let my parents know right away or give it time?"

Rachel bit her bottom lip. "Let me tell my friends and parents first." She wanted a bit of joy before all hell broke loose. She wasn't a hundred percent sure how her parents would accept the news, but their reaction would be nothing like Michael's parents. She was excited to tell everyone but them.

"I agree. We'll leave my parents for last." Michael leaned down and gave her a quick kiss. "Maybe we'll elope and send them a postcard from our honeymoon. Or maybe post it on social media and tag them in the post."

She gave a scoffing laugh. Both of them barely used their social media accounts because of their businesses. "I'm certain your father would hunt us down, demand an annulment, and deport me back to Cayman."

"I wouldn't allow it. You'd be my wife and there'd be nothing he could do about it. We're adults, not teenagers."

Wife. She liked the sound of the word. After her broken engagement, she accepted the idea she might never get married and was happy to focus on her career. After Michael stormed into her dreams, and then her life wreaking havoc on her ideas about relationship and love, she still hadn't considered marriage.

"I feel like a teenager." Rachel ran her hands over his chest and gazed up at him hotly. Their night together had been better than in her dream. The physical connection of their skin, hands, and body locked, making the experience hotter and heightened by their spiritual connection. To say there were fireworks would be an understatement.

"Me too." Michael kissed her long and slow, starting those fireworks again.

Sometime later, they lay on their backs, gazing up through the skylight in the bedroom. Hues of orange and gold streaked across the sky and Rachel realized he had woken her up before sunrise. "How about we go down for breakfast today? There's supposed to be a buffet with vegan Belgian waffles I'd like to try, and there's also an omelet station." She almost laughed at his pout. "We'll need all our energy for when we come back to the room."

His face lit up before he jumped off the bed and then pulled her with him. "What are we waiting for? I'm starving!"

They showered separately as Rachel knew if it was together, they'd never make it down for breakfast. Michael had pouted again but agreed. They headed toward the elevator hand in hand. When the doors opened a few doors down, she tried to pull her hand away. He smiled at the people in the elevator and led them to the free corner in the elevator. Two floors later, Ciara entered the elevator and Rachel tried to yank her hand away again, but Michael fingers tightened around hers.

"Michael. Rachel," Ciara greeted with her smirk that faded when she saw their linked fingers.

Michael nodded stiffly and Rachel managed a polite smile.

Rachel was relieved when they reached the ground floor and everyone poured out, including Michael, who relaxed when Ciara headed in the opposite direction from them.

"I forgot she was at the hotel." He sat at the table the waiter ushered them to. "What did she say?"

"She asked me if I was here alone, and I changed the subject and she left right after." Rachel nodded her thanks to the waiter after he set water on the table. They ordered coffee and spoke again after he left.

"No doubt to call my mother." Michael grimaced.

"I don't think so, since your mother never called."

Michael snorted. "They are probably plotting something as we speak. Especially now that my mother knows we're in a relationship."

"Maybe your mother never called because she knows we're in a relationship now and there's nothing to call about," Rachel offered, although she noticed the tension returning to his body. "You didn't seem bothered when I told you yesterday."

"That was because she hadn't seen us together. I didn't think we'd run into her. This hotel is enormous."

Rachel linked her fingers with his and pressed her frame closely to his. "Don't let her ruin our time together, especially today," she whispered.

Michael took a deep breath before caressing her cheek. "You're right. We're engaged and that's cause for celebration, not worrying about someone who's not part of it."

She was grateful he hadn't added, and who could make things difficult for them. Her brother was part of Michael's family's business, and she was certain Ciara had blurted the news of them here together with him.

They filled their plates with their favorite picks from the buffet after the waiter poured coffee in their cups.

"Are we going to have a long engagement? To get your family and business used to the idea."

"Now who's trying to ruin the moment?" A teasing smirk pulled at his lips.

Rachel poked him with the fork. "You're right. Let's just enjoy this moment together instead of thinking about what's going to happen next. Otherwise, our brains will explode, or we'll change our minds."

"Brains explode, maybe. Change my mind? Never!" He leaned over and kissed her.

"Good. Because I know where you live." They broke into boisterous laughter, drawing the attention of the tables around them.

She coaxed him into going for a short walk on the jogging trail after breakfast. "I didn't realize how much you enjoyed nature and being outside."

Her face lit up with a beaming smile. "It must be the island girl in me. I can't have the ocean, so nature is my substitute."

Michael gazed around at the large trees and beautifully landscaped pathway. "I can understand why. It's nothing like the ocean and sand in Cayman, but it's a decent alternative."

"I miss digging my toes in the sand and the sound and smell of the ocean, but I do enjoy the crunch of the ground and leaves beneath my feet, and the wind moving through the trees. It's like they're talking to me."

"Talking trees?" Michael gave her a sideways glance.

"Yes. Like when the birds are chirping and any other noises the animals make. It's their way of saying to slow down and savor the moment you're in."

"Really? I thought they were saying, 'Get the hell out of our neighborhood!'"

Rachel gave a throaty laugh. "You might be right, but I like to think of them as guides giving us signs for how to stay connected to nature and ourselves."

"That's deep.

"It's something I was learning from Sky before I left Cayman."

She'd mentioned Sky once or twice to Michael but never shared the details of their sessions. He was on his own spiritual journey, he told her how he took the route of meditation to calm, center, and heal. Not much more.

"I didn't realize since you never mentioned it before."

"I didn't want you to think you'd hired a crystal-wielding spiritual junkie."

Michael glanced at her sideways. "Have you not met my best friend?"

Rachel laughed. Connor was obsessed with everything spiritual. "But you don't work together. And he's not someone you're trusting with your family business."

He stopped walking and pulled her against him. "It wouldn't matter to me because I know it wouldn't affect the way you run the business. You've always been professional and would never do anything to jeopardize that. Besides, all these new age ideas are supposed to help with being a more happy and hence productive employee."

"So, you'd be open to hosting a work retreat with meditation, yoga, and stress detoxing?"

"Has Connor been pitching you his idea too?" He rolled his eyes.

She nudged him with her elbow. "Be honest. It's a great idea. I was also thinking about have a masseuse come to the office for an hour each day for the staff. We could use one of the empty offices. It wouldn't be full massages, just a quick fifteen minutes for their back and neck. That's usually where most people who sit all day hold the most tension."

Michael harrumphed. "You've definitely been speaking with Connor."

"Actually, I discovered that when I was in Cayman. I still have a knot in my shoulder no masseuse has been able to work out. I call it my Rick Knot."

Michael linked his fingers behind her waist. "Glad to hear it's not a Michael Knot."

She gave him a quick kiss. "No, that one's in my heart."

"A good knot, I hope."

"The best. The kind that links us together in a way I've never been linked with anyone else. And never will again." Rachel choked out the last words.

"Glad to hear it's not just me." Michael lowered his head and kissed her, long and slow.

"Wanna go back to the room now? I could use another shower." She glanced at him hotly.

"Is that a trick question?"

He took her hand and rushed them back to the hotel. They kissed and clung to each other in the empty elevator and ran to the room. Clothes flew in the air as they made their way to the bathroom and in the shower as hands touched bare skin and lips locked, tongues exploring and fingertips digging. The water of the shower flowed over them as their bodies joined and they cried out again and again.

"I can't stand anymore," she whispered in Michael's ear, and he picked her up, legs around his waist and carried them into the bedroom and laid her on the carpeted floor. "I'm going to get carpet burn." Rachel stated.

"Do you really care?" Michael asked as he thrust deeply. She moaned and grabbed his hips, giving him her answer.

CHAPTER 31

Rachel stifled a chuckle when the lady checking them out asked if they enjoyed their stay. "The food was excellent," Michael responded, giving her a scolding glance.

"Yes. The food was amazing. Especially the desserts," Rachel agreed, remembering last night when he ate dessert off her stomach.

"Have you no shame woman?" Michael asked after they walked away from the counter and headed outside to the car waiting to take them to the train station.

"Not when it comes to you," she whispered before licking his ear.

Michael gripped her by the shoulders. "You are so in trouble when we get back to my place later."

"Promise?" she teased, yelping after he squeezed her hand tightly.

The train trip back to the city seemed to take forever, along with the car ride. Liam watched them in the rearview mirror and smiled at Rachel when their eyes met. His, "Did you have a nice trip?" question when he opened the door for her, made her blush, along with Michael's comment.

"Yes, it was very relaxing."

While they had done some relaxing at the spa, the rest of the trip was far from it with them making love on every surface in their suit. She was going to need a vacation from her weekend getaway. When she glared at Michael after sitting, a cheeky grin curled his lips. She shook her head but didn't resist when he linked his fingers with hers.

Engaged. We are engaged. The words still sounded foreign in her mind, even without the weight of a ring on her finger, though she suspected it would still sound strange even with a ring. The first thing she had to do when she got back to her apartment was to call her parents, Arlene and Skylar, and then try to get a good night's sleep before work tomorrow. Although they'd only been gone for the weekend, it seemed longer. Between their activities, the heaviness of the conversations, and Michael's marriage proposal, their Friday at the office seemed like a lifetime ago. Excitement and dread coursed through her the closer they got to her apartment.

Fear crept across Rachel's skin and seeped into her bones as she thought about the people at work. She might have to start thinking about an exit clause before she and Michael got married or maybe consider a long engagement and get married after her contract ended. Rachel turned her gaze to the passing scenery outside which was shifting from tall trees, greenery, and scattered homes to clusters of houses and buildings as they got closer to the city. She needed to take a close look at her contract and maybe consider speaking to her lawyer.

Geez, Rachel. Talk about sucking all the romance out of your engagement! Arlene's voice echoed in her ears. While it wasn't far from the truth, she needed to protect her business, given her parents were investors.

Michael squeezed her and she leaned into him when his arm went around her shoulder. "Are you coming up?" she whispered.

"Yes, but just for a little while. I have some work to take care of before tomorrow. And I need to get some sleep. My insatiable fiancé kept me up all hours this weekend."

Rachel elbowed him in the ribs. It was one thing for Liam to know they were sleeping together, but it was another for him to learn they were engaged. That bit of news might be too enticing for him to keep to himself. Ciara seeing them at the resort together was bad enough. Rachel was certain that bit of news had already reached Michael's parents, since he ignored a few calls on the drive.

"I was going to kick you out after an early dinner anyway. I have a meeting with my annoying boss on Monday, so..."

"Ouch."

"Serves you right."

The car stopped and Liam got out to open the door for them.

"Thank you, Liam," Rachel said with a warm smile.

"My pleasure, Rachel." He smiled, and without any indication he'd heard their conversation. He unloaded their luggage from the trunk. "Shall I take the bags upstairs, sir?"

"We've got it. Thanks. I'll call you when I'm ready to be picked up."

"Yes sir," Liam closed the door.

Rachel and Michael grabbed their bags and walked through the entry way toward the elevator, smiling at the people they passed. Michael dropped his bag and pulled her into his arms when the elevator door closed. His lips captured hers in a heated kiss, and she clung to him as his tongue played with hers until the elevator opened onto her floor. He grabbed their bags and threw them inside a corner of her entryway and pulled her into the living room and onto the couch. Their hands moved to unbutton and unzip clothing until they were naked.

"I can't tell you how much I've dreamed about this moment," Michael rasped in her ear as he pressed himself inside her.

Rachel groaned. "Not nearly as much as me." She gripped his shoulders. Then they fell with a loud *thud* onto the floor when he tried to shift into a different position.

She laughed while Michael winced. "You really should communicate better what you want," she teased.

"I prefer to tell you with my hands, and mouth," he replied showing her what he meant by his words.

"I won't argue with you about that," Rachel moaned and arched her back to meet his thrusts. His mouth found hers again after making a trail from her breast to her shoulders and the spot on her neck she'd told him drove her crazy. The sounds of their moans filled the room until they collapsed on each other moments later.

"I am going to need to get some sleep in this relationship."

"You can sleep when you're dead." He teased, kissing her shoulder before helping her sit up. "I'm trying to make up for lost time. There are lots of other places in this flat that need our attention."

She winced as she put on her underwear. "I might have to get back to my yoga classes; otherwise, I won't be able to bend over." She raised a hand to keep him from answering.

"So close. I had a good one too," he winked.

"I bet you did. What do you want to eat for dinner?"

"I'm in the mood for Chinese," Michael responded, pulling up his pants but remaining shirtless.

"Chinese it is." She headed to the entryway for her handbag. After pulling out her phone, she placed their orders, since they both had the same thing every single time, plunked down on the couch next to him, wishing things could stay this way. She rested her head against his shoulder and linked her fingers with his.

"I wish things could stay like this," Michael said, as if reading her mind.

"What? Half-naked on the couch waiting for Chinese food?" Rachel's lips pulled into a teasing smile.

His grip tightened around her until she yelped. "Things are going to change starting tomorrow and not all of them in a good way."

"I know. We'll take it one day at a time," she assured him, even as flutters of fear nipped at her. They remained silent, holding each other, and enjoying the skyline of the city lights until the food arrived.

They laughed and joked while they ate and made love one more time before she walked him to the elevator. It was almost nine o'clock and she still had to call her parents, Arlene and Skylar and tell them about the engagement, not to mention prepare for her workday tomorrow and get a good night's sleep.

"I wish you could stay the night," Rachel said, even though it wasn't what either of them needed right now. Seeing his face in the mornings and lying around in bed was nice.

"Me too. I love waking up next to you." He squeezed her against him and kissed her one last time before getting into the elevator. "We'll be there soon enough."

After the elevator door closed, she checked her watch to figure out the time zone her parents were in to see if they were awake. They were. She dialed their number and grinned when they answered in unison with happiness and laughter in their voices.

"Hi, Mom, Dad."

"Hi honey. Is everything okay? You're calling late for your time."

Rachel smiled. "It's only nine o'clock here."

Her father checked his watch again. "Oh, never mind. Good to hear your voice."

Although they tried to speak at least once a week, the conversations lately had been short, due to both their busy schedules, hers with work and theirs gallivanting on a new excursion in whatever country they were visiting.

"I'm calling to give you big news."

Both of her parents' faces popped into the phone screen, their eyes wide with anticipation.

"I'm engaged."

They didn't try to hide their shock. "Engaged? I didn't think things were that serious between you and Michael." Her mother nodded in agreement. "I thought you just made it official as a couple."

Rachel hadn't shared that much about their relationship with her parents, other than seeing each other, which they had lectured her about, given their working relationship. But they were happy she'd found happiness after things ended so badly with Shawn.

"What do his parents think?" her mother asked.

"We haven't told them yet. We just got engaged yesterday. I wanted to call you. We haven't decided when we'll tell his parents, not to mention everyone else. It's very new and sudden."

"Are you happy?" her father asked.

"Ridiculously," Rachel said her lips splitting into a huge smile.

"Well, that's all that matters."

"It won't be easy," her mother interjected, "but if anyone can handle it, you can."

"Thanks, Mom."

The rest of the conversation with her parents was her mother making her promise to contact her once they chose a date, and to share the drama that would erupt once people at work and

Michael's family found out. Her dad shared the funny photos from the excursions they'd been on that month and all the strange food they'd eaten. When Rachel hung up, tears filled her eyes. She hadn't realized how much she missed her parents and wished she could stop by their house and spend time with them, hug them, especially now their relationship had returned to how it was when she was a child.

Arlene and Sky were the next phone calls and while she was looking forward to talking with her friends, she didn't know how they'd take the news. Rachel chuckled, imaging Sky's response, and Arlene getting annoyed.

"Hello?"

"Hi Arlene."

"I'm sorry who's this?"

Rachel grinned. "It's your best friend."

"Best friend? I don't have a best friend, cause if I did, she'd call me more often than you do. What, you leave the island and suddenly you no longer have time for me?"

"You know that's not true. I've been busy, and the time difference doesn't help either," Rachel argued.

Arlene snorted. "Those sounds like pitiful excuses to me."

"They're not and you know it," Rachel retorted, but couldn't help laughing.

"You're laughing at my pain? Some friend."

"I'm laughing because I forgot how much I miss talking and joking with you."

"You wouldn't have to forget if you'd call me more or return my phone calls."

"Then stop calling me late at night when I'm sleeping," Rachel shot back playfully.

"What kind of workaholic is asleep after ten o'clock?"

"One that's up at five in the morning. Why don't you answer when I call you?"

"Ha! Like I'm going to be awake enough to talk that early in the morning. It's inhuman."

Rachel broke into laughter and Arlene joined her.

"So, why did you really call me?"

Rachel took a deep calming breath. "Before I share my news, we need to get Sky on the call."

"Why? Won't she already know?"

Rachel let out a chuckle. "She doesn't know everything before it happens."

"Sure, she doesn't. How much you wanna guess she knows?"

"I'm not taking that bet." Rachel put her on hold and called Skylar.

"Hi Rachel, Arlene."

"Told you," Arlene said.

"I don't know everything, Arlene," Skylar shot back. "I just knew who was calling."

"I'm engaged," Rachel blurted out before they started arguing on their three-way call.

"To who?" Arlene asked.

"Isn't that obvious?" Skylar said.

"I know who, it's just an automatic respond, Sky. People do have them."

"I know that!"

"Ladies!" Rachel interjected. "I wanted to let you know right away, but if you're going to argue, I'm going to leave you here on the phone and go to bed."

"I know how you feel about him and I'm happy for you, but..." Arlene stated.

Here it comes.

"Does this mean you're going to stay and live in Ireland instead of coming back to Cayman?"

"I'm not sure. We still have a lot to talk about. We haven't even told his family yet."

"I don't envy you that conversation," Skylar said.

Rachel ran a hand through her hair and leaned back onto the couch. "You and me both. Maybe I'll let him do it by himself." She grinned into the phone.

They laughed, lightening the mood of the conversation. "You know I'm going to be your maid of honor, right?" Arlene declared.

"Depending on his family's response, they might be eloping," Skylar said. "How did your parents take the news?"

"They handled it the same as you. Happy for me but have their reservations."

"Then it's settled. You'll have the ceremony here in Cayman. You're not taking away my chance to be at my best friend's wedding." Arlene stated.

"And being her maid of honor," Skylar added.

"Exactly!"

Laughter erupted on both ends of the call. They spent the rest of the time on the phone reminiscing about all the crazy things they got up to in school and when they were coming to visit her in Ireland.

"I miss you guys." Rachel's voice cracked.

"Stop it or you're going to make me cry," Arlene said.

Rachel garbled, a cross between a laugh and a sob.

"That sounded terrifying." Arlene stated in horror and chuckled with Rachel and Skylar. "We love you and can't wait to see you soon." There was a pause before Skylar added, "We really are happy for you, Rachel."

"I know."

"Bye."

"Bye. And I love you guys too."

She glanced at her watch. The amount of sleep she'd hoped for was gone, but it would be more than she got over the weekend.

Rachel grinned as she remembered the moments they shared from their time in the room, and when he'd proposed. They were memories she'd treasure over the next couple of weeks when his family found out about their engagement.

Five minutes after she got into bed, her phone dinged with a message from Michael. It was a peach and tongue emoji, followed by heart eyes. The words, "Miss you," came through right after. A chuckle escaped her lips before turning into a dreamy smile.

CHAPTER 32

"Declan Murphy is here to see you, Rachel," Ashley said, sticking her head inside her office. *This is the last person I need to deal with.* She longed to blow him off, but the last time they spoke, he knew she was single. Who knew what the story would be now that his sister, Ciara, saw her and Michael together. Declan didn't strike her as the type to take no for an answer—no matter the situation. *Get it over with.* Fast, and like a bandage, she was certain it wasn't going to be painless.

Rachel didn't want to be alone with him, so met him outside. "Mr. Kelly." She addressed him formally knowing it annoyed him, as it kept him at arm's length. "What can I do for you?" She wasn't going to waste niceties on him.

The dazzling smile he gave probably charmed a lot of women, her assistant included by the way she watched him, but something about him grated on her.

"I've told you to call me Declan." He took a step, closing the space between them. "You can allow me to take you to lunch."

His arrogant tone made her stomach want to hurl. "Thank you, but I've got a full schedule this whole week."

"Fine then let me take you to dinner one night this week. I won't take no for an answer." He flashed another dazzling smile and ran a hand arrogantly through his midnight hair. "According to my sister, we have lots to talk about."

Shit. This is bad! She didn't trust what he might do with this kind of information. Nothing good, that's for sure.

"Why don't we discuss it while I walk you to the elevator?" She ignored the arm he extended.

When they were out of earshot Rachel said, "I think it's only fair that I tell you upfront that I'm not interested."

"Interested in dinner? Is that because of your relationship with Michael?" His sneer marred his otherwise attractive face.

Rachel stopped walking, glancing around to make sure no one could hear them, before she turned to face Declan. "Let's not waste each other's time and play games or beat around the bush. I know exactly why you keep inviting me out. Your only interest is in agitating Michael because of the history between you two, and I have no intention of participating in your games or being a part of anything so petty." She negated responding to his comment about her relationship with Michael.

Declan surprised her by laughing. "Ciara was right about you. You are direct—and shrewd. I can see why Michael likes you."

Rachel kept her reaction neutral.

Declan stepped close to her and whispered with a provocative tone. "And cool as a cucumber. I bet there's fire under all that ice." His hand gripped her arm tightly, keeping her from moving away from him. "I wonder if you'd burn me to keep your secret."

Her eyes shot to his face as she understood his meaning. He's an even bigger ass that she originally thought. She longed to blurt out the words, but Declan had Shamus's ears, along with certain members of the board. She had to remain professional no matter how vile he was acting, or how much she wanted to punch his smug face.

Rachel pried her arm aways from his grip and pushed him into the elevator. "Goodbye, Mr. Kelly." She walked back to her office without looking back.

Every time she encountered him and his sister, it only confirmed how rude, arrogant, and privileged they both were, to the point that they couldn't see outside the world they and their family had created for themselves. They were used to getting everything they wanted and didn't care if that meant hurting the people around them. Rachel wanted nothing to do with them, but she couldn't avoid them because of their connection with Michael's family.

Declan and Ciara knowing about her and Michael's relationship was a recipe for disaster, especially given her interaction with Declan. She shivered with disgust remembering his obvious blackmail words. *What the hell am I going to do?* She sure as hell wasn't going to sleep with him to keep him quiet and she was hesitant to tell Michael.

Their relationship was strained given their competitiveness and their family connection, not to mention the strain she created with Michael's parents over their relationship.

When she returned to her office, Ashley was smiling. "Should I book you a hair appointment for your date?"

"No need. There is no date."

"Why not? He's cute."

"Stay away from him," Rachel said, picking up her phone from the desk where she'd left it while walking Declan to the elevator.

"Why?" Ashley asked before clearing her throat and asking Rachel what she'd like for lunch, and if she needed help getting ready for her upcoming meetings.

"Ms. Miller will be having lunch with me today," Michael interjected from the doorway.

Rachel resisted the urge to grin with excitement. Too bad she couldn't make it.

"Do you have a minute to discuss an issue with me?"

She nodded and headed into her office. Michael followed behind her and closed the door.

His lips were on hers just as she turned, and she kissed him back feverishly, grateful for the blinds and that she had the lipstick she was wearing in her handbag.

"Mr. Doherty. I might have to file a complaint for sexual harassment for that kiss."

Michael grinned. "It'd be totally worth it!" He squeezed her against him and nuzzled her neck.

Rachel hugged him back just as tightly.

When they parted, she sat in her desk chair, and Michael in one of the chairs in front of it. "So, guess who just paid me a visit?"

"Who?"

"Declan Kelly."

Michael straightened in his chair. "What did he want?"

"To take me out to lunch, or dinner."

"What did you tell him?" The strain in Michael's tone was strong.

She told him about Declan's constantly asking her out, but it still put him on edge. The rivalry between them was the reason she always told him. She didn't want Declan to give him any wrong impressions about her or use it to hurt him.

"No, of course. However, Ciara told him about us."

"Shite!" he grumbled.

Rachel stretched her hand across the desk to him. "That's not all." Her voice was tense.

His brows narrowed, and his face lit with concern.

"He wanted me to sleep with him to keep our secret." The words rushed from her mouth, as if saying them would be easier for him to hear.

"Bloody bastard! I'll kill him!" he said through gritted teeth. Michael shot out of the chair and headed to the door. She chased after him, tugging on his arm roughly to stop him from leaving her office.

"He can't speak to you like that, Rachel!"

She pulled him into a tight hug. "I know that. But he didn't use those exact words. He merely implied. What do you think he'll say if you confront him?"

The rigidness in his body loosened. They both knew he'd deny it or claim it was a misunderstanding.

"This wasn't going to be an easy road, Michael, especially after this weekend." She released her tight grip on his frame and leaned back to look him in the eyes.

He raked a hand through his hair in frustration. "I know, but I still want to rip his limbs from his body."

She glanced at his taut jawline, and clenched fists. He wasn't just annoyed; he was angry. She'd never seen him like this before. "Wow. I really wish we weren't at work right now."

Michael gave her a quizzing glance.

"You being mad is really hot." Her hands traveled up his jacket until they were around his neck.

He tsked, a comical grin pulling at the edges of his mouth. It took him a moment to realize she was serious and his eyes darkened. "Really?"

She nodded, her eyes dancing across his face before settling on his mouth.

He cursed under his breath before lifting her off her feet and walking them to her desk. He placed her on the edge and stepped between her legs. His hands were in her hair and his mouth on hers while she tugged on his jacket, pulling him closer until she felt his erection against her core. She moaned when he gripped her hips and ground himself against her. "We can't. Not here," she whispered breathlessly.

Michael rested his forehead against hers, trying to catch his breath. "I know. We can't even go for a long lunch because we have meetings we can't reschedule."

"I say we do away with all meetings."

He chuckled and removed his hands from her hips while pulling her off the desk and back on her feet. He tugged at his suit, trying to return its neatness.

"I'll have lunch with you if you promise to keep your hands to yourself?" she said with a cheeky grin while pulling her makeup bag from her purse.

"I'll make no such promises." He leaned against her desk as he watched her smooth out her hair and refresh her lipstick.

"If you broke it, I suppose you could make it up to me later tonight." She tapped a finger against her chin.

"I'd be more than willing to make it up to you all night long," Michael pledged with a heated glare.

"Then I suppose that would work." She snapped her compact mirror closed and returned it to her handbag. Standing, she walked to the phone. "Ashley, please order Chinese for me and Michael."

"Ok," came from the other side of the phone before the call ended.

He pulled her into his arms and nuzzled her neck.

Leaning back, she gazed into his eyes, whose blue color she was starting to adore. "You know, even if I was trying to keep up the appearance we weren't together, I still wouldn't go out with that man." There was no need to ask who she was talking about.

"He's rude, arrogant, and a complete ass. And I don't like his sister either."

Michael relaxed and squeezed her frame. "I'm happy to hear that. I'm not fond of them myself."

"But you did date Ciara." Rachel tried to keep her tone neutral.

"I did for a short while because my parents were pushing for a relationship, but I didn't like her that way and never would."

"I'm happy to hear that." Her smile was one of relief.

"If he tries to escalate things, let me know."

"You know he will, but I can handle him."

"I know, but I also know Declan. When he wants something, he'll do whatever it takes to get it, regardless of the circumstance."

"Is that what happened between the two of you?"

Michael nodded and Rachel let the silence stretch out between them, waiting for him to explain further, but he didn't.

Michael started to speak, but Ashley's voice over the intercom interrupted him.

So close. Rachel answered the phone. "Yes?"

"Lunch is here."

Rachel grabbed their lunch from Ashley's desk. And they talked about work while they ate, determined to avoid talking about the threat of Declan and Ciara.

"We'll catch up later." Michael stood and put their empty food containers in the garbage.

"It'll have to be over dinner. I've got too much work to catch up on because my fiancé whisked me away for the weekend."

"Sounds like a keeper," he grinned.

"He is." She stood and walked with him to the door. She kissed him lightly before opening the door, then refreshing her lipstick again, she called Ashley to her office to prepare for her afternoon meetings.

After hours of meetings and playing catchup, Rachel was ready to crawl into bed before she remembered she had dinner plans with Michael. She was certain he wouldn't mind if they ate either at the office if he was still working or at her place. She walked to his office and was surprised to see Ciara there. It appeared that she and her brother were on a mission. Seeing them together at the hotel obviously hadn't discouraged Ciara.

As she stood in the doorway, Rachel longed to rush into Michael's office and tell her to take her hands off her fiancé, but it was not only a ridiculous notion, but not something she'd do. She trusted Michael completely, regardless of the scene before her. Ciara was pressed closely against Michael, who was backed against his desk, trying to pull away the arms she was trying to put around his neck.

"Come on, Michael. You know we'd be good together."

"I know for a fact we aren't. We tried already, remember? I just don't feel that way about you."

"You never gave it a chance."

"When you know, you know, Ciara."

"I think it's because of that woman."

"What woman?"

"The woman I saw you at the hotel with. The one who works for you."

"You know her name, Ciara. Rachel."

"Yes. It's because of Rachel."

"It's because of me and you, Ciara, and no one else. We'd never make a good match. You're just too stubborn to admit it."

Ciara pouted. "I don't like to lose, but I do like you." She ran her palms along the front of his shirt.

Enough is enough. Rachel knocked loudly on the door and stepped inside. She smiled at them both. "Hello, Ciara. Michael."

He tensed and Ciara pressed herself closer to him.

"I came for Michael. We have dinner plans."

"Well as you can see, he's occupied."

"Shall we reschedule, Michael?" Rachel inquired calmly, even though inside she was imagining yanking Ciara off him by the hair and throwing her out of his office.

"No," Michael almost shouted, stepping away from Ciara. "We have a lot to talk about." He headed out the door, shepherding Ciara out the door with his palm pressed against her back. "Let me walk you to the elevator. Rachel, I'll meet you in the garage. We'll take my car."

She nodded. "Goodbye, Ciara." The sour face she shot at Rachel was priceless.

She was standing by Michael's car for about five minutes before he showed up. "I really didn't expect you to head to the garage, but I needed an excuse to get rid of her quickly and it was the only thing I could think of."

"You didn't keep me waiting long, and this garage is safe and secure. Otherwise, I would've waited inside."

Michael put his arms around her waist and kissed her lightly. "Thank you for being so understanding."

"I overheard your conversation and trust you completely."

He cupped one side of her cheek. "I'll never give you a reason to doubt me."

Rachel wrapped her arms around his neck and kissed him. "You'd better not. Arlene knows where you live," she teased, "and Skylar will hex you."

He chuckled and opened the car door for her. When she was inside, he got into the driver's seat. Starting the car, he headed out of the garage into the city streets where a cascade of multicolored lights from the windows of the buildings reflected inside.

CHAPTER 33

"**I**'ve got a special surprise for you." Michael pulled her hand from her lap where she sat across from him in the car and linked their fingers.

"Don't forget we have dinner plans with Connor and Regan later."

A week had passed since they returned from their weekend get-away and other than the drama with Declan, he was pleasantly surprised to discover things had been quiet. No calls or meeting requests from his parents and nothing from Ciara or Declan. He was happy for it, but a part of him couldn't help but wonder if something bigger was brewing and would explode on them.

"We'll make it," he said with a warm smile. He put on the indicator and turned into a small parking space outside an old cottage-style building.

"Is this why you wanted to go lunch today?" Rachel asked when she noticed the words on the bright sign.

Michael nodded as he parked the car. They walked hand in hand up to the building, where an employee was waiting by the door.

"Welcome, Mr. Doherty." She smiled politely at Rachel and said, "Ma'am."

"Good evening," they said in unison. "Thank you so much for keeping the store open after hours."

"It's our pleasure, sir." The employee led them to a private area where trays of rings were laid out on the counter, with two cushioned seats before it. "Can I get you something to drink? Water, tea, champagne?"

"I'd love a green tea if you have it." Rachel took a seat.

He watched as she tried to contain the giant smile and obvious excitement that appeared to be bubbling up inside her.

She squeezed his hands when they were alone. "Thank you for doing this."

"I can't have my fiancé ringless." Not to mention, putting a ring on her finger would be a clear sign to Declan that she was off-limits.

Rachel being able to wear it to work or in public without questions from everyone didn't matter in that moment.

The employee returned with green tea for her and water for him and then proceeded to tell them about each ring Rachel liked and tried on. In the end, she settled on a yellow diamond, because it was stunning, and he suspected it looked the least like an engagement ring. That way she could wear it without anyone getting suspicious, although they'd ask questions. The ring was gorgeous and bound to draw attention.

As they headed back to the car, their fingers linked, Michael felt the ring press against his skin. It felt strange. *Is the sensation because there wasn't a ring there before or because of what lies ahead?* He was looking forward to their life together, but dealing with his family and everything that went along with it? Not so much. Maybe they could elope and run away to the other side of the world?

He kissed her hand to help push back the anxiety threatening to rush to the surface. She graced him with one of her warm smiles, the one that made him feel as if he was the only man in the room, one that gave him peace and caused his heart to stutter at the same time. That smile said, "I love you," and "Nothing else mattered."

He longed to believe it, but in some situations, love wasn't the answer to everything. Love wouldn't make his parents accept her overnight.

She turned on the car radio and rock tunes flooded the car before she turned down the volume.

Michael glanced over at his fiancé. The crease in her forehead screamed something was on her mind. He suspected it was the unavoidable meeting with his parents they needed to have. If the news leaked before they had the chance to tell them...he shuddered.

They'd decided to meet with Connor and Regan first as a gauge for how his parents would respond. While their opinions would be skewed, because Regan and Connor would be happy for them, they were also the only candidates for test subjects, as they'd provide honest feedback.

Michael turned into his driveway and shut off the car engine. He'd asked Connor and Regan to meet for dinner at his place. This was the first time Rachel had visited his flat. They agreed it was better she didn't because it would raise eyebrows for her to visit him, but not for him to visit her at the company-owned flat, which could be explained away as dinner meetings. Cold sweat spread across Michael's body as he opened the car door for Rachel and led her up the stairs to his flat. *Why am I nervous? Maybe it's because your future wife is about to see your home for the first time? Or that you're one step closer to telling your parents about your proposal to Rachel—a woman they aren't particularly fond of?*

Michael rubbed his hands along his pants to remove the excess sweat before opening the doors and turning on the lights. He watched as Rachel circled the immediate areas and peeked around corners to get a glimpse of the next room. He checked his watch. Connor and Regan would be there any minute. No time to ravish her in the kitchen or another room, as he'd fantasized about several times. Maybe after they left. Rachel gave his flat her smile of approval. "Expecting a bachelor pad?"

She grinned. "Honestly, yes, but only because you spend more time at work. I suppose your mother had it decorated?"

Michael chuckled. "No, but she did insist I hire one."

"I thought so." She placed her arms around his waist and kissed him. "Do we have time to..."

The doorbell rang before Rachel could finish her sentence.

"I guess not." They laughed but he gave her a quick kiss.

She stayed in the living room, while he went to welcome their guests.

"Mom, Dad," Michael said loudly so she would hear. "What are you doing here?"

"Visiting our son. We never see you anymore, so we thought we'd catch you here, especially since Regan said she was coming over for dinner."

Michael's mother kissed him on the cheek and gave him her coat, as did his father. "Why didn't we get invited over for dinner?"

"Because Connor was also invited."

Shamus's face soured. "I told you we should've called."

"You'll be fine," Moira assured him. "I'm certain Connor's face will have the same expression when he finds you here."

"Rachel's here too."

Shamus rolled his eyes. "So, everyone was invited except for the people who raised and cared for you?"

Michael was tempted to mention their nanny's name but decided against it when the doorbell rang again. When he opened the door, their actual guests were standing in the doorway. *Did they come together?* "Mom and Dad are here," he said quietly and smothered a snicker when Connor's face soured the way his father's had.

"You shouldn't have told him about tonight," Connor said to Regan.

Regan threw her hands up. "I know. It was just an impulse."

"You used to be better at dodging your parents. You're getting too honest in your old age."

Regan stuck her tongue out at Connor just as they entered the living room where their parents were standing with Rachel in awkward silence.

"The food should be here soon, so I'll have to order more."

"It'll be fine. We'll just share," Moira assured him.

The silence in the room was deafening, as if they'd already shared the news of their engagement and everyone was in shock.

"Can I get anyone a drink?" Michael asked.

Everyone gave their request. "I'll help you," Rachel offered, following him into the kitchen.

"What are we going to do now that your parents are here?" she asked, taking wine and Scotch glasses from the clear-fronted cupboard.

He grabbed a bottle from the wine fridge after handing her a bottle of Scotch.

"We go forward with the plan and tell them about the engagement. Knock everyone out with one shot."

"You sure that's a good idea?" Apprehension etched her face.

He wasn't sure, but he knew the longer they waited to tell them the worse things would be. He leaned closer and kissed her soundly. "No, but I say we do it anyway," he said with a chuckle when Rachel scrunched her face with dismay.

"Okay, but you get to tell them. I'm going to sit as far away from your parents as possible in case they decide to dive across the table and attack me."

He nodded, a grin tugging the corners of his lips. His parents wouldn't physically attack her, but words were sure to fly with the intent to mean harm, especially from his father. Thankfully, Regan and Connor were here to buffer him.

"Ready to go into the lion's den?" Michael asked, grabbing three glasses off the counter.

"No, but we can't stay in the kitchen all night," she replied and followed him into the living room. They sat after handing everyone their drinks. Connor and Regan chose to stand, while Moira and Shamus sat on the couch.

Painful idle chatter passed between them before Regan blurted out. "Wow. Beautiful ring, Rachel."

Panic raced across Rachel's face and her eyes darted to Michael before she mumbled, "Thank you."

"Yes. It's stunning. Where did you get it?" Moira inquired after taking a sip of wine.

The doorbell rang before Rachel could answer.

"That's the food." Michael rushed to answer the door. He placed the delivery on the table and started unpacking the bags and opening the boxes while Moira and Regan went about pulling plates from a drawer next to the dining table.

The conversation shifted to their meal as each person placed small portions on their plates, before sitting.

"You never answered the question, Rachel," Moira probed, before taking a bite.

A forkful of shrimp was suspended before Rachel's mouth, and she shoved it in quickly so she wouldn't have to answer. Connor and Regan's gaze shifted between each other before going to Michael, Shamus, and Moira, and then back to Rachel.

"The reason for this dinner together was to share news, and the reason why you weren't invited, Mom and Dad, was because I wanted to get Regan and Connor's reaction before sharing it with you."

"What kind of news?" Shamus asked.

"I asked Rachel to marry me."

"And I said yes," Rachel blurted out.

CHAPTER 34

Rachel hadn't planned to chime in after Michael's confession, but she didn't want him to share the biggest news of their lives alone.

Regan and Connor were the first to react by giving their congratulations. Regan shot out of her seat and hugged them with excitement. Connor sat next to Michael and patted him on the shoulder, grinning. "Good for you, mate."

Over Regan's shoulders, Rachel glanced at Michael's parents' faces. Moira's expression was calm, her face smooth. Shamus's was another story, narrowed and sharp, ready to attack. Rachel braced herself mentally as Regan moved away.

Shamus opened his mouth to speak, his face red, but stopped when his wife touched him gently on the arm.

"This news is unexpected, especially since you just told us about your relationship. Isn't the engagement a little fast?"

Michael took Rachel's hand in his and kissed it. "Actually, Mother, this relationship has been going on for the normal amount of time for an engagement."

"How do you think your coworkers or the board are going to take the news, considering your working arrangement and Rachel's contract with the company?" Shamus blustered.

"This news is just for your ears only. As for everyone else, we're still figuring that out," Michael replied.

"Figuring it out?" Shamus's voice rose.

"Yes. We wanted to share the news with you first and then enjoy our engagement time, whether that's a couple of weeks or at the end of Rachel's contract. As I said, we're still figuring out what's best for us and the company."

"No engagement is best for the company. Your relationship was bad enough, but this?" Shamus's tone sliced through the rising tension he'd created in the room, along with the volume of his voice.

"Shamus," Moira said calmly, urging him to sit back down. "The news is a surprise, that's all. Given your working relationship, however, I'm happy to hear you're considering all possibilities, along with the consequences."

The last statement was a knife plunged in Rachel's heart, even though it was true. *Why is this so hard?* She wished she and Michael had met under different circumstances and there was no work contract between them, or complicated family situations. *You can't get away from complicated family!* That last part was true, but right now, she'd take that over what she and Michael had to deal with. Unhappy relatives were one thing, but coworkers? Board members? *What I wouldn't give for a happy engagement where everyone is celebrating our relationship.*

"We recognize we have a lot of things to discuss, and we're in no rush to make our engagement public. We invited Regan and Connor here tonight to get their reaction and advice about how to break the news to you delicately, but it's better everyone showed up. It takes away some of the stress," Michael said, giving her a reassuring smile before glancing at his parents.

Shamus snorted. "I'm glad you're less stressed. The whole situation is a mess and will only get messier when your engagement goes public. Perhaps it's better you hold off until you're certain it's a good idea."

Ouch. And here I thought Moira's comment was hurtful.

"The engagement isn't a bad idea, Father," Michael interjected, "We just need to find the best way to maneuver it. That's all." He placed his arm around Rachel's shoulder.

"Can I just say how happy am I for you both? You're going after the love and the life you want, regardless of what others will think or say." Regan raised a glass to them.

"I agree," Connor chimed in.

Shamus snorted. "Of course you do. The two of you have never followed the convention of anything."

"I think it's best to wait until after your contract ends, Rachel. I thought that was your original plan when you decided to start dating," Moira said.

"Plans change, Mother. We realized we want to start our lives together, and not let any obstacles stop us."

"We?" Shamus glared at Rachel.

"Actually Father, I was the one who proposed, and I had to convince Rachel it was a good idea." He winked.

Rachel blushed. "I wanted to wait until after my contract ended before making anything public. A part of me still feels that way, but I want to start my life with Michael, whatever that means."

"What about the business? Have you discussed a prenup? You'll be required to sign one," Shamus stated, his hard gaze pinning Rachel.

"And he'll need to sign one to protect Rachel's business, Father," Regan added.

"Why would Michael want her business?" Shamus questioned.

Regan rolled her eyes. "Father, you're the only one from whom it escapes that Rachel has a successful business. While it might not be worth as much as ours, it is a multimillion-dollar company. I'm sure Rachel's family has advised her to protect it if things don't work out between them."

Rachel longed to kiss Regan for defending her. She gave her a brilliant smile instead.

The evening ended shortly after.

Connor and Regan hugged them and congratulated them again. Rachel mouthed, "Call me," to Regan before they left.

Shamus's face had remained sour, right up until the moment he walked out the door, while Moira's was etched with concern underneath her smile and well wishes for them both. Rachel wasn't sure if she was just being polite or genuinely meant the words. Either way, hers were better than Shamus's bitter silence.

They breathed a sigh of relief when they were alone.

"That went better than I thought." Michael plunked down on the couch.

Rachel gave him a sideward glance. "Seriously?"

"At least no one dove across the table to attack you. Or me." A smile crinkled the edges of his eyes.

Rachel punched him playfully in the arm. He grabbed her and tickled her until tears poured from her eyes.

"I'm so happy you're here," he said when her laughter died, and he held her in the crook of his arm.

Rachel touched his cheek. "Me too. You do realize this is the first time I've been to your apartment?"

"Really?"

"Yes. If I didn't know you, I might think you had a wife and kids stashed here whom you didn't want me to know about."

"I do. They're hiding in the bedroom. Should we go find them?" Michael teased with a wicked grin.

"And ruin their happy image of you? I think we should stay right here." She unbuttoned the top buttons of her blouse and reached for his shirt.

"Have I got myself a saucy maiden?" Michael asked, thickening his accent knowing it drove her crazy.

She pushed against his frame until she was above him and kissing him deeply as she held his face in her hands. Michael kissed her back with the same passion, his tongue playing with hers, slowly at first until she ran her hands along his chest and all reason left him along with control. Moments later they were half naked, their bodies partly on the couch and on the floor, their moans and laughter filling the room.

CHAPTER 35

R achel was smiling from ear to ear the next morning, from the time she woke up, all the way to work. The office was quiet as she headed to her desk, but she didn't think anything of it because she was usually one of the first to arrive. She stopped at the kitchen and made herself another coffee for the thermos she brought from home.

She hummed while waiting for the machine to finish.

Telling Michael's parents about their engagement hadn't gone smoothly, but she never expected it to. Rachel was just thankful it was out in the open and they wouldn't have to sneak around his parents, and she could wear her ring, at least outside of the office. Telling the board and people at the office would have to wait, maybe they would never tell them at all before they saw their picture on a tabloid site. Maybe not the board, but if they waited until after her contract ended, would the board have to be notified? Of course they would. As Shamus had stated last night, to make sure Michael's assets with the company were protected. Rachel's happiness slowly dissipated thinking about the negotiation of their prenups. She loved and trusted Michael, but she'd be a fool not to protect her own business.

After taking a long drink of her coffee, she stood by the window to enjoy the view, something she rarely did because she didn't usually have time. Downtown Dublin stretched out before her, a bright and beautiful mixture of the old and new world.

In that moment Rachel realized she hadn't really explored Ireland, a place that she'd longed to visit for years. She'd seen a documentary about castles and became fascinated by their stories and wanting to explore them to see if she could imagine what life was like when the castles were new and vibrant, to touch the stone walls and climb the stairs to the top and visualize how the land looked when the castle was thriving.

Rachel took a deep calming breath. She'd forgotten about that dream to explore and to have a life outside of work. Her heart ached as she realized she hadn't changed as much as she thought when she took this job halfway around the world. All she did was replace her old life of working too hard with a new one. Rachel wished she could remember the end date of her contract and if there was a clause that would allow her to escape it sooner on good terms. *Doubtful.* And there was her relationship with Michael and how the board would react to their engagement.

So many variables.

While she couldn't control all the unknowns, there were things she could do. Mainly, refresh her mind about the date her contract ended, every detail, and speak to a lawyer to see if there was an exit clause. Rachel pulled it up on her computer to glance at it before Ashley arrived and sent an email to Sky requesting an appointment. Then she searched for parks and museums close to her apartment. She would speak with Regan about finding a lawyer, one who wasn't associated with their family.

For the first time since telling Michael's parents about the engagement, no, maybe longer, she felt peaceful that she was taking steps toward the life she truly wanted.

All of it evaporated the moment Ashley arrived and placed an article pulled up on her phone before Rachel.

"Is Ireland's most eligible bachelor engaged to his employee?"

The photo was of them outside the ring shop. It wasn't dark enough to hide their faces, so both of them were clear enough to be recognized.

"*Shit!*" Rachel gritted out.

"OMG, it's true!" Ashley nearly screamed.

Rachel glared at her in disapproval.

"Sorry. I suspected there was something between you, but I never imagined it was so serious."

Rachel didn't respond. *The less said, the better.* "Please clear all my appointments for today."

"Yes. Of course."

Rachel left her office and headed straight to Michael's, surprised to find it empty. She called his phone. He answered on the first ring.

"I was just about to call you," he said. "I'm almost at the office. Are you in?"

"Yes. I'm in your office."

"Stay there. And Rachel? Please arrange for a coffee pot to be delivered to my office. It's going to be a long day for both of us."

"See you soon," she replied and hung up. *Long day was an understatement.* She texted Ashley to head downstairs to the coffee shop and pick up a box. They weren't going to need just any coffee. They were going to need the really good stuff.

Ashley was setting up the coffee along with fresh mugs when Michael arrived.

"Thanks," they said in unison as Ashley closed the door.

Michael hugged her. She squeezed him tightly, inhaling the smell of him she'd come to love, fresh spring soap with a hint of sandalwood. Calm settled into her bones for the first time since seeing the article.

"How are you holding up?" Michael stroked her face.

"Not sure yet. You?"

"Same. The good news is I don't think my parents have seen it, as the article was on a tabloid site. However, I suspect it won't be long before they find out...before I have time to tell them. I've been on the phone with the solicitors who put together your contract. I want to know where that stands before I call my father. Not to mention the board."

"Something we should've considered first."

"I wasn't thinking about contracts or anything other than wanting a life with you when I proposed, Rachel. I wouldn't change that moment for anything." He kissed her gently.

"Me either." Even if it did mean a shitstorm was headed their way, possibly from a legal perspective. If only they'd met under different circumstances. *They brought you to this moment in your life, Rachel!* She loved him, and once all this madness was over, they'd start their lives together. She ignored the twinge in the pit of her stomach. "I was going to ask Regan about a lawyer, one who isn't connected to your family."

"Great idea. The more eyes on this contract, the better. If I know my father, he's going to try and turn this to his and the company's advantage. I want to make sure you're protected."

Rachel untangled herself from his embrace and made herself a cup of coffee. A long sip followed. "I'm glad I ordered the good coffee."

Michael's laugh was as hollow as her smile. "One of the company solicitors will be here in an hour. Not Declan," he clarified.

She released some of the tension her body was holding. While it wasn't at the front of her mind that she'd have to deal with him, she was relieved. "I'll reach out to Regan now and grab a copy of my contract." She headed to her office.

When she returned a few minutes later, Michael was seated on the couch with their mugs on the mahogany coffee table. They went over her contract and managed a quick kiss before Michael's assistant announced the lawyer's arrival.

Rachel's heart sank as each minute ticked by and the lawyer went through the contract. Michael was right. The man's interest was clearly that of Michael and the company only. Not to mention the way he glared at her, as if she were after his family's money. It was only when Michael mentioned she would be having her own lawyer read through the contract to protect her company did his expression change. Rachel could see the wheels turning in his mind.

"I'd recommend a meeting with your father and the board also."

"That's the next step. Thank you for stopping by." Michael stood and shook his hand. So did Rachel, but he barely looked her in the eyes, even after she thanked him.

"One down. Two more to go?"

"Two?"

"One with my father and the board, and the other with the staff."

"Oh. Then I guess I have three," Rachel mumbled.

"I'd be happy to sit in with you and the solicitor," Michael offered.

"No. I need to do this alone. Not to mention you might intimidate him."

"Me?" Michael asked, genuinely shocked.

"Yes. You, Mr. Doherty. This is your office. Your company. And technically I'm your employee."

"Technically you're a consultant," Michael clarified.

"Either way. I think it's best I meet with them in my office, on my terms."

Michael leaned in and kissed her. "Agreed."

CHAPTER 36

Rachel plopped down in her chair physically and emotionally drained in ways she hadn't felt in months, just as Ashley came into her office.

"How did it go?"

Rachel's look was her answer, but she added. "I could use a week at a spa."

"That bad, huh?"

"Worse." She wished she could share the details with Ashley just to get it off her chest and out of her head, but the last thing she wanted was anyone knowing the details of her life any more than they already did, especially since she and Michael still had to speak with staff. Rachel prayed their reaction would be better than the board's and Michael's parents. Shamus didn't say much during the board meeting, but his stern expression and *I told you so* glances were enough.

Rachel was grateful Ashley didn't press her for details. She wanted to be friendlier, but given her contract, and her relationship with Michael, getting too personal was a recipe for trouble. *Solely excuses to keep people at arm's length, Rachel.* Sky's words taunted her. That was the trouble with your spiritual guide also having a degree in psychology, and being one of your closest friends.

"Is there anything I can do to help?"

A small smile pulled at the corners of Rachel's lips. "Could you please make dinner reservations for Michael and me? I'm starving, and I'm sure he is too. We barely had lunch."

"Of course."

She picked up the phone and called Michael to invite him to dinner.

"I'm sorry. I won't be able to make it. I've got stuff I need to catch up on. How about lunch tomorrow?"

"Of course, but you have to eat."

"I'll have Brian order something in. Night."

"Good night."

Rachel glanced at the phone after the call ended, feeling like he rushed her off. She pushed down the twinge she felt since she couldn't put an emotion to it. Was it fear, guilt, doubt? Whatever the reason for the twinge in the pit of her stomach, she didn't like it. In a way, it felt like a precursor to her relationship with Michael. She stood, packed up her laptop, grabbed her handbag, and left her office and the thoughts behind.

She told Ashley what she wanted for dinner from the restaurant and said she'd pick it up instead of needing a reservation and bid her a good night before Ashley had the chance to ask about food for Michael.

On the drive home, Liam shared polite banter with her after picking up her dinner, but he went quiet when her responses were shorter than usual. He was probably one of the only employees that she talked to, and she finally realized why. He wasn't a part of the normal office circle and was used to being discreet as part of his job. She wished in the moment she could find the words for how she felt and share them with him, but silence gripped her throat, and she stared out the window instead, taking deep but labored breaths to center and calm herself. A lot of changes lay ahead of them, with ebbs and flows they'd have to maneuver through, both in their personal and professional lives now and in the future. *Focus on you, Rachel.* The words were a combination of her own thoughts and those of Sky.

After arriving at the apartment, Rachel ate her dinner and had a longer meditation session than normal to silence the loud voices in her mind that created anxiety for her about the journey that lay ahead. It would be a journey with more lessons than she wanted. She wanted to be as prepared mentally and physically as she possibly could. Deep sleep settled over her and she drifted calmly into a dream state.

Her calm state was interrupted by an intense dream about Declan and Shamus. The kind she had as a kid when she saw Arlene being seriously hurt. It gripped her with dreadful details that came in blurs and clarity, making the meaning clear.

Rachel shot up in bed, drenched in sweat from head to toe. She reached for the phone with trembling hands and dialed Skylar's number.

Before Rachel could say a word, Skylar stated, "You have to tell him."

CHAPTER 37

Michael glanced at the five board members around the table. "You can't be serious?"

Their silence was the answer.

"This is an insane proposal." Michael's voice rose.

"No more insane than you marrying someone you have a business contract with. This is an alternative that fixes the problem from a scandal perspective, and the business side," the solicitor in the group said bluntly.

"I can tell you now that Rachel isn't going to agree with this. She isn't interested in a publicized wedding any more than I am, and she certainly won't be interested in your business proposal. There's no benefit to her."

"The benefits to her are outlined in the proposal, one we're certain she'll agree to with the right amount of pressure from us and you."

Michael glanced at his father. "You agree with this?" *Of course he does. Anything that supports the business.* Michael was surprised by his agreeing to putting their family on display for public scrutiny, but as the solicitor said, it was to avoid a scandal. Rachel was a consultant brought in to help the company for a specific time frame, one that ended in a few months. Not to mention their prior relationship. Michael was thankful he and Rachel had met before this whole fiasco with the board's proposal was presented to her, and that she was getting her own solicitor. He hoped it was one who wouldn't be intimidated by their family name.

"You convinced her to accept the contract to work with us. We're certain you can convince Rachel to agree to this proposal," one of the oldest members stated confidently.

"You're also forgetting one important element: Rachel's parents are investors in her company. Does your proposal include or benefit them?" None of the men in the room could look him in the eyes, including his father. "That's what I thought." Michael pushed the offer across the table. "I suggest you make some changes, otherwise, there's no way in hell Rachel will accept." He rose and strolled out of the room, wishing he could slam the door.

Shamus was at his side by the time he reached his office. "We had to do something, son," Shamus declared after closing the door.

"There was nothing to do but to make a quiet announcement and let us have the wedding we want. By turning our wedding into a big public spectacle, you're only shining a light on us and making everyone wonder why." Michael raked a hand through his hair after plunking down in the chair. He didn't mention the other portion of the proposal, knowing he wouldn't be able to contain his anger. The last thing he needed was a shouting match with his father for all of the office to hear.

"That was not my intention, nor was it my idea."

"But you agreed to it. You consented to something you knew I wouldn't want. I know the image of the business is important to you, but I'm your son." His eyes closed to hide the betrayal he felt.

Shamus stared at his son, stiffly at first, but then his face softened. "This whole situation has taken me by surprise, is all. You're moving so fast, and I'm worried you're making the wrong decision. Not to mention I don't know if Rachel is cut out for our world.

She's from a small island. While she didn't grow up poor, she has no idea of the pressures that come along with our family."

"And yet she's grown a successful company that's reaching international waters. She is stronger than you think. I know she can handle it."

"Really?" Shamus raised an eyebrow.

"Yes. Rachel knew, and that's why she was reluctant for us to get engaged. But ultimately, she realized as I did, that we love each other and don't want to wait to start our lives together." Michael stood and sat on the edge of his desk. He placed a hand on his father's shoulder. "Everyone thinks it's fast, but we have known each other for over two years. While we didn't spend all that time together, the times we did were special and gave us the chance to get to know each other. Really know each other."

"There no such thing, son. I've been married to your mother for almost forty years, and some days I feel like we still don't know each other."

A small smile pulled at his lips. "Agreed, but it's enough for us to start."

Shamus stood. "I hope you know what you're doing son, and that you're not making a decision that will hurt this family, our business, or you."

"I know what I'm doing." Michael assured him.

He sat back in the chair after his father left, the last words he spoke came back to haunt him. *Do I know what I'm doing?* He'd been so sure before he walked into the meeting with the board, now he wasn't certain. His doubts weren't about Rachel, but rather how they were going to navigate their wedding, the proposal from the board, and worse, if they would reach an agreement. What if they couldn't? What then? For once he wished his family and business weren't so closely tied together, and their problems could be easily solved with a prenup.

Michael called Connor and invited him to meet him for lunch. Connor readily agreed since they hadn't spent much time together since Rachel moved to Ireland.

They met at one of their usual restaurants. Michael hugged his friend a little longer than normal but knew Connor wouldn't hold it against him. It was their signal that a serious talk was needed.

"That was one long hug, mate. Must be bad," Connor commented as he gestured for the waiter.

"I just met with the board—and my father."

"I see." Connor was a victim of his family's board of directors, and knew firsthand how brutal their decisions could be. It had devastated not only Connor's life, but his family's. "What happened?"

"Let's order a drink and some food first," Michael said when the waiter arrived. They placed their order, and Michael shared what had happened since the night he and Rachel announced their engagement.

Connor leaned back in his chair and took a drink from his beer. "Shite."

"Exactly," Michael agreed.

"So, what's going to happen if the board and Rachel can't come to an agreement?"

"I honestly don't know."

"Do you think they're making it impossible, so you'll call off your relationship, or delay the wedding until you or Rachel break?"

Michael paused mid-drink. "I hadn't considered that. I figured they'd find another way to block our relationship, but perhaps this is their only plan."

"Do you think your father is behind it?"

Michael set his mug down and leaned back into the leather booth seat. "I'd like to think not, but I honestly don't know. I know he's concerned I'm being hasty, and says he's only looking out for me, but I know he can be ruthless."

"Have you spoken to Rachel about the proposal?"

"Not yet. I honestly don't know what to tell her."

"I don't envy you that conversation, mate."

The waiter arrived with the food, making Michael realize he hadn't eaten all day.

"Enough about me. What's the story?" Michael attacked his food before his gaze settled on Connor. He'd been so busy with work and his and Rachel's relationship, he felt a tinge of guilt for neglecting his friendship.

"Nothing much. Just focused on the bookstore."

"Seeing anyone?"

"Not really."

"All right," he stated, knowing Connor would tell him when he was ready.

The rest of the lunch was spent chatting about their football team, Connor's bookstore, meditation, and other topics not related to his engagement, his parents, or work. Michael didn't realize how much he missed hanging out with his friend and promised himself, and Connor, it wouldn't be so long until their next meet up.

Connor gave him a quick hug and reassuring pat on the back before leaving him in the parking lot. As Michael walked back to the office, he was grateful for the lightness that surrounded him now. Connor suggested some time ago that he protected his energy each time he engaged with people at work and his family. Michael hadn't fully understood what he meant until that moment. He made a mental note to study more about it when he got home tonight. He sensed he was going to need it in the coming weeks.

CHAPTER 38

Rachel threw her phone onto the kitchen counter in frustration. Another article about her and Michael had appeared, and portrayed them, or rather her, in a less respectable light. *What is this? The US?* She'd thought, or rather hoped, the news about them would settle down and be seen as yesterday's stale gossip, but she was wrong. While she and Michael weren't being followed around by paparazzi, it certainly felt like it when she saw her face pop up on her phone almost every day with a horrible headline. She had no idea Michael's family were that known—at least not in the social world.

She didn't think Michael gave the articles much thought or care. Maybe because he was used to them while growing up. The only time Rachel was in the news at home was when her business expanded, and a magazine called to interview her for their business section. Seeing her face and name associated with gossip was disconcerting.

The phone she'd discarded buzzed on the counter. "Hi Regan. Perfecting timing."

"Really? What's happened?"

Rachel laughed. "Nothing much. Just hoping you can recommend a lawyer who's not afraid of your family."

"I might be able to help with that. I know someone who wants to put her company on the map. She's smart...crazy enough."

"Please tell me it not Declan's sister!" Rachel shuddered.

Regan snorted. "Not even close. She's no solicitor. Nor would she ever go against my family. She tries too hard to be a part of it."

Rachel could see that given how strongly Ciara went after Michael.

"I'll share her contact information. Make sure to tell her I sent you. How are you doing otherwise?"

"Deliriously happy whenever we're not around other people."

Regan chuckled. "That's something I suppose."

"What about you? How are things going with Connor?"

Silence came from the other end of the phone before Regan asked, "How did you know?"

"I suspected at the Sunday brunch and from your statement at Michael's apartment the other night." Rachel flopped on her couch. "Not to mention the crazy sparks between you two."

"We have a complicated family history."

Shamus's obvious dislike for Connor was likely the reason. "Why doesn't your father like him?" She hadn't thought to pry before, chalking it up to Shamus's difficult personality.

"It has to do with his family. They were in business with our family and let's just say things didn't end well. Connor's father adamantly denied it but, in the end, it didn't matter, the relationship between our families was ruined. Unfortunately for Connor, my father insists on taking it out on him. His relationship with Michael is the only reason they remain civil."

She consider their interactions civil? Rachel hated to think what it'd be like if they weren't. She hoped never to see that side of Shamus.

"Connor's hesitation with our relationship, I think, is him getting around the fact I'm his best friend's little sister."

"I suppose that would take some time. But you've been an adult for a while now," Rachel joked.

"That's what I said. Men!" Regan huffed.

"Give him time. He'll come around."

"I suppose. Hopefully it'll be before I start graying."

Rachel giggled.

"Hang in there, Rachel."

"You, too."

Rachel called the lawyer after Regan hung up. After the first twenty minutes of speaking with Maggie, Rachel knew she was perfect for the job. She forwarded her a copy of her contract and set up their follow-up meeting. For the first time in days, Rachel felt hope for a resolution.

As she looked out at the city lights, her thoughts drifted to her dream. Her daily life had been so hectic, she didn't have time to think about it, but the meaning was clear. *Something bad is going to happen with Shamus and Declan.* For the first time in years, she was truly terrified.

As she sat on the balcony with a book and a cup of green tea, Rachel recalled her last conversation with Skylar.

"Look at how Michael reacted when he found out he was in my dream." She had insisted after Skylar's advice to tell him.

"What happens if you don't stop it?"

She raked her hand through her hair. If her dream was any indication, it was bad. But would Shamus believe her? Michael might convince him, but what if Michael didn't take her dream seriously? This situation was completely different from their dream experience.

"Wait for the opportunity to tell him, Rachel. It will present itself," Skylar assured her.

Rachel wasn't sure she was brave enough to take it.

Michael called her at ten o'clock to say good night and that they needed to meet first thing in the morning. She didn't press him about the topic, but suspected it was serious from his tone. *Does it have something to do with my dream? No, Michael wasn't there.* The earlier relief she experienced evaporated, and she had to extend her usual mediation by an extra thirty minutes before she finally drifted to sleep.

CHAPTER 39

"Is this a joke?" Rachel asked, laughing. The men seated around the large oval table glared at her. She knew it wasn't, but wanted to make sure they knew exactly how ridiculous their proposal was. *Did Michael agree to this?* They didn't get a chance to meet this morning like they planned, this meeting taking priority instead.

"I'm surprised you want to publicize our wedding considering you're so obviously opposed to it." Her gaze settled on Shamus who sat at the head of the conference table. "But surely you don't expect me to agree to the other part of your proposal?"

"It's in your best interest—and ours," Declan stated firmly.

When she saw Declan in the room instead of the first company lawyer she and Michael spoke with, she knew the meeting was going to hell in a handbasket. The man was sleaze incarnate. "And how is cutting my parents out of their portion of my business and being absorbed into the company in my best interest?"

"You would still have a share in the company, which you could assign to your parents or offer them to buy into ours."

"How generous of you to allow them to buy what they technically already own a part of." Rachel gripped the pen next to her phone to keep herself from stabbing Declan in the eye with it.

"You would become part of the family business and continue your position but on a permanent basis. Although I do believe you'll be busy with learning about all the charities run by the company and your involvement in them," Shamus offered, as if it made the offer more enticing.

"I thought that was Regan and your wife's responsibility."

"It'll now become part of yours."

"Because I'm a woman?" *Sexist pigs!* Just breathe and hear everything they have to say.

"That's what all the women in this family have done for generations." The tone of Shamus's voice was rising.

"I'm not marrying into this family with nothing of my own or born into it. I have my own thriving business, and only took this job because it would help me to expand into this part of the world. You're expecting me to hand it over and become your employee just because I'm marrying your son?"

"You'll own shares in our company," Declan said with a sly smile.

She resisted the urge to throw her pen at him, or better yet dive across the table and punch that smug expression from his face. "You offer that to all your VP and CEOs, Declan. I don't consider that a perk. Unless you're offering me fifty percent of those shares or more, then I might consider it."

Declan's face turned red, along with a few board members.

Since their last encounter where he tried to threaten her into sleeping with him, Declan hadn't shown his face, making her wonder if he and Ciara weren't behind the press getting wind of their relationship. Rachel wouldn't put it past them.

For the first time, Rachel realized Michael was remaining silent, his expression unreadable. That might be because she was so on edge herself. Rachel snatched up the proposal and stood. "I'll have my lawyer come up with a counter."

"The contract is non-negotiable," Shamus added before she reached the door.

Rachel resisted the urge to rip the contract into shreds and sprinkle it over their heads and storm out of the office. No one in their right mind would accept their offer, and they knew it. *They simply think I'd roll over and sign the documents? Over my dead body!* There was no way in hell she was letting it be absorbed into another company, and definitely not for the pittance they were offering. But, now was not the time to respond. Once she spoke with her parents, and her lawyer, then maybe they'd come up with a counteroffer, regardless of what Shamus said.

For the first time she doubted her complete trust in Michael. He might not have drawn up the contract, but surely, he knew the details. Had he even tried to go against his father? *He hired you, Rachel.* True, but it hadn't exactly been against his father's interests. While Michael owned the company she worked for directly, she had quickly discovered it was part of a larger parent company that was owned by his father.

Rachel didn't return to her office but instead took a walk outside to clear her head of anger and disappointment coursing through her. Pushback was expected, but what she hadn't counted on was the board going after her business.

She figured they'd want her to sign a prenup or something similar to prevent her from having access to the business or Michael's wealth. The board coming after her business was ballsy, and downright malicious. Tears stung the back of Rachel's eyes, remembering how Michael had remained silent. She hadn't expected or wanted to be rescued, but a word or two in her defense would've been nice. *Is this a glimpse of our marriage? Does he expect me to give up my business? To be part of the charities like his mother and sister?* The idea of giving up her business and career had kept them apart before and he'd wanted her to be happy, but what about now that they were about to get married?

They talked about so many topics around their lives together, but this was one she hadn't considered, not thinking it was a necessary conversation. *Boy was I wrong.*

Rachel called her lawyer with an update and was scolded for not having her there. She promised to send over their proposal and not attend any other meetings without her. She then called her parents to find out where in the world they were and how quickly they could get to Ireland. Surprisingly, they were calm about the news and said they'd be on the next available flight. *Did they expect this outcome? They couldn't have. No one could. They are just remaining calm for my sake.* That was the only explanation. Or maybe they weren't reacting until they devised a counteraction.

Whatever the reason, Rachel knew the response would be as volatile as Shamus's. She suddenly had an image of her parents and Shamus yelling around a board table and maybe even breaking out into a fistfight. Except for Moira, standing stoically in the corner trying to soothe everyone with her even tone. Until her mom slapped her soundly to shut her up. Rachel burst out laughing at the images and a scene that would never happen, but they did make her feel better. Taking a deep to-the-diaphragm breath, Rachel knew that everything would work itself out. She couldn't foresee how or know when but just knew it in her gut.

Rachel was smiling when she returned to the office, excited that her parents were visiting, and that they'd finally meet Michael and the rest of his family at Sunday brunch. She chuckled, thinking about the conversations between her parents and Shamus. Her father would match his intellect, while her mother would match his temperament. When she imagined the pained expression on Shamus's face, her steps were lighter all the way back to her office.

"Mr. Doherty is in your office," Ashley stated, handing her a stack of files.

"Thanks." Rachel checked her watch to see how much time she had before her next meeting. She was calmer, but she wasn't sure she was ready to speak with Michael.

Shamus was sitting on the couch in her office when she walked in.

Wrong Mr. Doherty. "What can I do for you, Shamus?" Rachel asked, placing the files on her desk before turning to face him.

"You can sign the contract."

She remained silent, choosing not to let him trigger her. That was his reason for showing up in her office?

"If not for me, then for Michael. I know he thinks it's in everyone's best interest."

Rachel didn't waver—not believing him.

Shamus adjusted his position on the couch. "I realize it comes at a loss to you but think of what you'll gain. A connection to our family and all that comes with it."

She sat on the edge of her desk.

"Signing those papers make it easier for Michael to retain his seat on the board when the company is restructured," Shamus stated with a pained expression, as if he'd given away a key piece of knowledge that was to his disadvantage.

"Restructured?"

"We're merging with Declan's family's business in a few months."

Those words got her attention. *Was this the opportunity Skylar mentioned?*

"Your business is more cash solvent and why we suggested the proposal to 'absorb' your company."

That's why their offer is so low. What she didn't have the answer to, one she'd have to ask him directly, was if Michael was included in the "we" to take her company. "Does Michael know about this merger?"

Shamus avoided her gaze and failed to answer her.

What the hell is going on? "Why not?"

"That's not your concern."

Is he for real? "It affects my business and my future husband's businesses so of course it's my concern, especially since you haven't told him. That leads me to believe he wouldn't agree with your decision."

"He and Declan have a difficult history, but I trust Declan and his family. The board agrees with me."

"Why are you telling me this when you know I'll tell Michael."

"That's why I'm telling you. Our business is in trouble, and this is the only way to save it. If you don't sign this contract, Michael will barely have a job, much less a share in the company."

Oh shit! That wasn't the response she expected. *Things have just gone from bad to worse.* Then she remembered her dream, but her gut told her this wasn't the moment. Besides, could she trust that Shamus was telling her the truth, and not manipulating her to sign the documents? She didn't know him well enough, but the shame on his face when telling her about the failing business was an indication he might be telling the truth.

"I'll take what you said into consideration."

"See that you do." Shamus stood and left not bothering to say goodbye.

The weight of Shamus's words constricted her chest until it was difficult to breathe while also making her doubt her relationship with Michael. Telling him meant finding out his father was all but betraying him and their family business. If she suggested they delay the wedding until after her contract ended, how would that affect their relationship and their businesses? Neither Declan nor Shamus would let her help. Could she? She had no idea what kind of trouble the company was in. The changes of Shamus or the board letting her anywhere near those company financials were slim to none. The thought of being the one to break Michael's family and possible business apart made her want to vomit. *Now what?*

CHAPTER 40

Rachel hugged her parents. So much time had passed since she saw them. While they video chatted all the time, it wasn't the same. Rachel hadn't pushed for them to visit as she was so busy with work, and they were enjoying traveling the world, a dream of theirs for as long as she could remember. The hug was long and tight, all of them needed it.

"I missed you guys. I didn't realize until now how much."

"We missed you too, honey." Her father squeezed her shoulder, while her mother wiped away tears from her face.

Rachel was so grateful that the relationship with her parents had turned into the beautiful one it was now. "How was the flight?" They meandered through the crowded airport.

"Pleasant, because it was first class," Karol said with a cheeky grin. Traveling outside economy was new to them—always the penny-pinchers.

"We can't take it with us, and you don't need it so..." her father reflected.

"I might need it if this deal doesn't pan out," Rachel joked, and nodded when they reached the car.

"Liam, these are my parents, Karol and Brian."

"Lovely to meet you." Liam shook their hands.

"Likewise," Brian said. Karol smiled.

After putting the luggage in the trunk, Liam drove them to her apartment. Rachel kept the conversation light and was grateful her parents took the hint.

The surprise on their faces when the elevator door opened into her apartment made Rachel smile.

"The videos from your phone really didn't do this place justice!" her mother exclaimed, staring out at the view from the balcony.

"Your mother's right. This place is huge and extravagant."

"Let me give you the full tour."

They oohed and aahed while she showed them around, and didn't make suggestions for changes, likely because it wasn't her place.

"Are you going to get your own place or live with Michael after you're married?" her father asked once the tour was over.

"We haven't really talked about it, but I'm sure we'll figure it out."

"You've got bigger things to worry about." Karol plunked herself down on the couch. "Do you have a copy of the contract so we can dive in, or did you want to talk us through it instead?" Her mother was always the more legally inclined one of her parents, enjoying it far more than her husband.

Rachel eased herself into the comfy chair across from the couch. "Why don't we order some food first? It's gotten a little more complicated since we spoke. *That is an understatement.*

"Sounds good to me. I'm starving. The sandwich and snacks on a three-hour plane ride are ridiculous!" her father declared.

"They had other food you could buy."

He snorted. "Ten dollars for a sandwich? I don't think so."

"It's not like you can't afford it." Karol rolled her eyes. "I told you we should've eaten at that restaurant at the airport."

"We flew first class. They should at least provide a hot meal. Besides, it was too far from the terminal. I didn't want us to miss the flight."

"We checked in three hours before the flight!" Karol bellowed.

"It's better to be safe than sorry."

Rachel almost laughed. It was nice to see some things didn't change and these interactions didn't trigger them but were embraced as fun.

After ordering the food they agreed on, their time eating was filled with stories from their trip they hadn't already shared, teasing, and lots of laughter. Rachel forgot her problems and lived in the moment with her parents, the joy of it, especially after her meeting with the board and the encounter with Shamus.

Karol's brows rose and fell several times as she read the contact. At one point she burst into laughter and Rachel knew what part she'd read because she'd laughed also. "You were smart to call us. What has your lawyer advised?"

"I haven't heard from her. She's likely trying to figure out either how to get me out of it with little pushback or devise a counteroffer that will please everyone. But after what Shamus told me after the meeting, I'm not sure that's possible."

"Why not? What happened?" Brian asked.

Her parents' faces reflected shock when Rachel relayed her conversation with Shamus.

"This changes everything," Brian professed.

"I honestly don't know what to do."

"You're screwed all around," her mother declared.

"I think you should tell Michael the truth," Brian said.

"I know, but that would mean destroying the relationship with his father and possibly the whole family, business...everything." She neglected to mention he might've been part of the decision making for her proposal. The fact that they hadn't mentioned it implied they figured he wasn't because she didn't say otherwise.

"You could delay the wedding until your contract ends."

"That wouldn't stop the merger from going through." Rachel longed to tell them about her dream, but she couldn't face their look of disappointment. "I'm not sure how I can explain it to Michael without having to lie to him."

"You could threaten to backout of the wedding and cause a real scandal if they don't meet your requirements," her father suggested.

"That move would only ruin my business opportunities on this side of the world, not to mention ruin my relationships with Michael, Connor, and Michael's family."

"Not to mention we don't operate that way!" Her mother swatted her husband with the edge of the contract.

"If they're going to play dirty..."

"Then we be the better people," Karol countered.

Brian leaned in to kiss his wife. "Right as always, honey."

"I know." Her mother smiled brightly. "What about the lawyer?"

"If I can't tell Michael, I'd say telling anyone else isn't an option, but maybe I could offer it as a hypothetical and see what she says."

They brainstormed a few counteractions to review with the lawyer, and Rachel did feel better. Between them and what her lawyer would recommend, she wished she felt confident they'd find a solution. No matter what ideas they came up with, it wouldn't solve the biggest problem: the merger and her dream.

Rachel said good night to her parents and called Michael to say good night. They hadn't spoken since the board meeting, both avoiding each other and the conversation they didn't want to have until a solution was found.

"I miss you."

"I miss you too. Did your parents settle in okay?"

"Yes. They just went to bed."

"So, you're all alone? What are you wearing?"

Rachel chuckled. "I'm still in my work clothes."

Michael faked a moan. "Oh yes, baby. I love it when you talk work to me."

She giggled and continued their banter while she got ready for bed.

"I wish you were here with me, especially now that I'm dressed for bed in my flannel pajamas."

"You know how those drive me crazy. I could be there in twenty minutes."

"Not with my parents in the other room."

"What? We're engaged, and adults. It's not like they don't know we're sleeping together."

"I don't think so."

"We could just cuddle?" Michael suggested.

"You know what cuddling will lead to."

"I know it's hard for you to keep your hands off me, but I can control myself."

"Really? Even with me curled up next to you, my flannel pajamas brushing against your bare skin?"

"You could take off those pajamas, so you don't torture me."

"I could, but then I'd be completely naked."

"Not completely. You'll have your underwear on."

"Will I?"

Michael groaned. "You're really trying to torture me now. Are you sure I can't come over? Maybe you could come to my place? I'm parents free over here."

"Tempting, but I'm already snuggled up under the covers and warm."

"I'll warm you up when you get here."

She fluffed her pillow. "How about I come over for *coffee* in the morning?"

"Coffee? I love coffee."

"Me too."

"I can't wait to press it against my lips and drink it in and lick the edge of the cup so not a drop gets away."

"You don't want to drink it too fast, or it could burn you."

"No chance. I like my coffee hot."

"Well, it's definitely going to be hot tomorrow. It's hot right now."

"I know the feeling. I wish I could kiss you good night."

She changed the call to a video call. Michael's face appeared and she pressed her lips against the screen.

"Not the same, but I'll take it until tomorrow morning when you come over for coffee."

"Make sure there's plenty. I might want more than one cup."

"I'm going to brew a whole pot." He wiggled his eyebrows. "Give me a glimpse of your flannel pajamas before I go."

Rachel started the camera from her legs and moved up slowly while her fingers worked on the buttons. The top of the pajamas hung off her bare shoulders.

"I think you missed a couple of buttons. They're obstructing my view."

"You know what they look like. Use your imagination until you see them tomorrow," she teased. "'Night!" She hung up the phone before he could respond.

A few seconds later her phone pinged. He sent her a weepy and fire emoji.

She chuckled before turning out the lights to meditate.

CHAPTER 41

Rachel glanced at her reflection in the mirror, but she wasn't focused on her image, remembering her *coffee time* with Michael. She'd left a note for her parents telling them she'd meet them later for lunch and had ordered them breakfast.

Michael did have the coffee he promised, but they didn't touch a drop until they'd christened the back of his entry door and the kitchen counter. Two cups of coffee had been consumed, along with breakfast, before they finally made it to the bedroom where they spent the morning holding each other and talking and reconnecting. They both had needed it after everything that was happening in their lives.

"We need to do this more often." She sighed, squeezing him.

"What? Coffee?" he joked.

She poked his side. "That too."

"Agreed. Let's make sure we have coffee time once a day after we're married, no matter what's going on in our lives."

"What if we're traveling?"

"Then we'll have Facetime coffee."

"Let's not forget date nights. We can't survive on coffee alone."

"I could definitely survive on your coffee alone, but date nights could be fun." Michael kissed her stomach.

"Even after we have kids?"

His body stilled. "Kids?"

Rachel propped herself up on one elbow to come eye level with him. They'd never spoken about them. "You do want kids, right?"

"Sure. I honestly hadn't given it much thought." Michael's eyebrows crinkled.

"Me either, but I figured we'd have them some day."

"How many do you want?" His hand caressed the length of her back.

"One might be best, given our hectic work schedules and my business."

"But they'll need a sibling to keep them company."

"Hmm, true. Okay, maybe two?"

"Not three or four?"

"And be outnumbered? And here I thought you were the smart one!" Rachel joked. She screamed when he rolled her over and started tickling her. She squirmed, trying to free herself, but he was relentless. "Uncle!" she declared.

"Say, 'You are the smartest one of us, Michael.'"

"You are. You're marrying me." She grinned at him.

He started tickling her again until tears were streaming from the corners of her eyes. "Okay, okay. You're the smartest one of us."

When their laughter died, he held her against his frame and cupped the side of her face. "I know there's a lot we haven't discussed, but life is unexpected, and we'll never know everything that'll come at us. The most important thing is we're honest with each other, communicate what we feel, and stay connected like this. Once we do that, there's nothing we can't handle…"

A knock on the bathroom interrupted her flashback to this morning with Michael. "I'm almost ready."

Moira had invited them to lunch at their home. Rachel was dreading the lunch and facing Shamus. She was grateful her parents were with her.

They headed downstairs to Liam who was waiting for them.

"Good morning," Liam greeted them warmly.

"Thank you, Liam." Rachel stepped through the open door he held for them.

When they pulled up to the Doherty home, her father let out a low whistle. "Swanky."

Rachel lost her breath when she saw that Michael was waiting outside. He opened the door, not waiting for Liam. She took his hand and marveled that his presence still had the power to make her tingle. "Hello, gorgeous!" His gaze caressed her from head to toe.

"Hello, yourself." Rachel said as her parents exited the car.

"Mr. and Mrs. Miller. Nice to meet you."

"Please, call me Brian." Her father offered his hand.

"And call me, Karol. We're about to be family after all."

"Very well. Brian, Karol." Michael shook Karol's hand too before leading them inside the house to the drawing room.

Rachel froze when she saw Michael's parents weren't the only ones there. Declan and Ciara were with them. "I thought this was family only."

"They were invited last minute." Michael said. "I'm not crazy about it either. It's my father's way of annoying us."

This sucks! Introducing her parents to Michael's was a big enough challenge without adding those two to the mix.

Ciara kissed Michael on the cheek and tried to cling to him, but he stepped back firmly and placed his arm around Rachel's waist. She neglected to extend Rachel the courtesy of a cheek kiss, but Declan was happy to oblige. Thankfully, Michael's escape from Ciara also aided her in escaping one of Declan's own clingy hugs. Since he'd stopped coming around her office, Rachel figured that he'd given up, especially given their tense interaction in the boardroom.

"I wish I could say congratulations, but honestly, I always thought we'd be the one's getting engaged," Ciara said boldly.

"There's no need for your congratulations," Karol chimed in. "They're getting married without it."

Rachel wanted to kiss her mother. For once, her boldness was appreciated. If nothing else, her mother was protective of her family if others tried to insult or hurt them.

"Ciara and Declan Kelly. I'd like to introduce my parents, Mr. and Mrs. Miller."

Ciara didn't even muster a blush at her mother's insulting words. "Are you also from a tiny island in the middle of nowhere?"

Brian laughed. "Yes, we are, but if you knew anything about banking or business, you'd know that we're far from just a tiny island. And thanks to my daughter and our thriving business, it's about to get a whole lot bigger. We've been able to retire and travel all over the world for over a year. What is it you and your little family business are doing? Continuing to suckle at the teat of Michael's family?"

The shock on everyone's faces, including Rachel's own, made the eventual blush that tainted Ciara's cheeks worth it. Her father rarely spoke so rudely to anyone, not that she'd ever heard, but in that moment, he was her hero. His cutting remark made all she'd endured from Ciara and Declan worth it.

Everyone was still in stunned silence, including Regan who was usually the one to stir up trouble, when Connor walked up. "What did I miss?" His gaze narrowed when he saw Declan.

"Nothing much," Moira mumbled, trying to regain her composure. "We were just about to head into the dining room."

Seeing Connor reminded her that his family also knew the Kellys. Maybe she could get some dirt from him that could help her. She released Michael's arm. "I need to speak with Connor for a moment."

Michael raised a brow but nodded and continued following the crowd.

Rachel linked her arm with Connor. "What do you know about the Kelly family and their business dealings? Tell me quickly."

Connor gave her a sideways glance. "They're terrible people who will squash anyone who gets in their way. Personal as well as business."

"That what I thought. You've been a big help."

Connor shrugged. "Glad to help."

He escorted her to a seat next to Michael and took his own.

Everyone made polite conversation as the food and drinks were served. All the while, Rachel wanted to scream. Even Ciara refrained from making rude comments and stayed mostly silent, only speaking to Moira and Regan. No one wanted to wake the dragon that was her father's temperament, which seemed crazy with Shamus in the room.

"Are you ready to sign the contract, Rachel?" Declan asked as dessert was being served.

"No business talks at the table today," Moira chastised.

"It a valid question that affects you, Moira. If she doesn't sign, then it could mean there's no wedding. Right, brother?" Ciara glanced at her brother, then gave Rachel a smug glare.

And...she's back! Before she could respond, her father spoke, ignoring Ciara completely.

"Are you the lawyer my daughter told me about?" Brian turned his attention to Declan.

"I am. I work for Shamus's company and I'm handling Rachel's contract."

"Isn't that a conflict of interest?" Brian inquired.

Rachel cleared her throat and shook her head at her dad. Michael visibly stiffened next to her.

Both men took the hint and dropped the topic.

"Me and my lawyer are still reviewing it as well as my parents now that they're here, since it impacts them also."

"Why would it impact your parents?" Moira asked.

"Because they're investors in my business."

"I see," Moira responded, but her expression made it obvious she didn't understand. "Why don't we head to the drawing room, where we can relax and get to know each other better without a dining table separating us?"

Everyone rose and followed her.

"What's going on, Rachel?" Michael whispered.

"We'll talk about it later," she assured him. *Would they?* She couldn't ignore the elephant in the room forever. She had to tell Michael at some point.

"Why wouldn't the wedding happen?" Regan asked when everyone was settled and holding a drink.

"Because Rachel could decide to walk away rather than sign the contract the company is offering her."

"Why does she need to sign a contract?" Moira asked. "Is it anything to do with the one she currently has?"

"In a way," Declan answered.

"Yes, why don't you tell them exactly what signing that contract would mean, Declan." Karol baited him.

"Now is not the time, Mother. As Moira said no business talk today," Rachel stated firmly.

"That's what happens when you get involved with your boss," Ciara mumbled into her drink.

"I'm a consultant, Ciara, not an employee of Michael's. There is a difference."

"Is there?"

Rachel released the tension and words that were bubbling below the surface and didn't respond.

"The contact will open Rachel's business up to new opportunities," Declan declared as if the statement was good news.

"Really. And how will that benefit us as investors?" Karol asked.

"You'll have the opportunity to buy shares in the Doherty companies."

"How generous of you. And what about our investment in Rachel's company?"

Declan's eyes darted about the room. "You have the money you've received as dividends."

"And our future dividends?"

"This isn't the time or place to discuss this. Perhaps at the next meeting with Rachel and the board," Declan recommended.

"Will that be before or after your merger?" Brian asked.

Rachel glowered at her father.

"What merger?" Michael asked.

"It's nothing, son." Shamus stated, flustered. "He doesn't know what he's talking about." He glanced at Moira for help, but her own expression was of confusion and concern.

"Then why did you tell my daughter about it as a means to sway her to sign?" Karol shot back.

"You what!?" Michael sputtered before gazing at Rachel. "Why didn't you tell me?"

"There's nothing for her to tell you, son."

"Stop lying! You're trying to swindle my daughter out of her company so you can use her money as capital to merge with the Kellys." Brian roared.

"Enough!" Rachel put her hands in the air. "This day was supposed to be about our families meeting and getting to know each other before we started our lives together and it's turned into business." The last words caught in her throat.

"It will be once you sign the contract," Shamus said with conviction, and a hint of pleading.

It was something Rachel never thought she'd see from him.

Arguments erupted from everyone in the room, either trying to argue their point of view or out of anger because of what her father had said. Rachel could feel the pain, anger, even hate swirling around the room growing heavy until it was suffocating her, reminding her of the dream. Images from that night flashed before her eyes like projector slides on repeat. Blinding light one moment and powerful dark imagery the next, overwhelming her. She slid to the floor.

"Rachel!" Michael was beside her helping her to a chair. "Are you okay?"

"No, I'm not!" She glanced at Micheal and then Shamus. "You can't merge your company with his family's. It will mean disaster."

"This merger is going to save us," Shamus insisted.

"It won't. I know."

"How do you know?" Shamus inquired skeptically.

"I—I dreamt it," Rachel stammered and braced herself for the inevitable reactions.

Declan laughed, while Shamus, Michael, and everyone in the room looked confused.

"Is this true, Rachel?" Karol asked, but her tone was not condescending as it had been in the past when she mentioned her dreams.

"Yes. And when my dreams are this strong, they're *always* true."

"You can't be serious?" Shamus asked incredulously.

"Deadly. You do this, Shamus, and your family and mine will be left nothing."

"Why didn't you tell me about the merger, Father?" Michael asked, his tone pained.

"I didn't want to concern you." He pointed at Rachel. "You don't believe this, do you?"

Rachel's heart sank when Michael wouldn't look her in the eye.

"This is ridiculous!" Declan stated. "Shamus, you've known our family for years. This merger is a good deal."

"Like my daughter's deal?" Brian argued.

"Or my family's?" Connor added. "I believe Rachel."

"Of course you would. You're just bitter about what happened to you," Ciara stated.

Rachel stood and walked over to Michael and took his hand. "Do you remember the day we met? When you walked into that boardroom?"

"Of course."

"I dreamed about you three days before that. You were there. You remember."

"Rachel. I—I—" His expression said he longed to believe her, but the doubt was glaring.

"Since I was a child, every vivid dream I have had has come true. Good and bad," she whispered. "It doesn't matter if you don't believe me. Your family will lose everything, and so will mine if I sign that contract. I can't do that. Even if it means walking away from our relationship. From you." Rachel's voice cracked, and tears pooled her in eyes.

Everyone was quiet before erupting into arguments again and Michael released her hand, shock, anguish, and anger tainting his face. She was grateful when her parents each took a hand and led them from the room and outside. Rachel was grateful that Liam hadn't left, but was hanging out in the parking area, chatting with one of the housemaids. When he saw her face, he said a quick goodbye and practically ran to the car, where he swiftly had the door open and waiting for her. His eyes filled with concern as he asked. "Is she okay?"

"No, she's not." Brian answered. "Take us home."

Liam's long experience as a driver told him not to ask questions and he nodded.

When they got back to Rachel's, she said good night to her family and went to her room to sob.

CHAPTER 42

Michael was picking up the pieces of the day hours later, still in shock from Rachel's declaration and departure. Then there was his father's betrayal. He'd expect this from Declan and that was why he didn't like working with him, but his father?

The ache from both betrayals stung. Rachel's was a reminder of the night she confessed he was in her dream. That fact that her dreams come true was so unbelievable he was still stunned and angry that she hadn't said something to him before today, about her dreams and about the merger, but worst of all, how easily she walked away.

His father's ran much deeper, making him feel that all his hard work and time to build the company had been in vain. His father still didn't trust or believe in him.

He was angry and broken when he finally left his parents, tears streaming down his face on the drive home. He longed to call Rachel, but the idea that she'd walk away from him cut deep. Even though it meant saving her business, it still hurt, because like his father, she hadn't trusted him enough to tell him about the merger, or her dream.

How are we supposed to build a life together when she is keeping secrets from me? And not small ones, but enormous ones that will impact our personal and business lives. Connor had tried explaining that certain people had special gifts, but his words didn't soothe the wound from Rachel's betrayal.

What now? Do I return to work on Monday as if nothing has happened and pray that Rachel won't leave me or try to convince her to stay even if it means we could both lose everything?

There was no winning no matter what they did.

He pulled into his driveway and headed inside his flat and poured himself a stiff drink. He wanted to finish off the entire bottle, but then what? He'd still be in pain, but with a massive hangover.

Regan and his mother had tried to defend Rachel while relaying their displeasure to Shamus for his deception. He still couldn't believe the business was doing so poorly, but then his father always kept parts of the company from him, encouraging him to only focus on the portion he gave him control over. Now he knew why. While his side of the business was doing well, it wasn't enough to keep the entire company afloat. If his father had told him sooner, maybe things might not have gotten so bad, and he and Rachel could've made different business decisions. *None of that matters now.* His father was determined to move forward with the merger, and there was a chance Michael could either lose Rachel or have to walk away from his family's business.

He raked a hand through his hair in frustration, wishing he could return to that morning when he and Rachel had been happy and laughing. Had she known about the merger and her dream then? She must've decided not to tell him. *Why? Does she not trust me? Or was she afraid of what I'd say or do?* Regret and guilt squeezed his heart when he remembered his reaction when she told him about her dreams. He had doubted her. *How could I not, especially with what she confessed?*

He grabbed his phone and started to call her but changed his mind. He was still angry and hurt, and talking now would only stir up more emotions, and words they'd regret later. They needed time. Would she come to work on Monday? *Of course she would, Rachel is a professional.*

Michael didn't have the answer when he finally fell asleep, or the next morning when his anger had cooled. He tried calling her, but she didn't answer. She was either still upset or hurt. If her parents weren't with her, he'd be worried, but he knew they would take care of her.

Michael's doorbell rang and he rushed to the door, praying and hoping it was Rachel.

Standing in the doorway was a slim, petite woman with bright purple hair that flowed down one of her shoulders. He'd thought she had the wrong flat, but then her face came to mind. She was the reader at the office party. He couldn't recall her name, but he remembered she was a friend of Rachel's. *What the hell is she doing here? Did something happen to Rachel?* His breath caught in his throat and fear raced across his skin. Before he could open his mouth to speak, she did.

"My name is Skylar. Rachel is safe, but she's far from fine."

"What the hell does that mean? Is she okay or not?"

"Physically, she's fine. Emotionally, she's a wreck."

Guilt pricked him. "She was the one keeping secrets. Not me," he responded with anger.

"Are you going invite me in, or leave me standing in the doorway?"

Reluctantly Michael stepped aside and watched as she strolled around his flat before she took a seat in the single chair.

"What are you doing in Ireland. In my flat?"

"I'm here for Rachel."

Michael eyebrows narrowed in confusion. "Why didn't she come herself?"

"She doesn't know I'm here. What I mean is, I'm here to explain why she didn't tell you about her dreams and about the merger."

"She told you about the merger?" *Did she tell everyone but me?*

"Not exactly."

"What does that mean?" Michael thrust his hands in his pocket in frustration.

"Do you really want to know?" Skylar leaned forward in the chair. "Because I don't think you can handle it."

"Stop talking in circles, woman, and get to the point."

"I sensed it the night she had the dream, when she called me."

"Sensed it? That's ridiculous!"

"As ridiculous as someone's dreams becoming reality?" Skylar asked. "Or meeting their soulmate in a dream before they show up in their life?" Her brow quirked.

Michael raked a hand through his hair. "Okay, but how are they connected?

She sighed. "Just as Rachel has her gift, I have mine. I can sense people's emotions, thoughts, and other things. And don't ask me what you're thinking because I don't read minds...most of the time." She winked.

"This is insane."

"No, but do you know what is? How people react when they find out. Rachel's own parents didn't believe her and forced her to hide her gift when they discovered she wasn't lying. She was ten when she saved Arlene's life because of a dream and that's why they're best friends."

"I didn't know that," Michael whispered. *That's why she didn't tell me. She was afraid I'd reject her, like her parents did. Like my father did with the pressure. I wasn't good enough or had to prove myself.*

"Your father is proud of you despite the way he acts."

"I thought you didn't read minds." *Did I just say that?*

A grin tugged at her lips. "That's my psychoanalysis of you. If he wasn't proud of you or trusted you, he wouldn't give you the responsibilities he did. Not telling you about the merger is about his doubts, not you."

"You're a therapist?" *Was that true?*

"A psychologist. And it is true."

"That's annoying," Michael stated.

"Rachel and Arlene tell me that all the time."

He plunked down on the couch in frustration. "This is a disaster."

"I know it seems like it is now, but it's all going to work out. I promise."

She's mad. Must be if she thinks this will be resolved. "How?"

"That part isn't important. It's the belief that it will that matters. And I'm not mad."

"I thought you didn't read minds?" Michael glanced at her from the corner of his eyes.

"I don't. I could tell from your expression."

He glared at her.

"The point is, you and Rachel need to trust each other. And you need to believe her about the merger."

Michael raked a hand through his hair. "How can I? And even if I did, the board wouldn't believe it. My father certainly doesn't, given how he reacted when Rachel told us. There's nothing I can do."

Skylar watched him intently, making him uncomfortable.

His phone rang. It was Declan.

"What the hell do you want? What do you mean they called an emergency meeting on Monday? I'll bet you had nothing to do with it. In our best interest my ass!" Michael threw the phone on the couch next to him after hanging up. "Things have gone from bad to worse."

Skylar remained silent for a few moments before standing up to leave. "Remember what I said," she stated cryptically before heading out the door.

Michael picked up the phone and called Rachel, but she didn't answer. Not that he blamed her. She had shared a secret in front of every person who could use it against her to save their future. *And what did I do? Rejected her with my doubts, the way everyone in her past has.* Earlier that day he'd promised they could make it through anything, and not even a day had passed, and he broke his promise. Michael wanted to fix it, but he had no idea how.

CHAPTER 43

Rachel stood in the corner of the conference room, not wanting to sit at the table until her parents arrived. They said they had phone calls to make but would be there in time for the meeting. She didn't want to go to her office in case Michael was there waiting for her. She emailed Ashley and told her she had an important meeting, and the rest of the day was a personal day. Ashley had assumed it was because of her parents' visit and promised to alert everyone who were scheduled to meet with her.

Michael had tried calling her several times over the weekend, but she ignored his calls. She was grateful he hadn't turned up at the apartment, no doubt still dealing with the fallout from her confession. Pain stung her each time she remembered the glaring doubt in his eyes. *He doesn't believe me.* While she couldn't blame him, she'd hoped he'd consider it, given how they met and their shared experiences. But most importantly because of what they meant to each other, and the trust they'd built by working together. *I was wrong. It was only one-sided.*

She, her mother, and the lawyer had come up with what she hoped was a suitable solution for the board. Her father didn't agree, but went along with it, given they needed an answer by Monday. Today.

Rachel checked her watch. Five minutes to go. Michael, Declan, Shamus, and a couple of board members walked in moments later, taking seats before they noticed her in the corner.

Michael's eyes devoured her as she took the seat farthest away from him.

Where's my lawyer? She is supposed to be here by now! Rachel glanced around the room, feeling outnumbered. She checked her phone for a message and when there wasn't one, sent a text.

Declan was grinning like a Cheshire cat who'd eaten the canary, along with most of the board members. Shamus and Michael's expressions were forlorn as if neither had slept the entire weekend. That should've made her feel better but instead worried her.

"We need to get started," Declan announced.

"We can once my lawyer arrives." *And my parents.* But Rachel didn't add that part.

Five minutes later, both her lawyer and parents strolled into the boardroom. Rachel visibly relaxed. "Now we can start."

"Given recent events, we created a new contract for Rachel to sign," Declan said smugly.

Rachel glanced at Michael, who was glaring at his father. *Does he know about this new contract?*

"What new contract?" Her lawyer pulled back the copy that was laid before her and started perusing.

"One that states Rachel will sign over her company to us, otherwise her 'disorder' will be made public."

"What disorder?" The lawyer glanced at Rachel.

This was low, even for Declan. They were going to expose what she said about her dreams becoming reality if she didn't sign her company over to them. It hurt deeply knowing Michael and Shamus knew and probably agreed to this, but if she were being honest, she no longer cared. She'd had a lot of time over the weekend to think about her life and what she wanted, and what she'd have to sacrifice.

"You don't scare me, Declan. None of you do. Go ahead and make whatever threats you want. I'm not ashamed of who I am and what I'm capable of anymore—even if others are. The only offer I'm making today is the full amount of my contract, including what you've already paid me. Consider it a gift for me forfeiting my contract. Hopefully it's enough so you don't have to merge with Declan's family, but I'm not giving you my business. My family's business," Rachel emphasized.

Declan laughed. "It doesn't matter what you say. If you walk away, we'll ruin you and your business."

Rachel smiled at Declan. "You and your family might have clout on this side of the world, but on my side of the world, my clients know who I am and what I'm capable of. They're certainly not going to believe whatever lies you come up with. I'll have to sacrifice expanding my business and life on this side of the world, but my family's fine with that." Rachel glanced at Michael. "I'm fine with that."

"We'll sue you for breach of contract," Declan added angrily.

"Do that, and I'll expose how your family has been doing business for years," Brian countered.

Declan smirked. "We've done nothing illegal. Besides, you have no proof."

"Don't I?" Brian asked. "I always like to know who my family gets involved with, especially in business. I've been digging into Shamus's business for months which uncovered some interesting tidbits about your family's business. You."

Real fear showed on Declan's face.

Brian gestured at the lawyer who handed him a large file. He pushed it down the table toward Shamus. "You should know who you're getting into business with."

Rachel, her parents, and lawyer stood.

"We're done here," Karol said.

They walked toward the door, leaving everyone glancing at each other and then at Declan, who threw the new contract across the room.

Michael rushed up behind them. "Can we talk?" he asked Rachel.

"We'll wait for you downstairs." Brian offered and headed to the elevators.

"There's nothing to talk about." Rachel crossed her arms.

"I didn't know that's what Declan had in mind with this meeting." Michael stated. "If I did I would've..."

"There was nothing you could've done. I understand that."

"I'm glad, and I'm so sorry for the way I responded at my parents' house. You took me by surprise."

"I know I did, and I'm sorry I didn't tell you about the merger. Your father revealed it the day before my parents arrived and I wasn't sure how to tell you."

"This whole thing has been a mess, but you found a way. I don't think the board is going to take any more action against your company. And if they do, I'm certain your father will find a way to stop them." Michael said with a grin. "I hope we can put this all behind us and get back to where we were. Planning our lives together."

Rachel touched his face. "I wish it were that easy."

Michael touched her. "I know it's not going to be easy, and it will take time, but I know we can make it work."

"I'm sorry, Michael. I can't be with someone who doesn't trust me, or who would doubt something about me. Something that is a part of who I am."

His hopeful expression faltered. "I trust you, and Skylar told me about your parents' rejection and how it hurt you. I'm sorry I made you feel that I was rejecting you."

"So, you believe me?"

His face scrunched. "I need time, Rachel. This isn't something that's easy to grasp."

She pulled her hand from his. "Take all the time you need."

"I'm glad you understand. We'll get through this."

"You misunderstand me, Michael. I'm giving you the space you need, but I'm not waiting around while you decide if you believe me or not. That will mean putting my life on hold, waiting and hoping another situation arises so I'll know for sure you don't doubt me."

"Rachel, I..."

"I understand."

"I don't want to lose you."

"I know you don't, but could you stay with me if I didn't trust you, or doubted everything about you?"

"No," Michael whispered.

"Goodbye, Michael."

Each step that Rachel took away from him felt like a knife stabbed into her heart, but she knew deep down it was the right thing to do. She meant every word she said in the boardroom. She embraced every part of herself and wasn't afraid of what other people thought, and that included Michael.

CHAPTER 44

Michael watched as the elevator door closed behind her. *You're an idiot, mate,* Connor's voice echoed in his head. He was. He'd just let the woman he loved leave, and for what? Because her dreams became reality? He made his a reality with hard work. *Not the same,* he could hear his father say.

She was amazing in the boardroom, giving up the money to save his family from the merger and walking away from her contract. *And me.*

She stared at him when she said that she could walk away from him and their future together. He'd felt a sense of pride mixed in with pain.

But I was the one who gave up our future. Those words hit him in the gut. He kept telling Rachel and himself that he needed time to wrap his head around her gift, but in this moment, he realized that wasn't what stopped him. It was doubt about himself that had plagued him his whole life. It started with his father and then he had piled more onto himself over the years. He never felt good enough, that he didn't work hard enough. Rachel's confession and actions in the boardroom made him feel he still wasn't enough because he'd been unable to protect her or their future together.

Raised voices in the boardroom reminded him the meeting was still going on. Shamus and Declan were arguing while the board members were going through the file Brian had left them and grumbling between themselves.

"Is the money from Rachel's contract enough?" Michael interrupted Shamus and Declan.

"No," Declan said.

His father's expression was one of shame, and Skylar's words came back to him. His father's failure to tell him about the merger had nothing to do with Michael. He'd made the decision before he came back into the boardroom, but it still amazed him how easily it came along with the words, "Is my business enough?"

Silence sliced through the boardroom.

"What?" Shamus asked.

"Is the money in my business enough for you?"

"No, son. I won't let you do that."

Michael glanced at the board members who nodded. He didn't bother looking at Declan whose answer would be in his family's best interest.

"I'll have Rachel's solicitor draw up the paperwork today so you and the board can make the decision you need without the merger."

"Son, this is my problem to fix, not yours," Shamus said adamantly.

"We're family, so we're in this together. I have faith in you that you'll turn things around but know that I'm here if you need me."

Shamus hugged his son, patting his back. "You're a good man, Michael."

"Thank you."

"Tell Rachel I'm sorry."

"Hopefully you'll have the chance to tell her yourself. Gentlemen, I have work to do."

"So do we," one of the board members said.

The last words Michael heard before the door closed behind him were "You're fired." He grinned knowing those words were for Declan.

Connor was waiting in his office. "What's up, mate?"

"There's something I need to tell ye."

"Can it wait?"

"No."

"Fine. Have a seat." Michael motioned his friend to the loveseat in his office.

"I thought you should know something before you doubt Rachel," he said nervously.

"Connor, I..."

"Let me say this before I change my mind," he insisted, clearly uncomfortable as he paced before the couch instead of sitting. "Rachel isn't the only one who has a gift."

"You've been speaking with Skylar."

"Who's Sklyar?"

"No one. Never mind. Who else has a gift?" Michael wanted to check his watch but refrained. He was eager to contact the solicitor.

"Me."

Michael's gaze snapped to the man who'd been his friend since childhood. *What kind of gift that he couldn't tell me about?* "Is it the same as Rachel?"

"No."

"Why did you never tell me?"

"Probably the same reason as Rachel. My parents didn't handle it well, especially when it affected my da's business."

Michael raked a hand through his hair. "I'm not your parents, Connor. We've been friends for years. We told each other everything." He stood and moved to sit on the edge of his desk.

"This is different, but it isn't about me. I want you to understand why she didn't tell you. It's difficult to trust people with this kind of secret when your own family don't accept you."

"I do understand, Connor. And I came to the revelation that my doubt had nothing to do with Rachel but my own fears and doubts with my father."

"I see." Connor gazed at him.

"You're not reading my mind, are ye, mate?"

"No," Connor grinned. "But I'm happy you've recognized your baggage and how it was affecting your relationship with Rachel."

"More than you know, but right now I must deal with something important."

"I understand." Connor headed to the door.

"This conversation isn't over." Michael held him with a firm gaze, implying they'd talk about his gift later.

"I know. We'll talk when you and Rachel smooth things over."

Michael called Ashley to ask her for Rachel's solicitor's number and then called her. She was surprised to hear from him and even more amazed when he hired her. She agreed to meet with him to discuss the documents he needed. Michael thanked her then grabbed his keys and headed to the garage.

CHAPTER 45

"Are you sure about this, Rachel?" her mother asked from her seated position on the bed.

"Yes. This is for the best," Rachel replied, folding another piece of clothing into the suitcase laid out on the bed. "I can go home and focus on my business."

"What about Michael?"

Rachel looked down at the ring on her finger. "He doesn't believe me, Mom. I can't be with a man who doubts me."

"He just needs time. He'll come around."

"I know, but I can't put my life on hold waiting, Mom." She paused her packing. "Look how long it took you guys, and you're my parents."

Karol squeezed her hand as an apology. "I agree, but you're moving halfway across the world."

"I don't have a job anymore, remember? This apartment comes with the job so technically I don't have a home either."

"I'm sure Michael isn't going to send someone to kick you out if you need more time before finding somewhere else to live."

"My business is on the other side of the world. I need to get back there."

"Our business," Brian corrected when he entered the room.

Rachel chuckled. "You're retired investors."

"That counts. And your mother's right. Don't run away."

Rachel sighed. "I'm going home to focus on our business and make you more money so you can continue traveling."

Karol's hand stopped Rachel from packing. "Honey. We don't care about the money. We care about you, and Michael made you happy. That's all that matters."

Rachel covered her mother's hand with her own. "That means a lot."

"I care about the money," her father mumbled. "These trips aren't going to pay for themselves."

Karol threw a pair of socks from the suitcase at her husband. "I think what your father is trying to say is that you've already been running your business from here. It won't hurt to continue to do so for a little while. You can find an apartment with an office and stay in Ireland for a few months."

"I can't stay, Mother," Rachel's voice cracked.

Karol put her arms around her daughter. "I understand. I'll finish helping you pack while your father orders us some food."

Brian looked at his wife and daughter. "Same restaurant?"

They nodded.

Rachel and her mother continued packing, with Karol sharing funny travel stories about a monkey who became attached to her father. They were laughing when Brian came back into the room.

"She's telling you the monkey story, isn't she?" Brian scowled at his wife. "I thought we agreed not to share that with anyone?"

"You agreed. I didn't answer."

"I'm your daughter. It was important to know," Rachel chuckled.

"We can laugh about it now, but it wasn't funny at the time," Brian defended himself.

"Yes, it was."

"You're a cruel woman, Karol." Brian shook his head at his wife.

"What's life without laughter, Brian?" Karol touched his scrunched face, then kissed him.

Rachel smiled at the shared moment between her parents. She was so grateful to witness them and be a part of these moments.

When the food arrived, they ate and finished packing all her things. Her mother went off to bed, while she and her father remained on the couch talking.

"Thank you for helping me today, Dad. It really meant a lot to me."

He reached over and squeezed her hand. "Fathers protect their family. Especially their little girls."

"I'm not so little anymore," she whispered. While she was the one who walked away from Michael, deep down she thought and hoped that he would show up at the apartment and beg her to stay.

Her father sighed. "I know I said don't run away, but if that's what you need to do honey, you do it. I'll support whatever decision you make."

"Thanks, Dad. I think leaving is the best thing. Being back in Cayman and focusing on my business is what I need right now." *Otherwise, I'll grow crazy waiting for Michael.*

"I understand, and don't worry about the things you can't take with you now. Your mother and I will stay in Ireland for a couple of weeks to take care of everything for you."

"You don't have to do that," she insisted.

He shrugged. "It's no problem. We'll see the sights and help you out."

She wanted to weep. Wrapping up everything is the last thing she wanted to do. It meant endless memories and reminders of Michael and the life they almost shared together. "Thanks, Dad."

"It's what we do." He patted her arm. "We better get to bed. We've got a long day ahead of us."

They both stood, and shared a long hug, before heading to their rooms.

Rachel put on her favorite flannel pajamas then broke into tears remembering her phone call with Michael. This is why she couldn't stay in this apartment. She knew he wouldn't expect her to leave, but there were too many memories here. It's another reason she needed to return to Cayman, back to what her life was before him. Her phone pinged on the nightstand next to her, but she didn't pick it up. It was him and she couldn't face whatever message he was sending her. Not yet. She'd check it in the morning once she got a good night's sleep and had the chance to clear her energy and her head. *Sure. Keep telling yourself that.*

CHAPTER 46

Rachel stood by the entrance of the elevator with her parents. The two suitcases she brought with her when she first arrived in Ireland were next to her. "I'll call you the moment I land."

Her mother pulled her and her father together in one last tight hug.

"We'll be in Cayman for a visit in a couple of months and you can fill us in on how the expansion is going."

He didn't add, and to see how you're doing, for which Rachel was grateful. She had no idea what she'd be like in a couple of months. She had walked through the apartment earlier to make sure she hadn't missed anything and nearly broke down in tears after being flooded with memory after memory of her time in this space with Michael. This is why she couldn't stay here. It was too painful. Especially when she slipped her engagement ring off her finger and placed it on the nightstand for Michael to find. The right thing would be to return it to him directly, but she didn't have the strength to see his face again. See the hurt and other emotions that had reflected in his eyes when she walked away from him. This was the best way. The coward way, but she was taking it.

The elevator door opened, and Liam stepped out. "Good morning."

"Morning," they replied in unison.

Liam strode inside and grabbed her suitcases, while she shouldered her backpack that held her laptop and her carry-on necessities. She hugged her parents and said goodbye one more time before getting onto the elevator with Liam.

They remained quiet during the elevator ride and the walk to the car. It was only when they were on their way to the airport that Liam spoke.

"I'm sorry to see you go, Rachel."

Their eyes met in the rearview mirror. "Me too, Liam," she said with a sad smile.

"Will Mr. Doherty be joining you on your trip?"

She swallowed the lump forming a tight knot in her throat, until she could only manage to shake her head. If she spoke, the tears that were burning behind her eyes would become an endless rainfall.

"Maybe next time," he said casually.

There would be no next time, but he didn't know that. No more trips, cuddles, or coffee time. Nothing. Two days had passed since the meeting in the boardroom and while she got a couple of calls from Michael, he didn't try to text her or come by to see her. She didn't answer, knowing that if she heard his voice, it would be over for her. He was her weakness.

She had called Ashley to say goodbye, because going to the office wasn't an option. There was nothing and no one left there for her.

"I'm moving back to Cayman," she said out loud.

The surprise in Liam's eyes was genuine. "I didn't realize. May I ask why?"

"Things didn't work out the way I hoped, so I cut my contract short."

"That's a shame. I thought you and Mr. Doherty made a splendid couple," a smile split his lips. "He was the happiest I'd ever seen him with you."

"Me too," Rachel whispered, wiping the stray tear that had escaped.

His expression said he wanted to ask more questions, but they had reached the airport. Liam pulled into a drop spot and opened the door for her. "Stay here. I'll fetch a trolley for your bags."

Rachel stood outside the airport, the cool air blowing her hair about her face. The structure was an architect's dream with all its angles and glass that reflected the rising sun. She took a long, deep breath as she stared upward, taking in the orange and yellows hues that splattered the sky and over the mirrors that made up parts of the building. *Goodbye, Ireland. Goodbye, Michael.*

Her flight didn't leave for a couple of hours, so she took this moment, hoping to make it a beautiful one instead of an agonizing time in her life. *Fat chance!*

Liam returned with a trolley for her bags and loaded them up for her.

She hugged him tightly and he squeezed her frame. "I'm going to miss you, Liam."

"Me too, Rachel. Take care of yourself."

She nodded and pushed the trolley inside the airport that would lead her toward her old life and away from the future she thought she'd have.

CHAPTER 47

The jerk from the plane landing yanked her from her deep breathing and she opened her eyes to look out the window. She'd taken a quick peek earlier when the pilot announced they were approaching but shifted her glance before her nausea got worse.

A mixture of excitement and misery coursed through her. She was happy to be back on the island she grew up on, and ecstatic about seeing her best friends again. Sorrow seeped in her bones with the realization that she was miles away from Michael and probably wouldn't see him again.

She pushed the thoughts of him away and focused instead on seeing her friends. Sky had texted while Rachel was in the Dublin airport to apologize for leaving without seeing her, but that she and Arlene would be there to pick her up.

Rachel smiled when she heard and then saw the two-person band playing Caribbean music for the people exiting the plane. Warm breezes raced across her face, and she removed her jacket and tied it around her waist as she walked to customs.

Several people who knew her parents waved from their spot in the line. By the time she got her suitcases and exited the building, she was exhausted from all their questions about where in the world they were.

Someone screaming made her smile because it could only be one person. Arlene rushed up to her and hugged her so tightly, Rachel swore she felt her circulation stop.

"Let her breath, Arlene," Skylar said, shaking her head.

"Shush. She is my best friend and I can squeeze her as hard as I want."

Rachel chuckled when Skylar rolled her eyes. "I missed you too, but we're holding up traffic."

Arlene lifted her head and glanced around before grabbing one of her suitcases. "Let's blow this joint."

Skylar shook her head. "Have you been watching old movies again?"

She shrugged.

They walked to Skylar's SUV, loaded up her bags and left the airport.

"Take me to my parents' house. There's still six months left on my renter's lease."

"I told you not to rent it out," Skylar admonished from the driver's seat.

"I know." It was one of the few times Rachel hadn't listened to her advice.

They all glanced at each other when her phone rang.

Heart racing, Rachel pulled it out of her bag. Not that it mattered if it was Michael. She had no intension of answering it. *Then why am I sad it's my dad calling?*

"I just landed," she told him, pushing aside the knot in her stomach.

"I'm happy to hear that, but that's not why we're calling." Her father's voice sounded hesitant, and unsure if he should share his news.

"What happened? Is Mom okay?"

"Your mother's fine."

"Then tell me."

There was a long pause before he spoke. "Michael stopped by today."

Rachel held her breath in anticipation of more words, but none came. "What did he say?"

"Umm. He was...upset you weren't here."

"Oh." She sensed there was more. "What did he say?"

"He was disappointed you left without saying goodbye or talking to him. And then angry."

She had nothing else to say to him that wouldn't turn into her changing her mind if she saw him again. "I'm sorry you had to deal with it."

"I felt bad for him. The hurt on his face was heartbreaking."

Guilt stabbed at her thinking about causing him pain. That wasn't her intention. She was trying to protect herself. She hadn't considered how her leaving would affect him. The only thought in her mind was getting away from him and the heartache she felt.

"Did you tell him where I am?" A small spark of hope bloomed in her chest.

"Yes. I thought he should know. I hope that was all right?"

"It's fine. Not like he can jump on a plane anytime soon," Rachel attempted to joke, but her voice croaked instead.

"I'm sorry, honey."

"It's okay, Dad. I'm going now. Bye and thanks for calling," Rachel said. She hung up before she started sobbing to her father on the phone, something she didn't want to burden him with.

Rachel burst into ugly blubbering tears. Skylar and Arlene remained quiet. Crying wasn't something they did together often.

"I know what we need," Skylar said when Rachel's weeps eased up.

"Margaritas and naked men?" Arlene blurted.

They all glanced at each other then erupted in laughter.

After they dropped her bags at her parent's house, Arlene and Skylar took her out for tacos and then so many margaritas, Rachel knew a terrible hangover was in her future the next morning. Too drunk to drive, they took a taxi back home and passed out on blankets spread across her parents' living room floor, something they hadn't done in years.

CHAPTER 48

FOUR WEEKS LATER

Rachel watched her team leave the conference room. They'd done an amazing job while she was in Ireland. The expansion was going smoother and faster than they planned. Angela was proving to be a great leader and manager, especially with the extra support Rachel needed to take time off. This was her second day back at work.

Coming back sooner hadn't worked out since she cried the whole car ride to work. She texted Angela and explained that she wasn't ready to return and would need more time.

Michael's calls stopped the day after she returned to the island, proving that he'd moved on with his life now that she was gone. Perhaps his parents had finally pushed him into Ciara's arms. Her heartache turned into agony as she imagined him kissing her, spending the night at his apartment in his bed.

She spent the extra time she told Angela she needed in bed ugly crying and yelling every curse word she knew when she thought of them together. She ate a shitload of ice cream and pizza, and watched romance movies that only fueled her spiral to the dark side of no showers and crusty pajamas.

Skylar was the one to pull her back to the land of the living, since Arlene thought she needed to wallow to my heart's content. "She lost her soulmate, Sky!" Arlene had argued.

"I know you lost Michael, but you can't lose yourself too. You're making the same mistake you did with Shawn."

Rachel had called her crazy for thinking her feelings for Shawn were anything close what she felt for Michael, but after avoiding work calls for over a week, Rachel knew she was right. Her business was one of the reasons she returned to Cayman, and she was neglecting it, and herself. In that moment, she knew she had to make a change, otherwise everything in her life was going to derail worse than it already had. She'd worked too hard and sacrificed too much, including the love of her life, to go backward.

She took the first step and deep cleaned her parents' home, took a brisk walk on the beach and stuck her toes in the sand. She'd taken a long hot shower and put on clean clothes for the first time in days. Then she meditated for an hour. By the time she went to bed later that night, she started to feel human again.

She returned to work the following day.

The road back hadn't been an easy one. She still ached for Michael. Saying she missed him wasn't a strong enough word for how it felt without him in her life. She stopped crying at night, but that was only because she meditated herself into a sleep coma. Some days were good and other days felt like she'd taken a million steps back. Skylar assured her it was part of the grieving process, but it still hurt like hell and felt like shit when she thought about him.

After work, Rachel placed an order for delivery from her new favorite place. She was trying to eat better since it helped her mood, and they had a lot of healthy options that didn't taste like crap.

She poured herself a glass of red wine and started reading a book while she waited.

Moments later there was a knock on the door. "That was fast," she said, walking to the door.

She gasped when she opened it. "What are you doing here?"

"I came here for you." Michael stood in her doorway, looking as magnificent as the last day she saw him.

"I thought you were my food," Rachel muttered, not sure what else to say after his declaration.

"Not food." His eyes raked over her face as if he were devouring every inch to memory. "Can I come in?"

Rachel stepped aside to let him in and closed the door.

He circled the room, taking in her parents' simple living room with a couch, single chair, and a bookcase that doubled as an entertainment center for their TV. She watched his every move as he studied the pictures from her childhood that were scattered on the shelves.

Her mind was screaming at her to run to him and wrap her arms around him, trying to convince her that he hadn't forgotten about her. About them. That he still cared. *He had to care if he flew all the way here, right?* Then she remembered he had a business on the island. *Is that why he's here? Is he just on a business trip and decided to stop by?* But for what? Closure? Her stomach lurched at the thought.

"I thought I'd have the words to say by the time I got here." He turned to face her and the sorrow in his eyes knocked the wind out of her.

"I don't think there's anything to say, Michael." The words felt wrong even as she said them. "I said everything there is to say. There's nothing more."

"No. There's so much more to say, Rachel."

Her heart was hammering in her chest as she crossed her arms. "I'm listening."

"Why don't we sit?" Michael gestured toward the couch.

Rachel felt her knees wobble as she followed him, but she sat on the single chair. Her mind was racing with questions, but she remained silent, waiting for him to speak. A tiny sliver of hope pierced her heart with anticipation.

"I want to apologize again for everything that happened. I never should've let things escalate the way they did. And I left you alone to deal with the fallout." Michael leaned forward. "When you shared your secret, I was shocked and thought that my doubts were about what you confessed, but it wasn't."

Rachel's heartbeat stuttered with excitement and dread at his words and in anticipation of what would come next.

"Your confession was a shock for sure, but the truth is my doubt came from feeling powerless to fix our problem. The bigger the issue became the worse I felt. Your business and our future together were slipping away and there was nothing I could do to stop it.

"I can't tell you how your words in the boardroom crushed me." He didn't need to say which ones. "And how easy they were for you to say and for you to walk away."

Rachel wrung her hands in her lap. *If only you knew how hard it was and how it's been without you.*

"But I'm grateful for them."

Her brows narrowed in confusion.

"They woke me up to the truth. And the decision I needed to make."

"What decision?"

Rachel stared at Michael in disbelief when he relayed what happened in the boardroom after she left. "Why would you do that?"

"Because my father needed more money to avoid the merger. And because I realized my business is a poor substitute for the woman I love. I just wish I'd realized it sooner."

Tears pooled in Rachel's eyes. "I can't believe you did that."

Micheal rubbed his hand on his jeans. "It was an easy decision to make the moment I lost you. Nothing else mattered."

"Then why didn't you come to see me? I didn't leave Ireland for two days?"

"You didn't answer my phone calls, and I was still working with the solicitor trying to deal with all the fallout from Declan, my business. Everything." He gave her a thoughtful glance. "I was also still hurt from you breaking off our relationship."

He slid to the end of the couch and closed the distance between them. "I was so angry when I found out you left without saying goodbye, without giving me a chance to make things right."

Rachel's breath caught in her throat when Michael got on his knees and crawled over to where she sat. He cupped her face with one hand.

"I've been going out of my mind without you, Rachel. Being without you this last month has been a kind of torture I wouldn't wish on my enemy."

The tears pooling in her eyes trickled down her cheek and he brushed them away with his thumb.

"I don't want to live another moment without you, Rachel. I love everything about you." He cupped her face with both hands. "Everything. All the good things, the broken things, and the things you keep from me. I don't want you to hide anything of yourself from me ever again. I want every piece of you. Forever."

Rachel gazed down at the man before her, breathless. Tingles raced through her veins from his touch and her body felt as though it would float away from the lightness that coursed through it.

"Being away from you was torture for me too, Michael. I thought about you every day, wondering if I hadn't made the biggest mistake of my life. When you stopped calling, I lost all hope for us, for a future together." She brushed away the stray tear from his face. "I love you with my whole heart, with all that I am. I want everything from you and with you. I want forever with you too, Michael." She wrapped her arm around his neck and lowered her face to kiss him.

The door knock in the distance stopped them.

"It's the food," Rachel said, and they both laughed.

She answered the door and set the food on the table before returning to the living room where Michael sat. She climbed into his lap and hugged him. It went on forever, as if making up for the time apart when they couldn't touch.

"Marry me," Michael said calmly as if he were talking about the weather.

"I already said yes," she murmured, scraping her fingers along his scalp the way he liked.

"As soon as possible. Here on the island." His nose ran along her neck. "I don't want to wait another minute to start our lives together."

Rachel shivered. "But..."

He dug into his pants pocket and pulled out the ring he gave her. The one she left behind. "You can have a big wedding or any kind of wedding you want later. I just want you as my wife as soon as possible." He slipped the ring back on her finger.

Rachel leaned in to kiss him again. "Yes. Every time, yes."

The End

I hope you enjoyed Michael and Rachel's story. If you fell in love with Connor and Regan, keep scrolling for a sneak peak of their story The Trouble with Empaths or ORDER THE BOOK now.

THE TROUBLE
WITH EMPATHS

CHAPTER 1

Connor cringed as the noise from the party hit his senses, loud and booming in his head. He usually prepared himself for large crowds with heavy meditation or breathing sessions, but that didn't happen because his best friend Michael showed up early for a quick drink.

Connor should've insisted they didn't drink, but Michael was about to lose the freedom he had in university when he went to work for his father in the family business in a couple of months, so saying no wasn't an option.

Next came the mixture of emotions that swirled around and over him like multicolored ocean waves rolling to and from the shore.

Excitement.

Annoyance.

Anger.

Boredom.

And a bunch more Connor couldn't process. Didn't want to process.

Not if he was going to make it through this party tonight.

The happy ones he could handle, but the strong negative ones were like knives in his brain. Focusing on them only made it worse.

"You all right, mate?" Michael rested a hand on his shoulder, concern etched in his eyes.

Beyond the open doorway where they stood was Michael's sister Regan's eighteenth birthday party. The room was decorated like every other charity event they hosted, instead of a young woman's party. Their parents' doing, no doubt.

"All good." Connor's lips curled with a fake smile. Michael wasn't aware of his "gift"—or curse, as his parents preferred to call it. Although his father had no trouble using it to his advantage when needed.

Empath was the word he'd learned years ago, but to him, it was too simple a word to describe it, in his opinion. No one else knew. Not since he was a kid. The possibility of losing his only real friends, and in some ways a second family, in his mind, wasn't worth the risk. Or having them use him the way his father did sour his stomach.

He learned his lesson the hard way that relationships ended when you didn't fit the box they put you in, whether it was your friends or their parents. Being different wasn't appreciated, especially in their social circles.

Michael laughed and clapped him on the back. "Let's go in there and get this over with. I'm sure Regan wants it to end as quickly as we do."

"You go ahead. I'm heading to the toilet first." Not enough time to prepare himself for the barrage of emotions he'd have to deal with once inside, but it was better than nothing.

This was why he tended to avoid large events.

At university, it was easy to block out the noise with alcohol but that wasn't an option tonight. Not for Regan's party, and definitely not with her parents watching them. Being an adult didn't matter to them if he and Michael made a scene.

When he returned to the party, he tried inconspicuously to find Regan, but she was lost in a crush of her friends.

Regan. Just saying her name shot a thrill through him that swiftly shifted to crippling guilt.

Like an idiot, he'd complicated their relationship by kissing her on the lips on her sixteenth birthday. It was silly, really, and something he hadn't planned. He never thought of her that way before. But after she hugged him as a thank-you for his gift and gazed at him with those stunning blue eyes of hers like he was the moon and stars, he couldn't help himself. He regretted it the moment it happened. She was only sixteen, for Christ's sake, and he was twenty-two.

What made matters worse was she was no longer the skinny little kid who followed him and Michael around. For the past two years, he'd sensed her watching him like a girl with her first crush, which didn't help. Neither did the fact that she was Michael's sister and off-limits for more reasons than their friendship and her age.

The annoying part was she was the only person he had difficulty sensing. As a kid, she wore her heart on her sleeve and in her eyes, so it wasn't necessary. He only sensed when she needed him and what for.

The thrill that coursed through him when she watched him nailed him with guilt each time. She was just a kid, and they were friends. Close friends, even though it wasn't the same as the friendship he shared with Michael. Her friendship meant everything to him.

Being at university helped. Talking and texting was easy and comfortable and kept their connection in the lane it belonged.

His life was complicated enough between the strained relationship with his parents and leaving university soon to get out into the working world to find a job. One that paid him enough to get out of his parents' house. Being away from them at university made him realize distance from them was the best thing to happen to him.

The last thing he needed was to develop feelings for his best friend's little sister—his other best friend. And a kid. Although she wasn't a kid anymore. And that's what bothered him the most.

THE TROUBLE WITH EMPATHS

CHAPTER 2

Regan Doherty had been in love with Connor McGrath for as long as she could remember. They'd been childhood friends forever. Well, friends by association because he was her brother's friend, but in her mind it counted.

When she was sixteen, he ruffled her hair and kissed her on the lips for her birthday, and hugged her the way he always did. But unlike the other times, heat and goose bumps had raced across her skin, and her heartbeat stuttered before speeding up until she was breathless.

Thankfully, he didn't notice, but she did. From that moment on, Connor was no longer the friend who brought her favorite books, really listened when she talked, and wiped away her tears when her parents were being unreasonable.

He became Connor with hair that glistened in the sunlight when they were hanging by the pool. Connor with the muscles and six-pack that stopped her breath. Her friend with the piercing blue eyes that saw into her soul.

For the past two years, the way she felt about Connor had only deepened. The distance of him being at university didn't dim but strengthened those feelings, and she planned to tell him tonight. He and her brother Michael were home from uni. It was the perfect opportunity. Never mind that her heart was about to beat out of her chest, and doubt stabbed every pore on her skin. This was Connor. One of her best friends, who, other than her parents and brother, was the most important person in her life.

Pining for him was never going to get her what she wanted. Those were the words she'd repeated in the mirror several times as she was getting ready for tonight.

Confessing her feelings could work in her favor, if he felt the same way, or she could massively crash and burn and ruin their friendship. But it was a risk she was willing to take. When he kissed her, the sparks between them were mutual. She was certain of it. The shock in his eyes clearly said kissing her on the lips wasn't planned, but that merely convinced her the connection between them was real.

Sparkling lights from every color of the rainbow reflected off the walls of the ballroom her parents rented for her party. People of all ages, from her friends to business associates of her father, were cramped into the space like finely dressed sardines.

Regan hated that she had to invite so many people, but there was no other option if she wanted a party. Business before family. Always. No exceptions.

On one side of the room were friends from school and her social circle under the age of thirty covered in bold colors and fine-cut suits and dresses, while the other side of the party was anyone over the age of forty and friends or business associates of her family or friends.

"Is this a party or a wake?" Ciara Kelly sipped her champagne, her heavily made-up eyes moving about the room until they settled on Michael. "You should invite your brother and Connor over."

Regan rolled her eyes. Ciara was less than subtle about her interest in Michael. He never showed one ounce of interest, but that never stopped her. Ciara was closer to their age and only befriended her because she was Michael's sister. "They'll come around once they've made the rounds."

Her eyes devoured Connor once Ciara wandered off to a group of her friends. He was dressed in a dark-blue suit that hugged his frame. A frame she had watched fill out from the lean one he had in high school to the thicker, more solid one while he was away at school. The body of a man and one she now drooled over even more.

His hair was slicked back so it looked almost black instead of the usual shaggy sandy-blond locks she itched to touch for reasons other than ruffling it in annoyance. It was as soft as it looked, but she wanted to run her fingers along his scalp as she tugged his face to her in a kiss.

As if sensing he was being watched, he turned, catching her staring, and graced her with one of his sexy smirks. One that made her heartbeat gallop and her knees tremble since she was sixteen.

She returned his smirk with her usual goofy grin before remembering she wanted Connor to start seeing her as a woman and not his best friend's little sister. His eyes swept her from head to toe; his eyebrow rose in question when her grin turned into what she hoped was a seductive smile. Or maybe it was the dress she wore.

She was showing a lot more skin than usual with the off-the-shoulder, shimmering silver dress that reached her ankles, but with a split that went nearly to her thigh. Her mother had been appalled when she stepped out of the dressing room and then annoyed when Regan refused to change it to what her mother thought was a more suitable choice. Most of this party—her party—was what her parents wanted. Her dress was the one thing she wanted for herself. Her mother had relented when Regan reminded her how often what she wanted was sacrificed for the sake of business.

He glanced around behind him, as if looking for someone else the smile was meant for.

Regan took a sip of champagne and, over the rim of the glass, blasted him with the sexiest stare she could muster. Would he take the hint? Her heart sped up when he excused himself from the circle of people around him and strutted toward her with an air of confidence and yumminess that sent quivers to places on her body that were hidden, even in this revealing dress.

As he moved toward her, his gaze raked over her from the tips of her open-toe shoes to the tops of her exposed breasts, up to her lips and finally her eyes when he stood before her.

Shivers danced through her veins when his cologne hit her senses. The same one she gave him every birthday. Sandalwood with a hint of bergamot. "Connor."

"Happy birthday, Re."

She flinched at her nickname. "Please call me Regan. At least in public. I'm not a little girl anymore."

His gaze traveled over her face, which was covered in makeup. Not as much as Ciara, but more than what usually covered her face.

"No, you're not." His voice dropped an octave before he cleared his throat and graced her with a friendly smile.

She tugged his arm. "Let's go on the balcony. I need some air." Regan had scouted the perfect spot outside already. One where no one inside would see them.

Connor followed her to the balcony doors, leaving her champagne glass on the tray of a passing waiter. "You're too young to drink."

Regan snorted. "Did you miss that today is my eighteenth birthday?"

He held open the large French door for her. "I'm just looking out for you, so you don't drink too much and do something you'll regret later."

She released his arm and faced him, making sure to stay close. "Is that what happened on your eighteenth birthday?" Her eyes twinkled with mischief.

"No. But I'm not you."

Her face scrunched in question. "What does that mean?"

"I'm not my best friend's little sister who is wearing a very revealing dress and attracting more attention than she realizes."

"Am I?" Regan placed her hand on the lapel of his jacket. Did he notice other men watching her? She couldn't care less about them. It was his attention she wanted.

"You are." He scanned her face, pausing at her lips before moving back to her eyes. "And wearing too much makeup."

Regan chuckled, sidestepping his comment. "So where is my gift?" They usually exchanged gifts in private, because they were often ones her parents wouldn't approve of.

"For someone who's not a little girl anymore, you're sure eager for your birthday present." Connor's lips curled with a smirk.

She ignored his comment, not letting his teasing get under her skin. Not tonight. Tonight, she was on a mission, and the window was closing quickly. There was only so long they could stay on the patio before someone came outside. "I know you're going to give it to me. You want to give it to me," she whispered seductively, and watched with surprise and awe when his eyes darkened. Her breath hitched in her throat.

His mouth opened to respond but closed. His usual blue eyes were gray under the artificial overhead light on the balcony. Silence stretched out as vast as the night sky blanketing their backdrop. The cool Irish night air swirled around them, forming goose bumps on her skin.

Tension sizzled in the small distance between them. Regan's hand caressed the lapel of his jacket slowly up and down, imagining it was his bare chest until his hand gripped hers, stopping her movement.

"Regan..." His tone held a hint of warning.

She lifted her face toward him and moved in closer. When he didn't step back, she pressed her lips against his, a feat she couldn't normally manage without heels.

She'd kissed a few guys before tonight, not wanting to come across as inexperienced to Connor, whose lips had seen more than his share of women over the years. To her delight, his arms went around her, pulling her against his frame, his fingertips grazing the skin of her back. She moaned and gasped when his tongue slipped into her mouth and he took control of the kiss.

Regan's knees weakened with every stroke of his tongue against hers, every brush of his fingers against her skin. He broke the kiss and attacked her neck with kisses, then trailed down her collarbone. She was grateful for his tight grip; otherwise, she'd be a puddle on the expensive marble floor. She arched her back as his lips kissed the tips of her exposed breast. "Connor," she groaned. "I knew it would be like this."

"Did you now," he whispered hotly as he nibbled on her shoulder.

"Yes. And I want you to be my first," Regan breathed. Her head spun from the intoxicating sensations spiraling through her body from his mouth on her skin, the smell of his cologne, and his own delicious scent just below the surface.

Connor's lips stilled and his body tensed.

Regan met him with desire-filled eyes. "What's wrong?" Why did he stop? Everything was going the way she hoped.

"I can't be your first, Regan. A sexual relationship isn't in the cards for us."

Her grip on his jacket tightened. "Why not? I love you. I've always loved you."

His hand slid into her hair. "You think you love me, but you don't."

Is he serious right now? "I know how I feel, Connor. I've known it the moment I was sixteen and you kissed me on the lips."

"That was just a brotherly kiss."

Pain pierced her heart. Why was he denying the attraction between us? One that still had her skin and lips scorched from the heat of their kiss. "My brother doesn't kiss me on the lips, Connor." She yanked his jacket.

His hand caressed her cheek. "This is just a silly crush that will pass."

She pushed against him. That's how he sees me? A silly little girl with a crush? It didn't matter she was old enough to drink now and do everything adults did. "So why did you kiss me?"

His jaw clenched. "I was caught up in the moment."

"I felt how caught up you were pressed against my leg. You want me." If only she could get him to see her as more than just his best friend's little sister, then he'd change his mind.

"Of course I did. Look at you, Regan. In that dress, with your soft skin, how was I supposed to react? Any normal guy would have the same reaction."

"I don't want any guy, Connor. I want you," she whispered, beginning to crush under the weight of his rejection and the painful realization his reaction to their kiss was just one to any hot, sexily dressed woman. It wasn't because he was attracted to her or was beginning to see her as a woman. Someone he could be with. She could see it in his eyes. He regretted kissing her.

"Regan."

Him using her full name was a death sentence. He only used it when he was serious, or if she pushed the boundaries of annoying him.

"When time passes, you'll realized this was just a phase. You'll meet someone and we'll laugh about tonight."

He was adjusting his suit where she'd mangled it with her fingers and raked his hands through his hair to fix the mess she made. It would be like their kiss hadn't happened. Like what she said and how she felt didn't matter.

She was used to that from her parents and even occasionally her brother, but never him. He'd always taken her seriously, or so she'd thought. His reaction only proved he saw her the same as everyone else—a little girl who didn't know her own mind. Rage crept over her, starting at the tips of her toes, making its way through her body like a fire in her blood.

She met his gaze. "The only thing time is going to prove, Connor, is that you're going to realize this attraction between us is more than friendship, and it's going to be too late. You're going to watch me move on with my life, with someone else, and you'll be wishing it was you the whole time."

The sadness in his eyes angered her more.

"You, Connor, are a proper wanker," she seethed before storming back to the ballroom. It was her birthday, after all, and she'd be damned if she'd let him ruin the rest of her night. Never mind that her heart was shattering into a million pieces.

Want to find out what happens next with Connor and Regan? Get your copy of The Trouble with Empaths.

338

ALSO BY ELKE

For the Love of Jazz
Book One - Deadly Bloodlines
Book Two – Deadly Race
Book Three – Deadly Family
The Renovation
Persuading Lola
The Trouble with Soulmates
The Trouble with Empaths

ABOUT THE AUTHOR

S he once dreamed of becoming the next Nora Roberts, traveling the world on book tours. These days, she's just as happy channeling her imagination into writing stories and compelling characters across multiple genres.

A mother of two, she loves superhero movies just as much as romance and thrives on structure, deadlines, and systems. Without them, her overactive brain tends to run wild.

Elke writes for readers who believe love is powerful, intuition is real, and hope can exist even in the darkest moments. Her stories blend romance, suspense, and spiritual depth—where love is tested, truth is uncovered, and healing is always possible.

When she's not writing, she enjoys connecting with readers at book events and sharing her love of storytelling. Elke loves connecting with readers like you! Find her on:

www.elkefeuer.com | Email her at elke@elkefeuer.com.